The Youth
& Young Loves
of Oliver Wade

stories

_____

Ben Monopoli

The Youth
& Young Loves
of Oliver Wade

They claim to walk unafraid.
I'll be clumsy instead.

— *R.E.M., "Walk Unafraid"*

(Age 13)

STAG

Stag.

I remember hearing that word, sensing immediately the freedom in it. Stag. It was a hard word, angular, macho, as navy-blue as military. And cool. Unimpeachable. It had no weakness, could not be questioned. It was strong.

The first of us to use it was Boyd Wren, and he used it well aware of its power. Someone had asked him who he was bringing to the dance.

"No one," he said. "I'm goin stag."

Stag.

Stag.

We whispered it, reveling in it, the five of us, the five bottom rungs on the eighth-grade ladder. Even those of us who'd never heard the word before understood its meaning. All except Dwight Macklin, who asked.

But it couldn't be explained; everyone else understood this. To provide a definition would be to reduce its power. It would be like explaining a magic trick.

So Boyd merely said again, "It means I'm goin stag."

When the word came out of his mouth you watched for his back to straighten and for his fists to press against his hips. You watched for his cowlicky blond hair to smooth.

"I'm going stag too," said Tyson Cordray.

"Me too, I'm goin staaag," said Michael Alonso, the weird one.

"How about you, Ollie?" said Boyd.

"Stag," I said.

My first choice — skipping the dance — wasn't an option. This was the big one, the Grad Dance, the last before high school. People like me who had successfully skipped three years of middle-school dances could not skip the Grad Dance. You went because everyone had to be there. The grade policed itself with the rigid enforcement of a grandmother making sure all the cousins showed up for Christmas. There was no way out. I couldn't even try. So I clung to the word.

***

"I'm going stag," I told my mother, only because she asked; I never brought up the dance on my own. I tried not to acknowledge it at all.

We were walking up the rickety spiral steps of the town's only seamstress. Certain preparations needed to be made for the dance, and my mother was intent on making them, even excited. My suit needed to be let out.

"Oh, Oliver, you should ask a girl," said my mother, looking down from a higher step. "What about Nadia Cummings?"

"All my friends are going stag." I held the word up at her like a shield.

"Or Jasmine Lorange?"

Names rained down. While we sat in the shop's

stuffy waiting area she listed all the girls I'd ever been on a soccer team with, all the girls we'd seen at gymnastics class and town yard-sales.

"No one is taking anyone," I said.

The seamstress, an old woman overworked in this season of dances and proms, sent me behind a curtain to put on my suit and then tugged at my crotch and my shoulders, taking measurements.

"Have you asked a pretty girl?" she said, smiling around the pins in her mouth.

"No," I said. "Going stag."

***

My four friends saw going stag as a way to polish the inevitable. It insulated them from being mocked for being the kind of boys who couldn't land a date. A boy going stag wasn't going alone, he was choosing to go alone. The difference between those things, for an eighth-grader, was everything.

For me going stag offered something more. For me it was a relief, a reprieve from a rite of passage I had come to understand I wasn't destined for. I whispered it to myself at every mention of the dance, like a spell to ward off suspicion. Stag. For me it kept things at bay.

***

Talk of the dance, all year a hum, grew to a buzz, a thump, a clanging in the school hallways. Girls talked about where they were having their hair done; boys talked about buying corsages. Invitations to go to the dance were delivered through the bolder proxies of bashful friends. At lunch, in classrooms, on the bus, notes were passed. I pretended not to see. That trick for monsters: if I closed my eyes and counted to three, would it all go away?

***

At the end of one day when I opened my locker a piece of paper fell out. Notebook paper folded into a triangle and decorated with hand-drawn orange musical notes. I closed my eyes and counted. One, two, three.

"What is that!" Dwight gasped from the cluttered locker beside mine. He was ready for it to be a treasure map, a ransom note, but I knew it was neither of those.

"Just from my mom," I said, slamming the triangle deep into my backpack.

One, two, three. One, two, three, one, two, three.

I thought about throwing it away without reading it. I couldn't be responsible for something I never saw. I owed no one an answer if I never saw a question. I was going stag, didn't they know? The note was an insult. But it was an armed bomb too. One I needed to defuse before it blew up.

I opened it on the bus, slunk down in the green vinyl seat with my knees pressed high against the back of the seat in front of me. Within the pocket of my lap I unfolded the triangle. In orange ink it read: *Oliver. Would you like to go to the Grad Dance with me? (Jessica Parson) Please check one and put this in Locker 341. __ Yes __ No. From Jessica Parson. PS: I'm good at dancing, you'll see.* Some, but not all, of the I's were dotted with circles.

Jessica Parson, only Jessica. A weight lifted; I exhaled and my knees slid down the green vinyl. Jessica was a girl it was OK not to want to go to this dance with. Any dance with. She was a girl no one would want to go to a dance with. My friends would excuse this, based on Jessica's ever-present kitten sweatshirts, her big buck teeth, her faded stretch-pants everyone said smelled like horse manure because she lived near a farm. They would reject it. To have help in rejecting a girl for not being good enough — this was a fine disguise.

"She asked you?" Tyson said, affronted, when I showed the guys the note. "That wench."

"I bet she's going to wear h-h-horse poop perfume to the dance," Michael said, laughing, rubbing the heel of his hand against his perpetually itchy chin. (Sometimes we called him Itchy Chin Mike.)

"I feel so dirty now," I whispered dramatically. "I need a chemical baaath."

"Let's see that note again," said Boyd, holding out a sturdy hand. I gave it to him. Using his knee as a table, he drew a blue X on the line beside *No*. Then he paused, touched the pen cap to his lips, then circled the *No*.

"Write on it *In your dreams Jessica*," said Michael. "Write on it *You smell like shit*." He had the devilish grin of a boy new to swearing.

"This is fine like this," Boyd said.

He folded the note in a series of halves and handed it back to me. Between first and second periods I raised it to the ventilation holes of Jessica's locker.

I closed my eyes and counted to three. Paper whisked against metal and it was gone.

***

As the days slid by everything started to become all

dance, all the time, an onslaught too overwhelming for my anti-monster trick. It came from everywhere—the obvious places, but even my own bedroom.

"We should buy you new shoes for the dance," my mother said. My suit was back from the seamstress and she'd realized it was still incomplete.

"I don't need shoes," I said, wedging the suit into the back of my closet, where I could better pretend it didn't exist. Plastic hangers clattered to the floor. "I can wear my church shoes."

"But those aren't very fancy. Don't you want to look nice? People are going all-out for this."

She was sitting on the end of my bed, cradling her chin with one hand while her elbow rested on her knee. She was looking at me as though I were the most mysterious thing in the universe.

"Who cares if I look nice?" I said, shutting the closet door and letting my hand slide damply off the knob. "Can I go outside?"

She sighed, pressed her knuckles to her lips. "You're going to have a lousy time at this dance, Oliver. Do you know why? Because you've already decided to have a lousy time."

"I'm going outside," I said, leaving her in my room and taking the stairs two at a time.

***

In biology class I had been thinking about my suit, thinking that if I didn't wear the jacket to the dance—if I only wore a shirt and pants—it might not seem so official, when a finger poked my spine. It was a poke full of intention, as though I were being summoned from a lower floor. I pretended not to feel it. I knew Amy Langley was sitting behind me. I looked toward the blackboard and closed my eyes. One, two, three one two—

"Oliver," she whispered, and after hesitating I turned a little in my seat. "Hi," she added.

"Hi."

"Are you going to the Grad Dance?"

"... Yuh."

"Are you going with anyone?"

I shook my head slowly, slowly, like a person trying to outwit quicksand.

"Taylor wants me to ask if you'll go with her."

"Oh."

"She really wants a flower, even just a little one."

"Oh. OK."

"Good! I'll tell her."

I faced forward, almost dropped forward. My fingers were leaving wet dimples on my textbook pages. What had just happened? What was happening? Why had I not told her about going stag, wielded it like the weapon it was?

After a few seconds with my eyes shut tight I felt another poke. When I turned Amy pointed to the far corner of the classroom. Taylor, blushing, looked up from her doodling, glanced at me, smiled.

At the end of the day when we were all in the hall putting on our backpacks she came over to my locker. She seemed to peek out from behind her brown bangs and long eyelashes.

"I'm excited we're going," she said. She looked happy. I couldn't fathom why. I wanted her to leave me alone. Why was she doing this to me? What had I done to her? "I heard Jessica was going to ask you, but then she decided to go alone instead."

"Oh."

"So."

"Yeah."

"So like do you want a ride to the dance?" she said. "My mom could pick you up?" She was biting her lip, clicking her Jelly-shoed heels together awkwardly.

"My mom's already driving me. So."

"Well... maybe your mom could pick me up, then?"

"We don't know where you live, though, so...."

"Oh. OK." She wasn't stupid, she was deciding not to press it. "So." Her heels stopped moving. "We'll meet up at the dance?"

"Yeah I'll just see you there, I guess?"

I hated her for making me act like a jerk but I didn't know what else to do. Was being a jerk better than pretending to want this? I knew only those two options: lead her on or scrape her off. The truth was too much. It was too much; I was thirteen. No one in this school was like me. No one in this town, as far as I knew, was like me. Bad people were like me. Dead people were like me.

"What was that?" Boyd Wren said after she'd walked away.

His voice made me realize there were other people around, people who were knowing. This was already happening.

"Not stag anymore?" Boyd added.

"She asked me, I didn't know how to say no."

"She's cool," he said casually. He scratched at my locker with his thumb. "Me, I figure I'll still go stag. I don't like to be tied down."

***

This was the opposite of Jessica. I was afraid to tell the other guys about Taylor. The reason Taylor was so devastating was that she would've been, should've been, exactly the girl for me. Cute. My height. Perfect. But when you're hiding, like I was, the sweetest girl is the most dangerous. Her perfection was like a looming spotlight three steps behind an escaping prisoner.

When the guys found out about her they found out through Boyd. I volunteered it to no one, including, especially, my parents. It felt like a secret, a perilous secret wrapped in a much bigger secret. It hadn't occurred to me that getting a fake girlfriend could be a good disguise. I was too afraid that if I tried playing a role I would fail so spectacularly that my secret would be laid open and made obvious to the farthest reaches of any audience. Better not to play, better just to stay the same, the same as yesterday and the year before, when no one asked questions, when lack of interest was normal and taken for granted and OK, when there was no pretending necessary and I was only me.

***

"I saw Tyson's mother at the bank today," my own mother said at dinner. The dance was just a few days away now and had invaded dinner too. "We talked about how we can't wait to see you boys all dressed up in your suits. She's going to take pictures. Oliver, I told her you'd kill me if I take pictures, but she says I should — as mothers we deserve to take pictures."

I felt sideswiped. Pictures? Posing? I hadn't

anticipated any of this.

"Oliver?"

"I don't want you to."

"Ollie," my father said, "let your mother take pictures. It'll only take up a minute."

"You can't. No one else's moms are going."

"*All* of the other mothers are going. I'm not going to follow you into the dance, I just want to see you and your friends all dressed up."

"No. No, you have to just drop me off and leave."

"Ollie, do I embarrass you that much? I'm not going to dress as a clown, for heaven's sake."

I finished my dinner in silence. I could feel my eyes were wide, frozen, too big to close.

***

As evening on Saturday approached, my mother reminded me again and again, with increasing urgency, that I needed to start putting on my suit. My last best hope had been to forget to go to the dance, but no one was letting me.

I pulled the suit out of my closet and dropped it on the floor, a small protest. Before closing the door I stood looking into the darkness at the other end, the good end. Tucked behind a shoebox of dusty G.I. Joes was a square of shiny contact paper with the name *Micah* written on it in block letters. The name-tag of a boy I'd known—just seen, really—at summer camp between sixth grade and seventh. I had rescued it crumpled from the trash, where Micah tossed it after walking away into eternity on the last day. I had smoothed it and pressed it to the inside of my t-shirt, rode home with it against my skin.

I had told myself I wanted his name, wanted his

looks, his smile, admired his skills with whittling sticks and heading soccer balls. That's all, and for a while I believed it. But I started telling myself about him, too, at night when I was in bed, when I pushed my pajamas and underwear down around my ankles and rubbed against the smooth sheets.

Now, crawling under hanging clothes and over scattered shoes, I sat in the closet holding Micah's name-tag. Its backside, fuzzy with t-shirt fibers and stray hairs, was no longer sticky. On the shiny side I could see my blurry reflection; his name in black went across my face.

From downstairs I heard my mother call again. I was running out of time.

***

"Try to have fun tonight, Ollie, OK?" my father said. I was standing in front of him, my back to his chest. He was tying my tie. I looked at him in the mirror. The top of my head was level with his throat. When the tie was tied he straightened my collar and put his hands on my shoulders and turned me around. He looked into my eyes. "You're so serious all the time. Loosen up a little." He punched my arm lightly. "It's a dance, not the end of the world. People actually have fun at these."

After he left the bathroom I looked at myself in the mirror. People had fun, but I wasn't people. The suit, the tie. They had dressed me up for my execution.

***

Here's what I knew: That I was in the car on my way to be the date of a girl and I had no flower to give her. Amid all my worries this was the most tangible, the one I was guaranteed to confront. But I couldn't get a flower because I needed my mom to buy the flower. And I couldn't tell my mom I needed a flower because then she'd know I had a date, and she'd know I didn't want a date, and why. And then? And then...? I couldn't see anything after that. There was nothing after that. It was gray static, like the end of a videotape.

My mom looked over at me. "I really wish you'd worn your suit jacket, Oliver."

***

We rolled to a stop in front of the school, in a lot full of kids and parents.

"I'll pick you up at nine," my mother said, but I was already out of the car. She sighed. "Are you sure I can't get out?"

I pretended not to hear. Reaching back, I swung shut the door. I wanted her to leave before she had a chance to talk to anyone.

Kids were milling around the playground, posing for photos while waiting to be let into the school. The boys in their suits were easy to recognize but I was shocked by how different the girls looked—their hair was up, they had makeup on, their gowns brushed poofily against the basketball lines on the blacktop. Why could we not have worn jeans?

And some couples were holding hands; I averted my eyes. My awareness of Micah, my awareness that I was aware of him, this had been private knowledge, an unfortunate fact, easy to keep under wraps. I thought I'd be able keep it under wraps forever. A perpetual bachelor. Why would anyone know? Why would it ever come up? But tonight it was being brought up, in supposed celebration. With gowns and balloons. Wait, what? Balloons? It didn't even make sense.

I spotted Tyson at the back of the playground, standing alone beside a telephone pole. He had on khakis and a wide argyle tie. He was kicking at the dirt as though his life depended on it.

"Seen Taylor?" he said when I walked over.

"Nope," I said while gazing around nervously. "This is stupid already." I hadn't watched my mother leave but our car was no longer in the lot so she must have complied. I still didn't see Taylor either. Maybe she forgot. Maybe she was sick. I found myself hoping she got in a car accident on her way here—then I felt funny and looked down at my shoes. This thing I was was making me wish things like that about someone like Taylor Corgan, who wore pink barrettes and was obsessed with butterflies in third grade. This thing I was made me want her to die.

Dwight and Michael showed up together. Michael's parents were flaky so Dwight's sometimes looked after him. We had to pose for photos.

"Are you boys all going stag?" asked Dwight's mom from behind the flash. The word was like a taunt now.

"'Cept for Ollie," said Tyson.

"Ollie's got a girlfriend," Michael snickered.

"Where is she, Ollie? Do you want to get her in the picture?"

I shrugged.

Mrs. Macklin pursed her lips. "You're still missing Boyd too," she observed, then snapped a few more shots.

Soon Mr. Allen, our principal, pushed open the double doors and kicked down the doorstops. Behind him the cafeteria was lit in a rosy glow.

"They're giving you dinner?" Dwight's mom asked, slipping the camera into her purse.

"Spaghetti," Michael said.

"Dwight, don't eat any ricotta, remember. I don't want you getting the squirts in your suit."

"*Mom*," Dwight said.

Locked in my group's gravity I approached the mass of students funneling into the cafeteria. Moments after I passed inside, a hand seized my wrist.

"There you are," said a girl named Erika. Erika was friends with Taylor. "She's been *waiting* for you."

She pulled me alone toward a row of windows, the kind with chicken wire between the panes. Taylor was leaning against one of them, her palms cupping her elbows against her chest. Her gown was yellow, patterned with sunflowers. These were the only flowers between us; when she saw my hands were empty, that I had neither a corsage nor even something wild picked at the edge of the playground, disappointment saddened her face. She quickly covered it with a smile.

"The streamers are cool," I said, looking around, flushed with my inability to meet her one request.

"You look handsome, Ollie," she said.

"Thanks." A reflex of manners made me want to add *You too*, but if I did that, what would be next?

Around us chairs were beginning to scrape across the tile as couples took seats at the tables we ate at every day, but which tonight looked glamorous, with white paper cloths and narrow vases holding roses and sprigs of baby's breath. The other half of the cafeteria was cleared, the extra tables and chairs stacked high against the walls to allow for a dance floor.

"Should we sit down?" said Taylor, waiting to be led.

"Um. I guess. I'm going to go make sure Boyd gets here OK first, OK?"

"Oh. But. You'll be back? Should I find us a table?"

I didn't know what to say so I tried to smile, but my face felt as stiff as my brain.

On my way to the door I passed the table Tyson and Michael and Dwight had chosen. It had a few empty chairs; Tyson was draping his suit jacket over the one beside his, I assumed to save it for Boyd.

"Going out to wait for Boyd," I said.

"Should we save you a seat?" Michael asked.

"What?"

I exited the cafeteria confused. Was I expected to sit with my friends? Of course not. But if Michael thought I could, then *I* could think I could. Taylor could sit with her friends and I could sit with mine. That would be OK. I realized my hands were shaking.

I sat down on the curb and watched the parking lot. Behind me someone—Miss Onedo—told me the spaghetti was on its way out.

"Just waiting for Boyd Wren," I told her. "It's important that I make sure all my friends get here."

I heard her laugh at me, even as I was realizing how stupid I sounded, how earnest. As if I had a goal, as if it were important—I wasn't hiding, I was working. I wasn't being hideous, I was being thoughtful.

I only had the luxury of waiting a few minutes before Boyd, in suit and tie, spilled out of his parents' red minivan. I walked him inside.

"My dad doesn't know how to tie a tie," he explained, smoothing the white silk against his black shirt, "so we had to get one of the neighbors." He looked around. "Where are you and Taylor sitting?"

15

"Taylor's probably with her friends," I said. A glance confirmed she was with Amy; both of them were looking at me expectantly. "I'll sit with you guys."

"Ollie, that's lame. You should go sit with her, you're her date."

"It's fine. It's just spaghetti."

It wasn't just spaghetti, though. Not to the hair-netted lunch-ladies who volunteered to cook it for us on the only night we were polite enough to say thank you. Not to the chaperons overseeing their charges' first tottering steps into adulthood. And not to all my classmates, in their suits, in their gowns, paper napkins carefully draped across their laps, spinning pasta on dented forks delicately so as not to spray sauce. Not even to me; it felt like a last meal to me. While I ate I felt like everyone's eyes were on me, willing me to get up and go sit with Taylor. Under that weight I twirled my spaghetti and breathed.

***

Stag.

Stag had offered me an escape, a chance even to have fun, the way Boyd and Michael and Tyson were having fun now, doing robotic dance moves under the colored lights. The only thing stag had required was that I commit to it. I had balked, I had failed to commit.

Now I was being punished. Now I was standing at the edge of the cafeteria beneath a tower of stacked chairs, seeing intermittently past dancing bodies the tears-moistened cheeks of Taylor Corgan glistening in the lights. Now I was feeling the weight in my chest, the breath I couldn't get a hold of. I had imagined that not sitting with Taylor at dinner would make her forget about me, lose interest, find someone better, but I was wrong, it had only made everything afterward more important. Not sitting with her at dinner was rude. Turning down her offers to dance was monstrous.

Yet I did turn them down, again and again—when the offers came from her friends, when they came from mine. Even when I saw in her eyes the dawning realization that the night she had so looked forward to was crumbling around her like a dream scraping into a nightmare. Even when she cried and pretended not to be crying.

My friends, realizing it was up to them to salvage things for a crying girl in a sunflower dress, turned on me at 8:30, when there was only a half-hour left. I was not only a monster then but an outnumbered one, which was the only thing worse.

"Ollie, jeez, *look* at her," Boyd said, directing my eyes across the dance floor with a stab of his hand. "You need to go dance with her while you still have time."

"She's been crying half the *night*," Tyson said. And it was true: Erika and Amy were ministering to Taylor with tissues and plastic cups of water, and casting furious glares at me.

"I'm waiting for the right song."

"Never mind the song. Just go dance!"

"I'm stag."

"You're not stag, Ollie, you're her date," Boyd said. "Stop being such a fucking wimp."

Having the swear word directed at me in anger for the first time startled me. And from *Boyd?*

"I'll do it when I'm ready, Boyd, so leave me alone."

I turned toward the chicken-wire windows and put my elbows on the sill. I was face to face with my own awful reflection. This time shadows of wire crisscrossed my skin but they might as well have been Micah's handwritten name. I closed my eyes tight and counted. Before I hit three something yanked me back toward the dance floor, a yank that closed my throat. Tyson was pulling me by my tie.

"Come, Ollie," he said, as though to him I were an obstinate dog. He dragged me a few feet, past a few dancing couples, before my struggling outweighed his commitment. And when he released me my instinct wasn't to punch him or scream, but to straighten my tie and get everything back to normal. No one could see how much my throat hurt or how much my heart weighed, but they could see my tie.

Then Boyd, from behind, grabbed my shoulders and started steering me toward Taylor. I stretched my legs out stiffly to brace myself but he was bigger than I was, and stronger. My rubber-soled shoes scuffed jerkily across the tile; the squeaking wasn't audible over the music but I could feel the rigid vibrations rattling painfully up my bones.

"Boyd!" I yelled, half crying. "Leave me alone!"

I wrestled out of his grip near the center of the dance floor and we stood there beneath the mirror ball, breathing hard, looking at each other, and I hated him. I hated him so much.

"Whatever," he said, lights playing over his face. "But see those tears?" He pointed to where Taylor was standing, though now she was facing the wall, unable to bear watching a boy resist so strenuously the possibility of being near her. "The last song is coming up. You better fix this."

"Fuck off."

I smoothed my tie and looked around. Tyson's face

was red and Michael had glasses-magnified tears in his eyes. He rubbed his chin helplessly. I spotted Jessica Parson dancing by herself, dancing like she had dodged a bullet. I put my head down and walked out into the hall.

There was a bulletin board out there that usually showcased school news and activities but tonight had been covered over with a giant sheet of white paper, beckoning autographs and notes from our class of graduates. I stood in front of it, hands in pockets, reading while I waited for my heartbeat to slow. Dwight was drawing a Ninja Turtle in the bottom corner, had been for a while. He hadn't seen any of the fight. He hadn't really been in the cafeteria since dinner. Why was he excused from it and I wasn't?

All around his drawing people had written things like *Best night ever* and *Paul hearts Melissa* and *LMS Class of 93 4ever.* Happy things, evidence of an ease I couldn't imagine for myself. Out of all the messages only one resonated with me: *I'm so sad I feel like crying,* a T.C. had written. Beside it was a heart with a sad face. I closed my eyes. It's your fault, Taylor, I thought. You did this. I was minding my own business. I didn't want to hurt anybody.

I leaned against the board. A handful of other kids were hanging out in the hall, bursts of elegance against the blue brick walls. Two girls examined their makeup in a compact they were sharing.

"Last song is coming up, Ollie," a voice bellowed. I turned and saw Erika at the second set of doors farther down the hall. "Are you really not going to dance with her?!"

I only shrugged, and hoped it carried across the

distance.

"What is wrong with you, Oliver Wade?" she yelled. "Are you a faggot or something?"

My vision blurred. Shadows of people around me raised their heads. Dwight stopped doodling and looked up at me.

"No!" I said. To me I sounded precisely like what I was, though: a person offended to be called out on a lie. "I just—don't—like to *dance.*"

Erika let out a ragged sigh and disappeared back into the cafeteria.

***

Outside the night air was cold on my face. The parking lot was amber-colored and silent; behind me music throbbed dully. I was shaking, my heart was pounding. I lowered my bum to the curb. I opened and closed my fists—my hands felt funny, twitchy, prickly; a numbness went up my arms, a numb buzzing. I was afraid I was having a heart attack. I had seen old people in movies grabbing their arms before keeling over. Superman's father. A sure sign. I grabbed my forearm, tried to squeeze away the buzzing. *Please don't die*, I whispered. *Please don't die.* Then it occurred to me that things might be easier if I did.

I rubbed tears out of my eyes with the back of my hand. I mocked the little yelps I couldn't contain. Stupid baby. Stupid fucking baby. I tried to get a handle on my breathing. I counted to ten, then twenty.

Would it always be like this?

***

Cars started to arrive. Parents sat idling. Some smoked, some got out and chatted among themselves. The music went silent. Behind me the school doors sprang open, placing me at the bottom of a rectangle of light that stretched a long shadow of me across the pavement. I was a dark form in a glowing box; silly, I had always dared to imagine it was the opposite.

Around me suited legs dashed past, gowns brushed against my shoulders, a river of eighth-graders high from dancing. Two legs stopped. I looked up. Boyd sighed.

"They're saying you don't even like girls," he said.

I didn't want to know who was saying it. "I like girls," I said. My throat was sore from holding back. "I just don't like to dance."

"Yeah, I can tell." He laughed, but it was a fake laugh. "Ollie, next time? Just go stag, man."

I looked up but didn't say anything.

I wanted him to apologize for pushing me, but he didn't. He smacked the back of my head and ran to the red minivan that was pulling into the lot. A moment later my mother arrived.

"Well?" she said cheerily as I slipped into the car and shut the door. "How was it?"

I shrugged and she frowned and we were quiet for a while. I pressed my mouth into a shape that might keep me from crying. My forehead bumped against the cool window. We waited in the traffic of exiting families. Ahead of us a bright red stoplight glowed.

"Did you not have fun?"

Again I only shrugged.

She sighed. It was an angry sigh. I could see in the reflection that she was looking at me, but I didn't look back.

Finally, as if having mustered it, she said, "It's your own fault, Oliver. What did I tell you? You decided a long time ago not to have fun and guess what? You have no one to blame now but yourself."

I raised my eyes to hers in the reflection. She really didn't know? She really had no idea? No, she thought I was just being a grouch. A curmudgeon. It seemed a good trade to be viewed that way. Better certainly than whatever she'd think if she knew about Micah. But how long could it last? For my classmates the events of tonight would blow over by Monday but they would never blow over for me. There could not be many more reprieves, I knew that now. People, a whole world of people, who used streamers and confetti to celebrate about themselves the very thing that in myself I most wanted to hide—these people would never stop pushing notes into my locker; they would never stop asking who I was taking to the dance. I couldn't keep closing my eyes to it. No. But when they asked, I could lie. I had done it tonight. First to Erika, then to Boyd. If someday my mother asked, I could lie to her too.

For a while we idled.

By the time the light turned green, I knew what the scariest part of this new lying life would be: that it had a flip side. That if I could lie, I could also someday tell the truth.

(Age 15)

Rainbow Subway

Somewhere down the line there was a disabled train. That's what the loudspeaker kept telling us. I didn't know what it meant by "disabled," though — whether the train had just run out of gas or had jumped the tracks and crashed through the front of a Dunkin' Donuts. All I knew was that I was going nowhere. Behind me the subway platform, empty when I'd arrived here a half hour ago, was getting crowded as passengers built up, bulky and monochrome in black and gray winter coats, hats, scarves. The city was weird.

Without stepping forward — because there was nowhere to step but into the open air in front of me — I craned my neck and looked over the edge of the platform, down along the snow-dusted tracks. No sign of a train. The people around me in their monochrome coats were mumbling to themselves, their gray breath like speech bubbles puffing past my shoulders. More people than you'd come across in a whole day in Lee. I felt pinched and all I could do was stand still.

Nervously I reached down and picked up my backpack, its padded straps stiff from the cold. I noticed my right foot was half on the bumpy caution strip that ran along the edge of the platform, so I repositioned to keep the tip of my sneaker just touching the strip. When I was younger I counted things, but these days I found comfort in clean lines that avoided bisection.

This weekend had made me want the comfort of clean lines. I had spent it with Dwight Macklin at his parents' condo here in Newton, a town right outside Boston, three hours east of Lee. Last summer when we were on our way to being sophomores, Dwight's father got a job and they moved here. Soon after that, Dwight stopped talking. He wouldn't speak anywhere, or for any reason. His parents, his new teachers, his doctor, everyone thought it must be because of the move, because he'd been ripped away from his friends.

"Dwight needs to see you, Ollie," my parents told me after Dwight's parents called them to plead for a visit. They had asked Boyd Wren and Michael to come too. (Tyson by that time was fully down the rabbit hole of St. Mark's, a private all-boys high school two towns over from Lee; we never even talked about him anymore.) Boyd flat-out said no, and Michael was starting to get popular and couldn't risk it. But they both knew what I knew: that whatever the reason for Dwight's mysterious silence, it wasn't because he missed us. We were his friends, so we knew Dwight didn't really have friends; Boyd, Michael, and me, we were just the guys he sat with at lunch. They thought I was stupid for agreeing to go. I told them my parents were making me, though they weren't. I guess I was curious.

Dwight was there at the train station when I arrived, standing gray and ghostlike beside his father. He looked different from how I remembered him. Six months will do that to a boy being pummeled by puberty, but this was more than that. He looked blank.

"Hi Dwight," I said. He didn't respond.

At his parents' prompting I gave him a rundown of what was going on back in Lee, at school, with the guys. It didn't take long—I was finished by the time we got to his condo—and the rest of the weekend I didn't say much else. Most of the time we sat at a drafting table in his bedroom and drew Ninja Turtles on big pieces of white paper. I was more into drawing race cars now but I knew the lines of the Turtles, the familiar curves of the head, the scars on the shell, the way the loops of the eye mask curled. My poses were static and statuesque, full of clean lines that helped me stay calm. Dwight drew them fluid and leaping.

"That's real good," I'd told him as I leaned over the drafting table examining his tumbling Donatellos. I was examining him, too. Dwight was not cute, had limp, pale hair and oddly-tinted glasses that made his eyes look small and bruised. But Dwight was a boy. I wondered what it would feel like to kiss him, if only because I thought I would get away with it. Dwight wouldn't yell at me or call me a faggot, because that would mean talking—and I knew that wasn't going to happen. So I had a small window of opportunity if I was going to try. Two days. Maybe it's why I had come. In Lee the boys wouldn't stay silent.

***

Shivering and jittery, I was carefully lining up the cuff of my coat sleeve with a horizontal stripe on my glove when I heard the honk of a train. Approaching headlights lit the polished tracks. Around me people started to chatter. "About time." "Not quite frozen to death yet." "Probably be packed." I looked behind me and saw how many more passengers were there than when I'd arrived, how many had accumulated. I started feeling more nervous. What if the people at the back got restless before the train pulled into the station? What if they pushed the whole mass forward and shoved me onto the tracks? I took a step backward and felt someone's elbow or bag or child push into my kidney.

I held my breath as the train rolled past, a scrim of snow on its windshield, and when it stopped and the doors folded open, I got on. There were a few open seats but I didn't sit down because I was afraid I'd never be able to fight my way off if I did. Instead I stood facing a window looking out at the platform while people poured in around me, like cereal pieces gathering around the prize. With half of the people still on the platform waiting to board, the doors started dinging and trying to close. I saw panic come into their eyes when they realized that after waiting so long they were losing their chance.

***

I had thought about kissing Dwight while we drew, while we watched TV, while we ate pizza. I thought about it when his parents gave us ten dollars and directions to an ice-cream place up the street. He wouldn't order, of course, and while I perused the menu for a sundae for him I wondered if I could mold him, this silent outline of a person, into a boy-shaped receptacle for these things I felt that no other boys felt. He had lips and a body and if I asked him to fall in love with me he wouldn't say no because he wouldn't say anything at all. And that, at least, would be something.

But through the long night I kept myself cocooned in

the beige sleeping bag on the floor near Dwight's bed. I knew I wasn't about to steal a moment, even from a boy who wouldn't protest. A stolen moment, even if it was good, would hurt because it would never be anything more. I doubted sometimes that I would even take one willingly if it was ever offered.

"Do you think you'll ever have anyone, Dwight?" I had asked in the dark. I wasn't expecting a reply and didn't get one, just the rustle of blankets when he moved his legs. "I can't imagine a single scenario where someone I wanted to be with would want to be with me."

***

Facing the train window, I could see my reflection. The reflection was a boy who liked boys, my only chance at seeing one who did. I looked to see what he looked like, this boy who liked boys. I looked at his eyebrows and his nose, at his wondering eyes that looked back at me, back and back to infinity.

Beyond my reflection the scenery started to slide sideways. The train picked up speed and rolled for a few minutes and then stopped at the next station, but only to trade a few passengers on and off. Angry people waiting on the platform shouted at us to move in, but we were already packed tight and there was nowhere for anyone to go. The people on the platform looked in the windows at us, inspecting for open space we might cavalierly be wasting. I wished for the train to pull away so they'd stop looking. I moved my hand to keep it from bisecting a streak of black-markered graffiti on the metal handrail. Then there was an announcement that we were standing by until further notice.

***

I rolled up the beige sleeping bag and put it on the bed beside Dwight, who was lying there looking out the window at the street, his untied shoelaces dangling off the end of the mattress. Watching him, I grew twitchy with an anger that came, I think, from knowing that my window of opportunity for kissing a boy had closed.

"If you never speak up you're going to be alone your whole life, Dwight," I spat, hating him for the thing that was so familiar in me. There was a sinisterness in my voice that made me feel bold. If I wouldn't kiss him, there were other, more common things you could do to someone who wouldn't try to stop you. "At least I hope you are, you fucking weirdo."

I punched my sweatpants into my backpack and zipped it shut. "I'm never coming back, just so you know," I said. "You lost your chance."

If he had looked at me with any regret or hurt or anything even human I may have put on my backpack and walked quietly out of the room. But when he didn't, I threw it down and jumped onto his bed, my sneakers sinking into the mattress on either side of his thin torso. I dropped to my knees and pushed one knee into his gut. His eyes bugged darkly behind his glasses and he gasped but still didn't speak. I grabbed his sweatshirt in my fists and knocked him against the mattress until his glasses fell off. I wanted to hear him hate me. I wanted to hear him acknowledge that he was lonelier than I was.

***

Motion on the platform outside made me lift my heavy

eyes. I expected it to be another irate would-be passenger, but they were all looking at newspapers or pacing or gazing longingly down the tracks the way we had come. Instead it was a boy on the platform—my age, a little older, probably fifteen or sixteen—swinging the braided strings that dangled from the ear flaps on his cherry-red hat. He looked taller than me and had big green eyes. He was wearing a blue Patriots jacket and lime-green gloves, a burst of rainbow brightness against all the bleak black and gray. He was already looking at me when I noticed him. He turned his head away, then looked back at me again and smiled with chapped lips. He raised his eyebrows and they went up under his hat—it was a conspiratorial look, as if our eye contact were a joke shared between us. Or something more?

I checked the people on either side of me (though I knew it was me he was looking at), then pointed to myself and raised my own eyebrows questioningly. He laughed. I couldn't hear anything through the barrier of window glass but a burst of breath bloomed around his face and his lips parted to show teeth that were railroaded with blue braces. He nodded. *Yes, you. Hi.*

My heart started pounding inside all my layers and I felt fully awake for the first time all day. The glass between us made me feel bold. I wiggled my nose like a rabbit. The green-eyed boy wiggled his. Then he tugged on the strings of his red hat, bobbing his head side to side and making a sound I could tell from his lips was *boop boop boop*.

Was he making fun of me? It was easy to think he was, maybe even comforting to think that, because that was familiar territory. But people don't usually smile and turn pink-cheeked when they're making fun of you, the way they do when they're flirting. I looked around again, afraid of who might be seeing us two boys blushing. The man on my left was reading a *People* magazine. The woman on my right was examining her fingernails. This might be a trick or a setup, but the boy's face was so friendly.

Now he stuck out his tongue, just the little red tip of it, like the end of a strawberry. When he pulled his hat down over his eyes, I did the same. In our shared darkness I smiled my biggest cheesy smile and bobbed my head side to side, not even sure he could see me. When I pushed my hat back up to check, he was gone.

***

"I really hoped you'd be able to get through to him, Ollie," Dwight's mother had said when she was driving me to the subway at the end of my visit. "But I guess it was too much to expect."

"I'm really sorry," I told her softly — it was almost a whisper. She didn't know it but I had made her son cry that morning — and myself too, while I had fixed his sweatshirt and his hair and put his glasses back on his face.

"Well Ollie, it's not your fault, you're not a therapist. We just thought...." She watched the road for a minute and then looked at me again, a kind of searching in her eyes. "He really didn't say *anything*? That whole time?"

I shook my head. "Maybe I'm just not the person he needs?"

***

As I leaned forward to try to see more of the platform outside, my glove slipped off the handrail and I almost

30

knocked my face against the window. The woman with the fingernails looked at me and smirked but didn't say anything. I couldn't see the green-eyed boy anywhere. How could he have just disappeared? I saw that the people on the platform were almost a mirror image of the passengers on the train. Same black and gray coats, same eyes gazing down. But it wasn't exactly a mirror image. There was only one me.

When I was starting to fear I'd imagined the boy, a lime-green-gloved fist rose up in front of the scratched glass. He must've been crouched against the side the train. One finger went up. Then two. A countdown. As the third was going up the rest of the boy bounced up too. The liftoff, like a spaceman. Smiling, as if this had been a great surprise (and it had been), he hopped on his sneakers a few times and then stepped closer to the glass.

"I thought you were gone," I mouthed.

He grinned, shook his head slowly. "Just fooling," he mouthed. I wished I could know what his voice sounded like. I knew it would be beautiful.

I stuck my tongue out and he stuck his out and smiled. All of a sudden I knew I was going to cry again today, though I wasn't sure why, because now I felt happy.

The boy took off his hat, surprising me with hair that was black as night. It stuck up in tall staticky spikes for a second before the breeze smoothed it. He pulled his hat on over his face like a feedbag and, holding the strings out at the sides by his ears, rotated them like antennae. I looked down and wiped my eyes with my sleeve.

Suddenly the train started to make noise, as if coming to a horrible kind of life. The boy yanked his hat off his face and stared at me. "Oh," he whispered, and his pink lips held the shape.

The snap on my shivering coat sleeve was clicking against the metal rail like an alarm. The doors dinged, opened and closed. The train lurched a few feet and the boy walked to follow it.

I didn't have time to think, so I just mouthed it. He was looking at me and I was sure he was seeing when I mouthed the three words I had come to feel for him in the small eternity of these last few minutes. I didn't think about what it would ruin for me, for my imagination, if he recoiled.

But his reaction was another smile, one maybe a little surprised and brighter than before. He looked happy. I'd told a boy I loved him and he looked happy.

So this was him. *So this is you.* A red hat, lime-green gloves, green eyes, jet-black hair: this was what a boy who liked boys looked like, too. He reached up and with two strokes of one finger in the dirt and salt on the window he drew a plump heart. Near the bottom point, near where the heart's curves would've met, his finger started dragging a horizontal line across the glass as the train started moving away from him. With his other hand, the boy waved.

A moment later I couldn't see him anymore.

"I need to get off," I gasped, crying, pushing against people who weren't moving, who wouldn't move for me, who had no space for me. "This is my stop. I need to— It's my only—"

"Kid, you missed this one," said the guy with the magazine, barely raising his eyes. "Next one's not far."

Not far. He had no idea what *far* was. This chance, this boy, I couldn't, I didn't even know his *name*. He was here, the other one like me, the one who wouldn't merely not say no but who had said *yes*. I discovered him only to lose him? How could that be?

I tried taking a deep breath. The landscape sped by, cars, trees, buildings, streetlights, all of it filtered through the crosshatch of gray streaks on the window, jagged like bolts of lightning. Lines were crossing everything everywhere. I was afraid I might faint.

But the heart was there, too. I focused on it. The smooth curves in the grit. He'd drawn it smiling. He'd known I was leaving and still he'd drawn it smiling. How could the boy like me afford to let the boy like him go, without tears or agony, without an explosion of the loneliness I had long been sure would define my whole life?

How? I was suddenly sure it was because he'd already learned the thing that was dawning on me now, that was coming to me like a sunrise: There were others. There were *others*. I was only one of them. He was only one of them, too.

At the station Dwight's mother had told me to take a series of trains that would get me from Newton to Worcester, where my mom would be waiting to drive me the two hours back to Lee. I had thought that trip would be as bleak and gray as Dwight's bedroom, as the subway platform, as everything I knew. But what ended up happening that day was that I rode the green train to the red train, to the purple train, to the orange and silver city, where my mom was waiting in our white car to drive me through all of the snow-blue hills, to the yellow house in Lee, home.

(Age 16–17)

Dial Up

All I wanted was to get to Boyd Wren. And all I kept hearing was "Goodbye!"

It was delivered in a robotic monotone that after all this time sounded dickish to my reddening ears. Every time I heard it was a surprise, too—and not a surprise. Because how many times had it been?

Entwined in a net of telephone cord and mouse cord and laptop power cord, I slammed back against the living-room couch and raked my hands through my hair. The shitty bastard of a service would not connect. Again and again, over and over, I heard the dial tone, the chirpy grind of the modem, the epic pause teasing the possibility that I might finally be allowed online... then that too-cheery "Goodbye!"

Eighty-six times so far tonight.

Busy signals. Too much traffic. Fucking America Online. Why did they mail out those trial CDs by the truckload when they couldn't handle the customers they already *had*? Didn't they know I depended on this, that this was my lifeline? No, of course they didn't, and I would've hated them—anyone—knowing.

"Ollie," my mother called to me from the kitchen, where she and my father were making popcorn or something, "why don't you give it a rest and go do something else for a while? You're making us crazy."

I ignored her. I was thinking of Boyd, not her. I sat up and chose a new phone number from the list of local options (much more of this and I'd start trying long distance). Again the dial tone, the chirpy grind—but the pause that followed the grind this time seemed longer, long enough to give me time to reposition the laptop perfectly along the edge of the coffee table, for a little extra luck. Then I got smacked with another "Goodbye!"

I punched the couch cushion and screamed.

"Ollie, language," my father shouted.

My mother added, "You could try *calling* your friends if you're so anxious to chit-chat with them."

"They're already *online!*" I screamed. I was losing it. "That means you *can't* call them. And it's not *chit-chat*, it's *chat*. Why won't this fucking thing *connect?!*"

"Ollie, Jesus, *language*," my father yelled amid bursts of popping corn.

The screen in front of me blurred as tears pooled in my eyes. Quickly I slapped them away with my sweatshirt sleeve. I took a breath. I needed to remember: I couldn't let my parents see how this was killing me. There was no acceptable reason why I should be this desperate to chit-chat, as my mother called it.

Again I clicked *Sign On*. I'd been doing this for forty-five minutes now. Dial tone. Modem grinding.

"Oll-*ieee*," my father groaned.

The pause was long. I held my breath. This time the yellow cartoon man lit up, started jogging, told me "Welcome!," ushered me through the sign-on screen to the home screen.

"Thank god," I heard my mother whisper from the dwindling edge of my consciousness.

Onscreen my buddy list drew itself alive and overwrote all other things. The only name on it—the only name *ever* on it—was the only name I cared to see: BoydyBoy. Leaning forward, I clicked him. And connected.

OwOw0: Yo yo yo yo yo
BoydyBoy: hey
OwOw0: It took me 88 tries. Almost 45 mins. I was going fcukin insane in the membrane
BoydyBoy: AOL blows donkey dick. but here you are.
OwOw0: Here I am....
BoydyBoy: I hope its worth it, haha
OwOw0: Hahaha. you better make it worth it.
Boydyboy: so much pressuuure.

My cheeks were flushing; they always did. It *was* worth it—the waiting, the agony—just knowing Boyd Wren was there on the other side of that screen, at the end of a short trip through some wires. Even if he had no idea why. It was enough just to see his name: Boydyboy. The letters were blue and seemed to bounce.

OwOw0: I kinda thought you wouldve logged off by now though.

I'd been terrified of it. Sometimes the busy signals only delayed me getting to him; other times they made me miss him completely.

Boydyboy: Nah i've been poking around
OwOw0: Cool cool

I dared to wonder, like always, if he'd been waiting for

me. Every night, in my deepest, secret, closeted hopes I imagined him watching his buddy list the way I watched mine whenever his name was missing from it. It was intoxicating to imagine. And scary.

Boydyboy: how goes your science fair project *cough cough* bullshit?

OwOw0: It's driving me to Nervous-breakdown City, Boydyboy.

Boydyboy: mine is not too shabby if I do say so...

OwOw0: fuck you and your liquid nitrogen demo. haha. has anyone ever used liquid nitro in thier project and not won their science fair?

Boydyboy: it's comin out good. after i'm done using it to freeze everything in site i'll use some to heat up your cold cold heart.

Without thinking I flopped over on the couch and looked dreamily at the laptop screen from the cushion where my cheek rested. I pulled the laptop onto my chest.

OwOw0: you know nothing could warm my lump of pulminary coal.

Boydyboy: Hahahaaah

OwOw0: Meanwhile i'll be there with my friggin zoetrope project!!

Boydyboy: Hahaha. yes. so what did you build exactly?

OwOw0: Well I built the zoetrope, which is a ring of posterboard (like imagine a lampshade) with a little window cut in it. inside the ring is another ring with a series of pics drawn around it..... The inner ring spins, and you see the pics through the window. and the movement makes them animate, like a flip-book. IN THEORY! However, I made the inner ring too big, so it's too tight. and the bastard does not SPIN.

Boydyboy: so what! Mr gruber is a lightweight... as long as you made the effort he'll grade you OK. it sounds somewhat cool.

OwOw0: HAHA! "Somewhat." Eat a dick, Boyd.

Boydyboy: haahahaha

OwOw0: everyone is gonna look at it and say "What's a zoo-trophy?" It's pitiful, you'll see. However: the way I wrote "Zoetrope" on it is fucking awesome!

Boydyboy: That should get you a B+ right there.

OwOw0: I don't even care. I've got other more important things to worry about in life than zoo-trophys.

Boydyboy: seriously. fucking sci fairs. we'll be out soon though. i can't wait till college, Ollie bolly bo bolly.

Yeah, everything Boydyboy said made me happy. The way he gave me shit about stuff, the way he bounced my name across the screen like a rubber ball: *Ollie bolly bo bolly.* The way he almost never talked about girls and the way he griped if I logged off too early. At the end of our chat sessions, which sometimes went three or four hours, my face hurt from smiling.

***

At the science fair Boyd froze a wart off the vice principal's thumb but his project didn't win. Probably that was because his liquid nitrogen sat undemonstrated for most of the fair while he hung out at my table, on the other side of the school gym, playing with my zoetrope.

"Look," he said, showing me how he'd gotten the inner ring to spin more freely. The little animation was flowing better. "Your car cartoon actually moves now."

"How did you do that?"

He handed me the zoetrope and I saw that he'd folded a wrinkle into the posterboard to make the ring smaller.

"Well aren't you a genius, Professor Wren," I groaned.

Smugly he crossed his arms over his thin chest and perched his butt on the edge of my table, behind which I sat like I was having a yard sale. I looked at his back, at his thin yellow t-shirt, and the butt of his favorite pants, brown corduroys he'd had since freshman year. I had watched, over time, those corduroys grow worn spots on the bum and knees that eventually opened to holes that showed underwear and skin. I thought of them as my holes: I'd been around when they were born and I'd loved them as they grew. Sometimes when he was sitting I could glimpse pale white moons of his skin through the holes in the thighs.

Scratching his blond, cowlicky hair he said, "It looks like I'm being judged."

I looked over to his table across the gym. Mr. Gruber was standing beside it with a clipboard. "You should probably go over there," I said.

"Eh." He sighed.

He went, though—stopping on the way to tie one of his black Adidas soccer shoes. I watched him explain his project to Mr. Gruber, while with one finger I idly spun my zoetrope.

***

Because Boyd seemed to like my little animation of a car chase, I spent the whole next weekend creating a real-life, stop-motion version on my bedroom floor. Using a feature on my family's camcorder I filmed Matchbox cars I had dusted off from childhood skidding across carpet, zooming around bureau legs. Frame by frame. It took me hours to create fifteen seconds of video. There were small plastic animals involved, and an explosion made from crumpled scraps of yellow and orange construction paper. On Monday at school I lent him the animation on videotape and that evening suffered through thirty-one disconnects waiting to hear what he thought of it. When I finally got online he was there. A message popped up.

Boydyboy: i watched your lil movie 6 times

Six times. I could feel myself glowing. At some point he had become someone I wanted to impress.

Owow0: Oh yeah? Cool. you like it?
Boydyboy: yeah, its fuckin awesome. those explosions must've been impossible!
Owow0: Hehehehhe.... Thanks! How about the billygoat that showed up at the end? Did you like him?
Boydyboy: yeah... especially when he pulled the guy out of the burning reck...
OwOw0: That was the hardest part to animate, making all his legs move right... not to mention the flames.
Boydyboy: it was Spielberg level shit thoguh Ollie.
OwOw0: Hehehe...*grin*

After that he kept the tape for weeks, forgetting and forgetting to return it to me. When he finally did, the inner air of the cassette and its paper box smelled like his bedroom. Like his deodorant and his t-shirts and his socks and his sheets. In the dark of my own room I inhaled the Boyd-smell from the inner guts of the cassette and felt my heart swell as well as my penis — a combination so perfectly yin and yang I knew it was love.

Sometimes after saying goodnight and logging off I would lie in bed wondering when all these feelings for Boyd started happening. It felt recent, but it wasn't as if I'd just met him; I'd known him since at least kindergarten and we'd been best friends since third grade. Even before we'd gained and lost Dwight, even before we'd gained and lost Tyson (who went to St. Mark's) and Itchy Chin Mike (who hung with the popular kids now), even before there was *OwOw0* and *Boydyboy* or even an Internet to dial in to, there was *Ollie and Boyd*. It was how life was. We were juniors in high school now and I knew that at some point my mind had twirled our "and" into an ampersand, and then started wanting to shape it into a heart.

Maybe I couldn't remember the exact moment it happened because it was still happening — daily, nightly. Falling in love isn't like jumping out of an airplane; it's not like taking a leap. It's like opening your eyes one day and discovering you're already in the air.

***

In real life, loving Boyd was an easy mixture of longings and satisfactions. A longing to see his Jeep pull in beside my Civic in the school parking lot; a satisfaction when it did. A longing to stand with him in the lunch line; a satisfaction when he would show up and roll his blue eyes at lumpy mashed potatoes. Seeing Boyd in school was a fact of life as old as we were, and the days were reined in — even when we were alone together — by habit and precedent, by customs and boundaries it felt impossible not to observe. You know? I wasn't going to say anything in school. I wasn't going to take chances. A boy with a secret is a conservative boy.

Online—that was new territory, a Wild West into which a new Ollie & Boyd appeared fresh at age sixteen. Often we were groggy, silly, giddy there; crude and lewd and snarky. School nights soared past 1:00 or 2:00 a.m., weekend nights went till dawn, when it felt to me like we were the only two people awake in the world. Online the boundaries were so much looser, had to be felt out and decided upon one at a time, IM by IM. Online my longings were untethered from routine. I dared to want more than just to see him. I dared to want to tell him things. I dared to want him to know things. The one big thing I increasingly wanted to tell him was beyond any boundary, even here, but I came out with little things, the saying of which was probably half the reason the big thing had come to exist in the first place. Things like:

OwOw0: but anyway i'm feeling sad today I guess.
Boydyboy: lets hear it. I'm here..........

I was learning what everyone with a modem was learning: that communicating through text, going through the middleman of a chat window, was easier than talking face to face. In short, online I opened up.

OwOw0: well my dad is still cleaning out my grandma's house and he's having some trash guy come and get her mattress, and I had to help him carry it out into the yard tongiht. It's been a year since she died but it seems like last week. I still miss her a lot, it was weird. I didn't like seeing my gram's bed laying in the leaves... I don't know...the finality of it got to me or something. ...I don't know why I just told you that........

Boydyboy: because it was bugging you Ollie. why do you think i tell you all the shit that bugs me? it helps to tell.

OwOw0: Yeah, it does....... I guess it's a minor thing, a mattress. But I didn't want to let it hit the floor when I was carrying it through the garage, like I didn't want to get it dirty... I was like, Careful careful. Then seeing it just laying there in the leaves... It was the worst thing, Boyd.

Boydyboy: i understand

Online—when at any moment we could be slapped with a disconnect that could take an hour or more to fix—I ached for him. I imagined us as two isolated outposts connected by a fragile wire in a frozen void. I felt like I was reaching out, saying, *Still there?* And each word could be the last.

OwOw0: i know you understand Boyd. that's why you're my best friend.

***

After I hit a telephone pole on early-morning ice in November—probably because I was driving on three hours' sleep and a learner's permit—Boyd drove me to school for a week while my car went in for a new bumper. Bleary from our late nights online, we rode together those mornings side by side silently, almost silently, as though we hardly knew each other, like a cabbie and his passenger. The connection we were forging online didn't seem to be carrying over into real life. It made me wonder how much of what I thought was building between us was genuine and how much I was manufacturing. In chat sessions words were just words until I filtered them through desperation and hope.

In real life, when I could see the holes in his corduroys and hear his sleepy voice in the mornings, when I had Boyd Wren, we didn't talk about grandmothers. We didn't talk about dreams or how we were feeling. Instead I would say things like, "I've really been getting into the band R.E.M. lately." "Cool," he would say, his hair slicked back, still wet, if it was the morning; cowlicky again if it was the afternoon. "Yeah they're pretty cool," I would say. That was how we talked in person. The rest I would save for the night, when I had Boydyboy.

OwOw0: honestly though i think this band is changing my fuckin life Boyd

Boydyboy: REM? Do tell..

OwOw0: have you heard the song Losing My Religion?

Boydyboy: of Course. i think every one has heard that song.

OwOw0: i guess i had too because it was familiar but i never thought about it. but it came on the radio whlie I was driving around last week and it almost made me cry for some reason. the lyrics. he has something to confess and he can't say it. I almost had to pull over. it was like, wow. i went and bought the album immediately. when i listen it makes me feel like my body is being opened up and Michael Stipe (the singer) is personally nursing my wounded soul

Boydyboy: "deepness follows"

OwOw0: Hehe what?

Boydyboy: joking. you know the REM song Sweetness Follows. haha

OwOw0: I just have the 1 CD so far. Out OF Time. I'll have to get that one!

Boydyboy: why is your soul wounded Ollie?

OwOwo: haha what?

Boydyboy: you said your soul is wounded, why is it woudned?

OwOwo: i dunno just stuff I guess.

Boydyboy: "stuff"?

OwOwo: just some stuff I guess.

Boydyboy: hhmm. well get the CD with Sweetness Follows, it's good. and pay attention to it. maybe it can help to you know yourself better than you do now.

OwOw0: you think it can?

Boydyboy: i feel it will.

Sometimes he was cryptic like that—and god I could pack so much hope into anything cryptic. The more IMs we sent back and forth, the farther I felt we were breaking from real life, into a place that roiled with secret possibility. What if Boyd was like me? I knew there were others. What if he was one? What if Boyd felt the things I felt? What if Boyd was interested in my wounds because he had them too?

OwOw0: hmm I feel like i know mysefl too well sometimes. Just no one else knows me.

Boydyboy: it's the opposite for me. I see everything....... except maybe what's right in front of me.....................

OwOw0: how so?

Boydyboy: i don't think i have to explain it to you. i

hope i dont
OwOw0: No. I think I know how it is.
Boydyboy: ys. yes. i believe you do Ollie.
OwOw0: It's nice to have someone just "know" what you're talking about without needing some huge explanation.
Boydyboy: i know

Sometimes there seemed to be something hiding in his words, alluding to a deeper connection that was only ever one unsent IM from coming out. Mysterious things, things he hoped he wouldn't have to explain to me, things he hoped I would just *know*. But it was fleeting.

Boydyboy: so anyway, work sucked so much today. it's only been amonth but this Big D job sucks. Lady today was like make sure my eggs don't break and i was like i know how to bag your fuckin egg.s
OwOw0: Sorry to hear that. she sounds like a huge ass. ar eyou OK?
Boydyboy: I'm tired and frustrated. But mostly frustrated
OwOw0: Frustrated about what?
Boydyboy: oh, you know, life and love and STUFF. *sigh*

Love? His IMs could set me ablaze with hope. But although my hope was roaring, it was fragile, like the hottest fire that can nonetheless be snuffed out with a carton of old milk. I was always afraid of hearing too much. It was dangerous to ask for explanations or clarity. Instead I would agree with his vagueness as if I were catching his drift loud and clear. I could live with not knowing whether Boyd loved me, but I was terrified of finding out for sure that he didn't.

OwOw0: Yeah i'm frustrated too.... *sigh*

Boydyboy: life is frustrating overall.

OwOw0: at least you have a job though. and some money!

Boydyboy: what's the point of money if you dont have someone to spend it on.... i'll be back. I need a beer.

OwOw0: haha, really? Where do you get a beer??

Boydyboy: my dad won't notice, he has moooore than plenty. Who cares anyway. be back.

OwOw0: OK.

Boydyboy: back.

OwOw0: hi. did you get one?

Boydyboy: yup

OwOw0: My dad is away tonight. and my mom. their anniversary weekend.

Boydyboy: really? you didn't mention this. let's have a drinking party at your house then.

OwOw0: hahahaha. that would be amazing.

Boydyboy: you know it would. :-)

OwOw0: but a bad idea. who knows what we would say if we lost our inhibitions..........................

Boydyboy: oh? what might we say exactly>?

OwOw0: be right back

Boydyboy: OK..

Sometimes I would say things accidentally and panic, and wonder if it had really been an accident. I would look at the screen while my brain scrambled for excuses. Excuses that were codes that could lead to openings that could lead to everything. But only if he was looking.

OwOw0: Back.

Boydyboy: hi

OwOw0: I mean we're perverted enough when we're sober hahaha. Remember that would-you-rather thing where I told you I'd rather get fucked by a wolfhound than get fucked by Mrs Doyle with a strap-on dick?

Boydyboy: uh yeah. But I'm not feeling perverted now.

OwOw0: No i guess I'm not either.

Boydyboy: actually I'm kinda in a "why does the world have to be so hard" kind of mood.

OwOw0: I'm always in that kind of mood....I just try to push it back. I listen to REM

Boydyboy: yeah you've always got your REm don't you.

OwOw0: it soothes the pain.

Boydyboy: Is there someone out there? i always wonder. there might be someone........

I would imagine him looking, sitting in his room, in the dark, in his holey corduroys, nursing the beer with tears in his eyes.

OwOw0: I think there is boyd. I think I'm sure of it.

Boydyboy: i feel like it's too much to ask. can't raise hopes too high...

I would want to drive over to his house and put my arms around him, kiss all his cowlicks. I would — if I wasn't so afraid of him wanting me to.

OwOw0: I know how you feel...................

Boydyboy: Whatever. I don't even know what im talking about.

OwOw0: don't you?.... "Strange things I have in head, that will to hand / Which must be acted, ere they may be scanned."

Boydyboy: haha. did you just quote fucking Shakespeare at me?

OwOw0: we're reading MacBeth in English. i like that line.

Boydyboy: uh huh

OwOw0: :-(

Boydyboy: I'm going to get another beer. then hit the sack. I'll see ya

The near-miss moments in our chats always reminded me of that teasing pause the modem made when I was trying to get online—that moment of potential that fizzled into a failure to connect. Boyd and me, we kept getting the *Goodbye* instead of the *Welcome*.

***

OwOw0: Want to hear a secret?

Sometimes my strategy was to try to plant in his mind the notion that a secret existed. To get his hopes up, in case there were hopes to be got up. And, if I'm honest, if there were hopes, to make him slip and reveal them.

Boydyboy: Of course i want to hear a secret.

OwOw0: It's potentially embarrassing

Boydyboy: the best ones are.

I would let it dangle. Then I would yank it away.

OwOw0: .... I want to see the new Chucky movie, in all its killer-doll cheeziness. Oops... Did I really admit that?

A bait and switch. I felt bad doing it. It was mean. Secrets can make you mean.

Boydyboy: i thought it was going to be something juicy. :-(but those movies are good... you shouldnt have movie shame.
OwOw0: You like juicy things you perv. :-)
Boydyboy: HHAHaha. the juicier the better.
OwOw0: Hehehehe.
Boydyboy: hooheeheehaha!
OwOw0: Hoohahahahaha!!!
Boydyboy: BWUHAHAHAHAHA!!!!!!
OwOw0: Haha you win, I cant top that one.
Boydyboy: what the hell is wrong with us Oliver?
OwOw0: A good question Boy-o-Boyd.

And sometimes he would seem to do the same.

Boydyboy: want to hear a secret?
OwOw0: Is it juicy?
Boydyboy: :-/
OwOw0: Tell me.
Boydyboy: i will
OwOw0: Haha. tell meee!
Boydyboy: don't get pushy, ya pushy bastard.
OwOw0: just tell me boyd.

Sometimes he would take my breath away.

Boydyboy: Did you know that I'm in love?

Sometimes he would reduce me to a shivering mass in a world so suddenly silent my ears would ring. I would look at the screen, rub my eyes, wonder if I was reading him right.

OwOw0: Really? you're in love?

I would see the bait and wait for the switch.

Boydyboy: yes really.
OwOw0: OK
Boydyboy: I can't say who. nothing funky, no animals or objects or shit because I know how you think.. you perv.
OwOw0: you can tell me who it is.
Boydyboy: i don't know.... i know i can trust you not to say anything to anyone. but maybe it's me whose not ready yet.
OwOw0: you're right i wouldn't ever tell anyone.
Boydyboy: i need time............ but if i ever did tell anybody it would be you.

I suppose if there was a specific moment when I discovered I was in love with Boyd Wren, it was this one, the one when I suddenly believed he felt the same way. What he had said took more than my breath away now; it took all of me, everything I had understood about the world and myself and our friendship and what the rest of my life was going to look like.

Adrenaline coursed through me and I felt dizzy. There was no time to think through my response, no time to settle on a code. I had to go on instinct, and I was weighed down by my fearful unwillingness to gamble, however small a gamble I thought in that moment it might be, with this last piece of ambiguity between me and the end of my lifelong secret.

OwOw0: I really appreciate you feeling like you can tell me though.
Boydyboy: do you?
OwOw0: well my list of friends isn't huge, as you know. i'm glad we're that close.
Boydyboy: i'm gladwe are too. means a lot to me.

And then something happened.

OwOw0: I'm glad you specifieid that it wasn't an object because otherwise i would've said your Jeep. haha
Boydyboy: haha no it's a human.
OwOw0: because you never let me eat in that thing. HAHA

Even as I typed I couldn't believe I was turning it into a joke. If this was the moment I knew I was in love, you could say I wasn't ready to be in love. I was too filled with doubt to deal with being in love. I was exhilarated, but I was afraid. It wasn't only a fear of coming out and being out, it was a fear of losing him. Because the closer he got to saying who it was, the closer he was maybe getting to saying it wasn't me.

When I logged off, after we'd detoured away from the topic of his secret love and spent a few minutes talking about R.E.M., the chat window disappeared and I was left with nothing but my memory of the conversation to turn over in my mind.

***

The possibility of Boyd loving me was like a werewolf in my brain: comforting and plausible by day but a full-blown monster of delusion by the light of the moon. Yet I couldn't leave it alone. I threw up three times after he told me he was in love and my crooked-line ticks were ticking like mad, but I couldn't leave it alone. The next night when I logged on he was there. I started typing.

OwOw0: so I was pondering about who you might be in love with. heh.

He could see the laugh. *Heh.* The little giggle. He couldn't have known that I was shaking, that my guts felt twisted, that the weight of the world was on my fingertips as I pressed the keys. That I was looking for a way to break this open, in the most careful way I could find. That on second, third, and fourth thought, I needed an answer, even if it meant giving up my fantasy. I needed to know if it was me.

Boydyboy: oh really? pondering?
OwOw0: So are you gonna tell me who it is? C'mon, c'mon.... Who? Hehehehe.
Boydyboy: i can't tell...
OwOw0: Sure you can tell me.... I mean, remember the would-you-rather thing with Mrs Doyle and the strap-on? Surely this can't compare to THAT, in terms of embarrassing confessions.
Boydyboy: i don't know.... How about this. if you can guess right i'll tell you.
OwOw0: You want me to guess?

My fingers froze. I was suspicious of guessing. It seemed to blow away whatever upper-hand I had here.

Suddenly he disconnected without warning—his name disappeared from my buddy list. I thought about using that chance to slip away, to log off too to let the situation cool. But almost immediately, he was back.

Boydyboy: parents tried to dial out!!
OwOw0: Aaahh! I hate that. Ive got mine pretty well trained. They know to ask me before they pick up the phone. i keep wanting to get a second line but they say it's too expensive.
Boydyboy: so do you want to guess.
OwOw0: oh. well, why don't you just tell me? haha
Boydyboy: I told you i can't tell.
OwOw0: is it someone from your work?
Boydyboy: ...I have seen the person at work.
OwOw0: is the person in our grade?
Boydyboy: :-/
OwOw0: What?
Boydyboy: Ollie there are 81 kids in our grade, that's too narrow
OwOw0: Ok, is the person in our school then?
Boydyboy: Yes
OwOw0: Is the person in our grade? haha
Boydyboy: Ollie. Whatever. yes.

I didn't know where to go now. I knew no way to hint at "me" without flat-out saying "me." I wanted *him* to say it. My hands were leaving sweat smears on the keyboard and I felt like I was breathing too much, or not enough, or not at all. The chat window on the screen looked crooked, as though the words would all slide out and end up in a pile even more confusing. I was counting my eye blinks. I was afraid I was going to be sick again.

OwOw0: I'm stumped.
Boydyboy: You barely guessed.

OwOw0: Is it Jasmine Lorange?
Boydyboy: wrong
OwOw0: Mrs Doyle? ahahahaha
Boydyboy: god! no! not that mustached yeti!
OwOw0: I don't want to guess anymore
Boydyboy: why?
OwOw0: because.
Boydyboy: Because why?
OwOw0: because I think i know who it is but i don't want to say.............
Boydyboy: why don't you want to say?

I could feel myself slipping and I'd lost sight of the idea that if I did slip, he might catch me; there seemed no chance of it now. It was all in my head, all along — of course. All I felt was the hot dank breath of exposure breathing on me, like a vicious dog on a fraying leash.

OwOw0: Because if I say and i'm wrong i'll be VERY wrong
Boydyboy: what does that even mean??
OwOw0: if I'm wrong it'll change everything and we might not even be friends any more
Boydyboy: it's not going to change shit
OwOw0: Boyd. fuck..........
Boydyboy: just tell me who you think it is Ollie.
OwOw0: I can't...
Boydyboy: why?
OwOw0: whatever. i'm done guessing. You can tell me if you want, and if you dont' want to that's fine.
Boydyboy: Ollie. Do you think its you?

Time stood still. The world stopped. You could hear a pin drop. There are moments in life so big that phrases were invented for them because nothing that existed at the time could do them justice. I have my own. For me, forever after, to this day, this is how I think of those kinds of moments: *It was as though Boyd asked me if I thought it was me.*

OwOw0: what?

Boydyboy: do you think it' syou?

OwOw0: I don't know what to say to taht

Boydyboy: I asked a question.......

OwOw0: if I did think it ws me I wouldn't want to say it because that woudl be implying i thought youwere gay

Boydyboy: so you thought it was you

OwOw0: well from what you were saying like if you ever told anybody it would be me.... it sure sounded like it was mee boyd.

Boydyboy: OK......................

OwOw0: but obviously if I said that and I was wrong you woudl think I was gay and that i just WANTED it to be me which is why i said if I was wrong i would be very wrong

Boydyboy: all right.......

OwOw0: i don't know...

Boydyboy: don't worry. I don't think your gay ollie :-/

OwOw0: I don't think you are either

Boydyboy: because i'm not

OwOw0: I know

Boydyboy: this got fucked up fast

OwOw0: see I told you not to make me guess.

Boydyboy: i think i"m going to log off now, i'll see you tomorrow.

***

Because I'm not. The words flayed me. After disconnecting I cried, on the floor beside my bed, with a pillow covering my mouth so my parents wouldn't hear. It was all the worst things to cry about, too, all at once: fear, vulnerability, exposure, regret—my broken heart was only the tip of the awful iceberg. I had been sure, hadn't I? Almost sure. So close to sure. But I'd been wrong. Now the wrongness had been driven into me like a railroad spike and I swear to god it felt like I was dying.

***

I didn't know how I would face him in school after that, and I had no one else but him. The flip side was that he had no one else but me. So in real life, where boundaries had always been obeyed and we'd never talked about things like this, we remained status quo. School continued to be physics tests and tater tots and standing around in the parking lot at the end of the day waiting for the popular kids to drive away first. But online things were changed. We were in an *after* where I felt lonely and disconnected. The *Boyd & Ollie* ampersand I had wanted to shape into a heart had bunched into a tangle. I did what I could to reshape it but every time I thought I'd found a loop, Boyd seemed to tighten the knot.

Time went by. Winter came. The nights got cold.

OwOw0: I've been doing some soul searching for the past few weeks.
Boydyboy: that sounds deep.
OwOw0: why is everything so fucked up? i wish life was easier.

Boydyboy: well don't we all.

OwOw0: I'm being held down, like. I feel like I'm always on the verge of doing something I have no business doing.

Boydyboy: what is that??

OwOw0: I can't say.

Boydyboy: uhh... well how does not-saying help you at all?

OwOw0: Not-saying just might help me a lot.

Boydyboy: why bring it up then?

OwOw0: I dunno. Never mind...

Boydyboy: Jesus. well hang in there!

OwOw0: Sometimes I wonder, you know....

Boydyboy: I'll tell you about my dream to distract you.

OwOw0: OK.

Boydyboy: it was a nice one, you'd like it.

OwOw0: then tell me.

Boydyboy: well there's this girl at work who i like.

He could make me feel very silly. He could pound on the railroad spike of wrongness.

OwOw0: OK.

Boydyboy: and last night i dreamed we were on a date.

OwOw0: A sex dream?......

Boydyboy: we didn't actually have sex. but we were sitting on a rock in the river and holding hands and kissing etc. it was nice and she's amazingly pretty and nice and it didn't even matter that we didn't have sex.

OwOw0: ....

Boydyboy: what?

OwOw0: Nothing.

Boydyboy: it was nothing like a lot of sexy dreams i've

had. it wasjust pure solid nice.

OwOw0: Yeah it sounds nice.

Boydyboy: you should try it some time!

I could tell he was angry at me and I didn't know why, though I knew what I feared. I feared he hated me because he saw through to what I really was. He hated me for being a fag. All signs pointed to that, and could I blame him? Yet still, in the light of day when I could see his blue eyes and his pale knees framed by the holes in his worn corduroys, I let myself believe he was angry at me not because he was disgusted, but because he was hurt.

***

More and more, hurt was what he seemed to be. Maybe. *Maybe.*

Boydyboy: well i'm drunk drnk drunk and drunk and more drunk.

OwOw0: You sound it. Where d you get it this time?

Boydyboy: dear old dad. i noticed he doesn't even fuckin notice, i can take all i want and he must think he's gushing it down himmself cause he doesn't notice. dad oblivious = Boyd drunk. :-)

OwOw0: Wonderfull.

Boydyboy: i have something to tell you but I can't....

OwOw0: Uhohh.

Boydyboy: Many things going on in my head. dangerous things

OwOw0: I'm not guessing.

Boydyboy: HAHAHA! That was so fucked up up when you were worried i was gay for you.

OwOw0: Yes.

Boydyboy: you wer e worried i was touching myself to thoughts of you every night in the moooonlight

OwOwo: Boyd.

Boydyboy: i'm sorry. really realy sorry. :-(

OwOw0: What are you sorry about?

Boydyboy: RREALY sorry.

OwOw0: You're drunk and messed up.

Boydyboy: really sorry you don't deserve to put up with a drunk bastard like me. i'm sorry for being like this and for being shitty.......

OwOw0: Boyd its OK, i wouldn't be here talking to you if I didn't want to be.

Boydyboy: I can't stay awake anymore. falling asleep

OwOw0: Ok...... Take care of yourself please.

Instead of trying to push him for more information I would log off and listen to R.E.M. in my room in the dark. I would let Michael Stipe sing to me, and there was always just enough hurt in his voice to ease my own. I would sit on the floor, my back against the foot of the bed, and in the strip of light that filtered in through the space under my door I would shape perfect ampersands with the headphones cord until the CD ran out or until I fell over asleep.

***

Mid-terms came in January and I failed a lot of them and had near misses with others. The guidance counselor, Mr. Bowen, called me into his office to see what was up. I couldn't tell him the real reason I was so preoccupied these days, and I didn't want to bring up my ticks again, but I had to give him something. Although I never was a great student I was not one who failed.

OwOw0: so i told him I was spending too much time online.

Boydyboy: well you do.

OwOw0: I spend the same as you!

Boydyboy: and yet I'm not flailing.

OwOw0: failing.

Boydyboy: failing / flailing, whatever.

OwOw0: I told him I liked who i was online better than offline. :-/

Boydyboy: oh CHrist that was like feeding blood to a shark. he'll hav eyou in therapy.

OwOw0: I told him i was more comfortable online and that offline I felt like a different person.

Boydyboy: ooookkkk who are all these different Ollies? explain to me.

OwOw0: something happened to part of me and that apparently is starting to influence the part of me that people see and who walks around. grades, etc.

Boydyboy: what happened?

OwOw0: if I have to tell you then I don't even want to talk about it.

Boydyboy: what's this cryptic shit.

OwOw0: I guess I'm just sick of being other people's Ollie so often.... doing the things people expect and afraid to do what i want to do. i'm like 90% to being like Fuck it all.

Boydyboy: i bet. why do you even think there are two ollies. There is only 1 Oliver Wade. that is defintely a sign that you're not being true to yourself. and yourself = happy

OwOw0: And you are captain Honest Abe over there all the time? i think you're two Boyds the same as i'm two Ollies.

Boydyboy: nevermind, what the hell do i even care what you do. i have homework to do.

***

Sometimes when I got disconnected from America Online an error message popped up right away; other times it happened quietly in the background and I would be typing and sending IMs for two or three minutes unaware that Boyd wasn't getting them. Our entire friendship had come to feel like that second type of disconnect. My words, which at one point had seemed to find him as though they were magnetic, now flew right past. Or maybe he was dodging them.

OwOw0: It's snowing pretty hard out.
Boydyboy: Let me look.................................. yeah.
OwOw0: Think we'll have school tomorrow?
Boydyboy: I fucking hope not, i still have homework i'm not going to finish.
OwOw0: Maybe I'll go outside and make a snow angel... :-)
Boydyboy: ... and that would be gay
OwOw0: Sometimes it's nice to at least pretend you're a kid again don't you think? When you looked at snow and thought it was so great instead of thinking, "Fuck! I have to drive in this shit!"
Boydyboy: brb. dad needs phone
OwOw0: yeah, fine.

Now at night I lay awake wondering when it fell apart between Boyd and me, if there was one specific moment. Or if falling apart, like falling in love, was just something you suddenly found yourself in the middle of.

***

Spring started hinting at summer. By now the tangled ampersand between us had replaced itself with a comma that was half on its way to becoming a period.

OwOw0: i nominated "Nightswimming" by REM for the official song of the junior prom. all those dumb shits better vote for it

Boydyboy: i thought you weren't going to that thing

OwOw0: i'm not going. but if the song is there i'll be there, in a way.

Boydyboy: yeah your record with school dances is RATHER POOR hahahahah

Ouch.

OwOw0: I just can't be bothered.

Boydyboy: by the way, Nightswimming sucks. it will get 1 vote! :-)

OwOw0: I think it's you who sucks.

Boydyboy: i think it's you who WISHES i sucked!

OwOw0: I think it's YOU who WISHES I WISHED you suck!

Boydyboy: Uhhhhhh. no, actually.

OwOw0: i'm so confused.

Boydyboy: that's because all that fuckin REM is rotting your brains out.

OwOw0: ....I don't even know what to say to that........

Boydyboy: well go ahead and take 20 or 30 mins and see if you can come up with something.

OwOw0: You know how I feel about REM. What is this,

beat up Ollie night or something?

Boydyboy: hehehehehehehehehheheheheheh

OwOw0: whatever.

Boydyboy: wait are you really mad at me? i was just fooling around.

OwOw0: are you drunk again?

Boydyboy: :-(no. i feel bad. I'm sorry.

OwOw0: Sure you are.

Boydyboy: I won't do it again.

OwOw0: you promise?

Boydyboy: promise what? ;-)

OwOw0: Promise not to bash REM again.

Boydyboy: yes...

OwOw0: that giant flood of periods makes me skeptical. I'm logging off.

***

Since I was spending less time online nowadays my grades had improved — there was solace in the clear-cut bullshit of textbooks — and I was able to get through my junior-year finals cleanly enough to get Mr. Bowen off my back. But still most nights I was fighting through the busy signals and stalking my buddy list like a brokenhearted ghost. Boyd's name no longer bounced but seemed flattened from a weight I could not lift.

Boydyboy: why are you still online? its so late ugh

OwOw0: what else am i Going to do?

Boydyboy: how about ANYTHING ELSE.

OwOw0: whatever. Are you going to the end of year talent show thing tomorrow?

Boydyboy: Fuck no. it's the last day of school, i'm not even going in, i'll be long gone already. are you?

OwOw0: ......they're usually pretty cool but if you're not going i don't really have anyone to sit with!

Boydyboy: it's all singing. you would want to go to something like that hahaha.

OwOw0: so you don't want to go?

Boydyboy: Nope.

OwOw0: OK.

Boydyboy: but that reminds me. there's soemthing i want to tell you Ollie.

Even though I was tired I felt myself pop to full alertness. After all these awkward months, he still had me — even when I was confident he was only teasing.

OwOw0: you always want to tell me something. what is it now?

Boydyboy: it involves.... homosexuality.......... :-/

Still he could make my pulse pound. And feel quiet at the same time. It had taken all year but now here we were, the last day before summer, and I was ready. I wouldn't lie again. I held out my hands. They weren't shaking. I typed.

OwOw0: I'm here Boyd.

Boydyboy: Someone you like is gay.

OwOw0: Is it who I think it is?.....

Boydyboy: Maybe. you might already know who.

OwOw0: i might have known for a while.........

Boydyboy: It's Michael Stipe your precious fucking REM god.

I looked at the screen with my eyes squinted and, like coming out of darkness into light, I knew that in spite of what we had always been, in spite of what we may have almost become, Boyd and I were nothing now.

OwOw0: shut up.
Boydyboy: he's a giant fag. i thought you knew. I thought that's why you were so in love with him. hehehehehe.
OwOw0: I only have the CDs.
Boydyboy: well he's gay. It's public, he admits it. What do you have to say about that?
OwOw0: Your lying.
Boydyboy: whatever, sure i am. search for his name on the web and youll see for yourself.
OwOw0: no.......
Boydyboy: Are you still going to listen to him now that he's gay...
OwOw0: well i still listen to you and you're a giant fucking faggot right?
Boydyboy: fuck you faggot................. I'm going to fucking block you now before you say something you'll regret.

He did, too. He beat me to it.

***

That summer I got a job cleaning oil pans at the auto-body place in the center of town. With my first few paychecks I bought a weight bench and set it up in our basement. I spent hours every night that summer lifting weights and listening to R.E.M. At least something Boyd had told me was true: my rock-god idol Michael Stipe was a gay man, and had been out for a while; I'd never known. Songs that had only pulled at my heartstrings before now made me cry, because now they were more for me than they'd ever been. I wanted to be like him. I wanted to be proud, and confident, and bold. I would've settled for being not so afraid.

Lifting weights was a good excuse to be alone, and before long I had something to show for it. I put on muscle easily, and the ticks I'd always had with things like numbers and lines lent themselves well to lifting. Every quarter inch my chest grew felt like a fuck-you to Boyd and to anyone else who would call me a fag.

At night after leaving the bench I would crawl up the stairs to my bedroom and go online (my parents had finally installed my own line). I would look at porn, I would go in anonymous chatrooms and talk to anonymous men. I would watch my buddy list, too. I had long since unblocked Boyd, but since his name never appeared on my list I knew he hadn't unblocked me.

***

Senior year brought a new blankness and a deep friendlessness. Then in late November, one year or a million years after he told me he was in love, Boyd's name reappeared on my buddy list. Boydyboy—I'd forgotten what it looked like, doubted sometimes it had ever been real. I watched the name but didn't message him, and after a few minutes it went away.

For three nights that same thing happened. I didn't know if it was a signal. We hadn't spoken in school all year. After some timid and unsuccessful attempts to rekindle things with Itchy Chin Mike (now prom king), I had fallen in with the stoners, at least during lunch when I needed a table to sit at. The rest of the time I imagined my muscles were much bigger than they were and I

hulked silently down the halls, keeping to myself. Boyd
and I barely even looked at each other. Now this. On the
fourth night of it I clicked his name.

OwOw0: hi boyd.
Boydyboy: hello Ollie.
OwOw0: how's it going...?
Boydyboy: up to my fuckin eyeballs in college essays.
OwOw0: already??
Boydyboy: I'm trying for early admission
OwOw0: oh, cool. what colleges are you looking at?
Boydyboy: something far from fuckin Lee is my main
    priority.
OwOw0: I haven't even really thought about colleges
    yet. I'll probably go to UMASS I guess if they'll take
    me.
Boydyboy: that's way too close.
OwOw0: I guess. or maybe someplace in Boston.
    Northeastern or Shuster.
Boydyboy: still too close. I have this high suspicion that
    my future is going to really suck and the only way i
    can hold that off is to get the fuck out of here.
OwOw0: why do you think it's going to suck?
Boydyboy: if the past is any indication.........

I could push him to say more, or I could leave it alone.
Maybe I had learned to leave things alone.

OwOw0: so where are you applying?
Boydyboy: Oregon state, a couple places in CA.
OwOw0: wow you weren't kidding about going far.
Boydyboy: nope.

For a long time we said nothing more and I sat watching

the cursor blink on my screen. I was sure nothing was going to come of this chat but for whatever reason I was reluctant to let it end. Maybe if I kept it going pure momentum would lead us to some kind of conclusion.

OwOw0: what are the application essays to these places like?

Boydyboy: the worst. I'm facing some serious bullshit.

OwOw0: what's an example question

Boydyboy: hold on.

OwOw0: Sure

Boydyboy: I got one. here: "Tell us about a time when you encountered someone who helped you discover yourself and your place in the human community.'

OwOw0: Yikes. Deepness follows.

Boydyboy: I know right.

OwOw0: so basically someone who helped you to know yourself more clearly than you did before?

Boydyboy: basically yea.

OwOw0: Who is your someone?

Boydyboy: I don't have one yet. :-(

OwOw0: do you want to know who mine would be if i was writing it?

Boydyboy: shall i guess? ha

OwOw0: you don't need to guess. it would be you Boyd.......

So was Boyd Wren ever in love with me? I still have no idea. When I bring all my experience to the question, I think he probably was. And that makes me angry. Having the world fuck you out of your first love is a hard thing to bear. By rights Boyd should've been my first kiss. He should've been the first person I touched without clothes. Most of all I should've been able to look into his blue eyes knowing he felt the same. In a different, more perfect world I would've had those things.

Boydyboy: OK. i don't see why it would be me but ok.
OwOw0: you don't? sometimes i wonder if i'm completely insane or if i've ever known you at all.
Boydyboy: we've known each ohter since preschool Ollie.
OwOw0: that's true. I'm sorry for things going so bad between us after all that time.
Boydyboy: well that's just another brick in the wall now isn't it Oliver.
OwOw0: everybody hurts. that's what michael stipe says and it's true.
Boydyboy: still with the stipe. somethings never change. i need to log off now, i'm expecting a call.
OwOw0: yeah. good luck finding your someone.
Boydyboy: you too.

But like I said, I have no idea. Everything I believe about it now is filtered through my own unreliable memories of hastily typed words read off a blurry laptop screen when I was going on seventeen. Maybe it was all in my head. Maybe he's married to a woman now, a woman who had once been the girl he was talking about when I believed he was talking about me.

Maybe, but still—I have what I had. I had the tingles, I had the desperation, the butterflies, the lust, the happiness. I had the fuck-up, I had the miscommunication, I had the fallout, and I had the broken heart. That's what first love looks like for almost everyone, right? No, I never kissed him; no, we never connected that way. But it's hard to deny that these were all the moments of love, and there were a lot of them. Love is a perpetual discovery, and for part of it you're discovering that it's coming to an end.

***

After his name disappeared from my buddy list that last time, I signed off. "Goodbye!" I wound up the cord and shut down the computer. In bed I let my mind wander.

It wandered to Boyd and me, back when the ampersand was at its most heart-shaped. We were in physics class, a few weeks into junior year, outdoors on the football field, sitting on a modified seesaw attached to a motorized turntable Mr. Gruber was using to demonstrate centrifugal force. I was on one end of the spinning plank, Boyd was on the other; we'd been paired because we had similar mass. While we spun, everything was a blur of nonsense and confusion—classmates' onlooking faces like some kind of abstract painting; the school, bleachers, trees just smudges that didn't seem to fully exist. It looked like my life, a confused mess. But across from me, almost within reach, was Boyd, crystal clear, laughing, the only thing that made sense in the spinning.

But it couldn't stay that way; it was simple physics. When the force got too strong we both tumbled backward off the plank and went careening in opposite directions onto the grass.

OwOw0: I felt pretty nauseaus after that spinning thing today..... Still do...... *blows chunks*
Boydyboy: yeah that was so nauseating... but fun though!
OwOw0: Yeah, it was fun.

Boydyboy: do you want to do it again monday??

OwOw0: Hahaha. I don't know if i can!

Boydyboy: you have to. i want to do it and i'll only do it with you Ollie bolly bo bolly.

OwOw0: Fine, then yes.

Boydyboy: :-)

OwOw0: If I can handle it first period.

Boydyboy: Baby :-)

OwOw0: hey my mom needs to use the phone. Will you still be online later? I can't promise itll be soon with all these fucking disconnects

Boydyboy: If you're here i'll be on.

OwOw0: Cool.

The Weight Lifter

Knuckles knocked the hollow door as my father's thin shadow slid across my bedroom wall. I was hidden but not hiding, not exactly. I was lying on the floor beside my bed, on my stomach like a kid, writing — re-writing, re-re-writing — the speech I hoped would make me a man. It was afternoon, August, the day before college.

"Ollie," I heard him say, "I was thinking—" He stopped when he didn't see me in the room.

I pushed pen, paper, clipboard into the newly empty space under my bed and raised one hand over the mattress to signal my presence.

"Oh," he said, coming closer and peering across the mattress at me, "I— What are you doing?"

"Pushups," I said, doing two and counting "Seventy-four, seventy-five" before standing up and shaking out my arms. And from this I knew of course I'd been hiding.

"Good warm-up," he said. "Lots of stuff to move in the morning."

He meant the boxes, the duffel bags, the big Tupperware containers bulging so much I had to shut them with duct-tape. I knew it was too much; I knew my dorm room would strain to contain it all, and I had no intention of bringing most of it with me. It's just that once I started packing I couldn't stop. Everything I packed and stacked seemed like the counter-weight I needed to lever myself into a new life. The final weight was under the bed, a sheet of lined paper covered in ink that weighed ten million pounds. Reading the words to my parents tomorrow would be another billion. But I couldn't really start fresh until they knew, until I knew I was strong enough to tell them.

"I was thinking," my father said, rubbing his finger along the dusty part of a now-empty bookshelf, "that we could do a little fishing this afternoon. Since tomorrow you're heading off. Just the two of us."

"I guess?" I said. I reached to align a Tupperware crate a little straighter atop its bottom neighbor. "I kind of have a lot to do still, though."

He frowned, just slightly, and wiped his dusty hand on his pants. "It's an invitation you can't refuse, Oliver. Put on some shoes. Then help me with the boat."

I watched him leave the room, and when he was gone I knelt and pulled my speech out from under the bed. The time for hiding it seemed past, the time for delivering it not quite here, so I folded the pages into a square and put them in my pocket.

My dad's back was shit, and when he said *Help me with the boat*, what he really meant was *Put the boat in the pickup while I stand around holding the end*. When I was younger, smaller, it meant powerlifting the front end of the flat-bottomed rowboat up to the edge of the pickup truck's bed, jiggering it enough so my dad could push it forward and in. But after spending all of senior year on the weight bench in our basement, I hopped up into the bed, reached down and heaved the boat up with one hand, easy. At the other end my dad tripped forward as I pulled the boat away from him faster than he was expecting. Inside of it poles and tackle-box rattled against its green plastic floor. I spread an oil-stained blanket across the end so it wouldn't scratch up the cab. Then I put a hand on the side of the truck, swung my legs over, and landed smooth in the gravel of our driveway.

"Well look at you," my dad said, putting in the oars. I came around and lifted his end of the boat with one hand so he could close the tailgate underneath it. I could tell he wasn't sure if I was showing off or was just enjoying being strong.

We rode to the lake mostly without talking; the radio played at a volume that excused our silence and the fishing equipment clattered in the boat behind us. I was busy thinking about the speech in my pocket and was eager to get home and re-write it again. That morning when I was cleaning out my closet I had found the handwritten name-tag of a boy I'd been obsessed with in middle school, plucked from the trash and saved all these years as a secret keepsake. I'd decided I needed to include him in my speech. It felt important to me that my parents know how far back this went, that this was not recent, that I had carried this.

"Your mother's going to be a basketcase starting tomorrow, you know," my dad said with a laugh as we turned into the lake parking lot. The tires crunched across the sand. "We should've had another kid to replace you." He paused. "She's going to want a puppy."

"I'll only be like an hour away," I said. UMass was not far from Lee.

"Distance is different for mothers, though," he

replied. "It's like dog years. There are mother miles." He smirked; he liked this. "Mother miles," he said again, pleased, and he turned off the truck.

Together we carried the boat down the concrete slip and set it on the still, honey-colored water. When I was stepping aboard he snapped his fingers and said, "Oars! We can't go far without oars."

Holding the boat in place with my foot, I turned and watched him walk back up the slip toward the truck. He was rubbing his spine with one hand, the place just above his butt where he'd had back surgery last year. I wondered if he'd tweaked something getting the boat down.

"Dad, hold on," I called, tugging the boat back onto the concrete enough to keep it from floating away and then jogging up the slip. I found him trying to shut the tailgate with his knee while balancing the heavy oars across his shoulder. I took them from him, then put my palm on the underside of the tailgate and lifted as he was lifting. I don't think he noticed.

Water lapped the flat front of the boat while I rowed. I always rowed; rowing had always been my job. I rowed fast in the general direction of his pointing, and soon my shining biceps were straining my t-shirt sleeves. I hoped he was noticing. I liked my muscles; they made me feel good, secure, someone to be reckoned with no matter who I was.

The lake was quiet. There was no one else here as far as I could see, only us and the water striders that skittered across the surface on needle-thin legs. When I was younger we often had to share the lake with lots of other boaters, but over the years many had stopped coming. The lake had grown weedy and too full of the types of fish nobody wanted to catch. We hadn't been here in a long time either. I wondered why he had wanted to come.

My dad casted here and there; he never seemed to have a strategy. He would watch the bobber for a minute or two and then reel it in regardless of whether it had bobbed, though it often did. Within a half hour he'd caught a couple of kivvers, thrown them back.

On one cast I saw him wince—maybe because it was a bad cast, but probably because his back hurt. The line went half as far as he was probably aiming for, and ended up stuck in a patch of lily pads. He worked the pole for a minute trying to get it free, then he sighed and said, "We're gonna have to go over there."

I rowed us while he reeled in the slack that grew in the line. It was a sunny day, hot but not extreme, with a touch of breeze, enough to cool you but not enough to push the boat. When we arrived at the patch he handed me his pole and then, leaning over the side of the boat, he started pulling at lily pads. I leaned the other way to balance us, though in flat-bottom boats like this tipping was practically impossible.

"Goddamnit," he grunted. "Can't see where it's hooked." One hand went to his back while the other yanked at weeds.

He wasn't enjoying himself very much, I could tell—his back hurt and now he was going to lose a lure somewhere in that slippery green tangle—but I didn't get the sense that he wanted to go back to the truck. He had wanted to come out here with me today; the fishing may have been an excuse. It seemed reasonable that if there were mother miles, there were father miles too.

Maybe they weren't quite as long—cat years to dog years—but they were there. I wondered if he felt they had always been there.

While I watched him, thin and struggling, I began to feel like I should tell him about me right here in this boat, on this lake. For the first time it felt possible not to do it with a speech, not to wait for the car ride tomorrow, not to say it to the backs of my parents' heads while we drove, so near to being safely an hour of mother miles and father miles away.

He heaved a mass of lily pads up into the boat—their stems pop-pop-popped as they snapped beneath the bubbly surface—and pulled them onto his lap. Slimy green stems dangled against his legs and shoes.

"You're getting wet, Dad."

"This is a good lure."

I knew I'd be prouder of myself if I told him here, if I did it face to face and man to man, if I acted as strong as I looked and as strong as I wanted to be. Prouder if I found I didn't need to *act*, if I was simply *up to it*. Then the hardest part of my life would be over. Forever after, no matter who I had to tell, it would always be easier: I would know I was brave enough to tell my dad, and what could compare to that?

I felt as still as the water all around us, but inside I was a wave rolling in, getting ready to break. No other place or time could be right now that I understood what telling him here and now would give me, and so I felt a sudden desperation to get the words out. I felt them— there were only two; pages of them had been reduced to only two. I felt them start to journey from my mind to my voice, words on paths familiar from a million mental rehearsals but never once ever said out loud, not even in the dark, not even in front of a mirror. I knew I would cry but I didn't want to cry until afterward, when I would know the tears would not be tears of fear but tears of relief, and of pride.

They were on my tongue, those two words. I swear they were. I swear.

"Ollie," my dad said without raising his eyes. His fingers were busy working the clump of fishing line and lily-pad stems, though I could tell the lure wasn't his real focus. His voice was serious. "Your mother and I, we—" And he paused.

Startled, my words had retreated and I was imagining the hundred possible ones he might say next. *We're selling the house. We're having a baby. We can't help you with school. We're getting a divorce.* I could tell from the look on his face that whatever it was it was big. And so he had hijacked my moment. I was angry but my anger told me how much I wanted the moment back, how much more with every passing second. If I couldn't tell him right now I would tell him in the truck, because I wanted to tell him. I wanted to know that I was strong.

He looked up at me then. His fingers were entwined in the tangle but all of his attention was on me. "Ollie, we know you're a gay man, son."

I flinched. It was as if he'd hit me. Lily pads were rocking in the waves that rippled away from the boat. My breath fled me in a hot cloud and tears spilled out of my eyes as if they'd been waiting there, and maybe they had been. I can't say there was no relief in that moment, in hearing those words said with that voice, in knowing I was finally out. And yet these were not tears of relief. I was still holding his fishing pole and it slid through my fist up to the reel and the other end dipped to the water.

"OK," my father said gently, "then I was right." He

put a hand on my knee and gave it a squeeze. "We wanted you to know we know, so you won't have to go into your college life with a secret. Secrets will hold you back, Ollie. I mean, we have some concerns. We have some worries about this. This is new terrain for your mom and me. But all of that is better than—" He narrowed his eyes. "Ollie?"

"But I was.... I was...."

"Ollie?"

I squeezed the oars to keep my hands from shivering. "How did you even...?"

"Know?"

I nodded, shrugged, something, it didn't matter. I felt tiny.

"One morning," he said, as though he were reading me a bedtime story, "I was trying to print something. And the printer already had something in its memory. It was that old printer, remember? It was so bad. When I was trying to clear the print jobs three pages came out, the same picture three times." His eyes returned to his fingers as he worked the tangle of stems. "It was of two men. With no clothes on. It wasn't *dirty*, exactly. But— Well, I guess it looked *sweet*. *That's* how I knew. By the sweetness. If it was a raunchy picture I might've thought it was a joke, something you were going to use for a prank on your friends. But— And I was surprised, Ollie."

"We got rid of that printer two Christmases ago."

"But then, *not* surprised. When you're a parent you notice things, I guess. Maybe you don't notice you're noticing at the time, but in a flash you'll remember it all. Dots connect. That dance...."

"You knew since two Christmases?"

"We wanted to wait. To give you a chance to tell us

on your own."

He looked out across the lake, again giving me a chance to say something, and when I didn't he continued. "Am I right that you haven't told anybody?"

I nodded. No one.

"I hoped maybe you and Boyd— For a while there during your junior year, you two seemed— You really seemed—"

"I thought we were— Maybe. Daddy— But I couldn't...."

He cleared his throat, nodded, looked again across the water at the sun. "The reason I bring it up now. Why we decided not to wait anymore. Your mom wanted me to. And I wanted to, of course. But the reason I bring it up, Ollie, is because I don't want you to miss out on anything. Not anymore. College is too important and it goes by so, *so* fast."

We looked at each other for a long time and I didn't know what to say. Finally he took out a pocket knife, opened it, and cut the fishing line in his lap. Then he flung the wet clump of lily pads, with the lure still lodged in it somewhere, back into the water.

"Telling your father you're gay," he said, "I guess that's about the hardest thing you'd ever have to do." He wiped the knife on his sleeve, folded it and put it back in his pocket, then reached and took his fishing pole back from me. "Everything after that's a piece of cake, right? So I figured I'd do the heavy lifting for you. I didn't know how to make things easier for you when you were younger. But there. I've done this."

"Yeah," I said, and I looked down at my hands, at the callouses from the weights.

There are home movies of me learning to swim, in this

very lake, back when the water was clearer and it had a beach. My dad shot them from the shoreline, his pant legs rolled up and his feet submerged, and you can watch me almost drown repeatedly, dozens of times, as I tried to swim from one red buoy to the next in the shallow water. Coughing, snot on my lips, I would stand up after each failure and wade back to the starting buoy and try again. When I was older, around twelve, I asked him why he'd been taking movies when he should've been in the water helping me. I remember he was quiet for a few seconds, then he pointed at the TV—at the moment, famous in my family, when I suddenly was no longer drowning. At the cartoonish grin on my face as I swam.

"I wanted you to know you could do it," he said.

Our row back was quiet and I felt like a stranger to him now, and to myself—a new person I had no practice at being, in a different life I hadn't earned. Did he think I could not have done it this time? Did he see some weakness in me he knew I would've come up against in the last moment, just as the words were touching my lips? Why else would he have stepped in just as I was going to show him? Did he know, surer than me, that I'd have nothing to show?

"I was going to tell you," I wanted to say as I rowed, "really," but that would almost be meaningless. All it would mean was that I hadn't.

The wind picked up and made my cheeks feel cold where the tears had been.

My dad leaned over the side of the boat and dangled his fingers in the water. He looked serene and unburdened, his fatherly duty done. Somewhere in the past ten minutes he had stopped rubbing his spine.

He looked at me and smiled, and I smiled back as much as I could. I was out now, yet I felt small and unsure of myself despite my biceps, my legs. In fact there was no connection at all between my muscles and my courage. I had imagined they were one and the same, or could be. Although I knew exactly what I could lift on the bench, the rest of it— Really, I'd never know.

(Age 18)

So Long Eucalyptus

Lots of things come to mind when I think about Wesley.
One of the first is eucalyptus. Eucalyptus-scented oil he
would pour from a little vial — *plink plink plink* — into a
spray-bottle of water and then spritz around our dorm
room. From wherever I was sitting I would watch him,
often backlit against one of our two big windows,
spritzing.

Picture the misty puff of the stuff in the sunbeams.
Picture the clear plastic bottle, a finger on its trigger,
clasped in a thin bony hand. Picture a spindly wrist,
tattooed on the veiny side with a blue lighthouse. Picture
his twiggy arm and his slightly hunched shoulders, his
boyish face with blue eyes and constellation of freckles
across the nose, framed by shaggy, honey-colored hair
he was trying to grow long. Picture him tall and slim. If
he were a tree he'd be a willow, though he was often
lying down. His bed, against the whitewashed wall
across the narrow room from mine, was made up with a
faded paisley quilt, fitted tight on the twin-long mattress
like a military cot.

Wesley was spartan but thoughtful, eccentric in an
understated way: He'd brought only his most important
possessions from home but considered a vial of

eucalyptus oil to be among them. Our room, perfumed with the potion he spritzed everywhere, was all Wes, from the tapestry he purchased at a Tibetan store and spread out on our floor to cover the drab carpet, to the chunky olive-green curtains he sewed himself to give our room a more homey feel. He had done it all with my help, and although I was never offered a choice it wouldn't have occurred to me to suggest anything different. Wes was like that, and I was like me.

I had arrived on move-in day a quivering freshman, intent on getting to the dorm early and first to get dibs on the better bed, if there was one; the better desk, if one was preferable. My new roommate, who had introduced himself in a letter two weeks earlier, was coming to UMass from California; I was only coming from Lee. I expected to have the place to myself for at least a night.

But instead of the empty room I was expecting, when I opened the door I found a suitcase spilled open on one of the beds, as if it'd been dropped to earth from a passing plane. Push-pinned to the wall above that bed was a curling Kandinsky print, though I didn't know who Kandinsky was at the time. Colored circles in colored squares.

My shoulders slumped. The strap on the duffel bag I was carrying slipped down and settled around my hips like a yoke. I stumbled across the threshold dragging it behind me, with a nineteen-inch TV in my hands and a laptop bag dangling from my arm. Without getting too close, as if something might pop out, I peered into the open suitcase, looking for clues about this boy I'd be living with.

"Oliver?"

The voice came from behind me. I turned, already

knowing it had to be my new roommate — who else here would know my name? He had on jeans, a faded blue t-shirt with the word *Sennheiser* in white across the front. A hand towel was draped over his shoulder as though he'd been doing dishes or something somewhere. I was simultaneously relieved and disappointed that he wasn't hot.

"That's me," I said. "Wesley?"

"Hi."

"Hey."

He entered the room with his hand held out to shake, then he seemed to realize my arms were full.

"Need some help with... anything?" he asked, eyeing the TV and then lifting my laptop bag's strap from the crook of my elbow instead. Shifting the TV to one hand, I extended my arm so he could slide the laptop bag off. "I guess you don't, really?" He was looking at my muscles; people looked at them. "Glad you brought a TV," he said, "I couldn't fit one in my carry-on."

He put my laptop — the most prized and intimate of my possessions since it was the only place I'd ever really been me — gently on the desk he'd chosen to be mine.

"Thanks," I said.

He added, "My parents are shipping out some more of my stuff, but I had to be choosy."

"Mine are down at the car, with pretty much everything else I own."

He laughed, crossed his skinny arms across *Sennheiser*. "Did you bring a stereo?"

"Of course."

"Can I use it sometimes?"

"Sure. Yeah."

"Cool."

That first afternoon after my parents drove away I had an almost throbbing awareness of being in college. A deep sense that my life had lurched irrevocably forward whether I was ready or not, and that now everything would be different—whether I was ready or not. Alone in my room unpacking, I listened to the voices of Wesley and some of our new hallmates in the lounge next door. I listened for clues about whether I would fit in with them, whether I would belong here. A pair of girls—freshmen roommates from down the hall—had already popped into our room to introduce themselves as Kaitlyn and Amy. They had wanted to know where I was from, what my major was, was I *so excited*. In the background of my every answer was the secret that had been a secret to everyone until a fishing trip with my father twenty-four hours ago. I didn't want to bring the secret to college but one slip, one deflective answer to a question like *Do you have a girlfriend back home?*, and then it would be a secret here, too.

Rarely would I ever miss high school but that afternoon while the sun lowered across the Quad and I listened to these new kids in the lounge I missed high school and the anonymity that twelve years with the same kids in a small town affords you. By high school everyone in Lee had learned everything they wanted to know about me, and I could stalk the halls unquestioned, basically invisible. No one was going to ask me anything. Here at UMass they were already asking; they were curious; I was as new to them as they were to me. So I unpacked slowly alone in my room, maybe to give them time to be less new before I had to talk to them.

After a while Wesley returned to our room and shut the door—an action that had a flavor of intimacy I wasn't prepared for. As an only child I had never shared a room with anyone, let alone a boy. I was standing barefoot on my bed amid a clutter of unpacked things, hanging my R.E.M. posters on my wall and on my half of our tape-cratered ceiling.

"You should've come hung out with us," he said, looking past me up at my posters. "They all seem really nice. That Kaitlyn is nutso."

"I will. Definitely. I just want to get unpacked first. It's hard for me to relax until things are—you know, settled."

Wesley said, "You must really like R.E.M." He turned and took a single long step toward his bed and sat down. He leaned against his wall under the Kandinsky print and cupped one knee in his threaded fingers. Everything he'd brought was already put away. He seemed so organized and sure of himself. I was spilling out all over.

"Yeah. I do like them." I looked up into the wrinkled paper at the face of my idol. I had wondered so hard what would give me my first opportunity to come out here, what twist of conversation, what sudden question—and now that there was one right above me, like a gift from the sky, it felt fitting. Years ago I had found something and now in this important moment it was with me. Looking at the ceiling I said, "Michael Stipe is gay and he's a rock and roll god and so am I."

"A rock and roll god?" Wesley said without hesitating.

I looked down at him. "Gay." My knee almost buckled, but held firm.

"Ah."

The firmness turned quickly to rigidness. "Is that going to be a problem for you?" I said. It was too defensive, but I didn't know how this was done. I tensed my shoulder muscles and inhaled, a bull ready to charge if Wesley flashed a cape.

He just smirked, though. "I'll survive. To be honest it'd be cooler if you were a rock and roll god, too."

Relaxing a little, I said, "You don't care?"

"About what?" He had turned and was straightening his Kandinsky.

"My... gayness?"

"I don't have a problem with it. I'm from San Francisco, it's old news. I care if you snore, I don't care who you date. Unless I guess if you bring a guy home to get busy while I'm trying to sleep." He laughed.

I turned to the wall and pressed the puttied corners of another poster. I felt my cheeks flushing. I was going to be able to get busy with people here — Wesley had given me permission, just by suggesting it. He expected me to meet boys.

"So he's a gay guy? Michael Stipe."

"He calls it queer," I said.

"I didn't know."

"Rooming with me you'll pick up a few things about R.E.M.," I laughed. I stepped back to admire my posters and laughed again in sheer relief. I had come out to my new roommate and now I was laughing! And I thought, *Dear young Ollie. Dear lonely, scared young Ollie: There's a time in your future — years, weeks, minutes into your future — when you'll have come out to your new roommate and then you'll be laughing. You can't imagine this but it'll be true.*

I jumped happily off the bed and landed in a squat on the floor.

Wesley said, "Now that the ceiling's decorated it makes me realize how bland this carpet is. Maybe I'll try to find us a tapestry to put down, give the room some spice."

I thought, *Dear young Ollie: There's a time in your future — years, weeks, minutes into your future — when you'll have told your life's most tortured secret to your new roommate, and seconds later he'll decide the room needs more spice.*

Wesley was almost a vegetarian, he said, but he had an inescapable love of pastrami. Picture him that first night sitting cross-legged on his bed, a pastrami sub and a sheet of curling white deli paper open on his lap. Picture him saying, "I'm not even going to feel guilty about this," before biting into it. On the stereo was R.E.M., the *New Adventures in Hi-Fi* album. He'd invited me to put one on.

Later when we turned out the lights it occurred to me that this was my first sleepover since that one with Dwight Macklin sophomore year. Dwight hadn't talked. Wesley did the opposite of not talking. Among the things he asked me in the dark was what I thought about Allen Ginsberg. I said I'd never heard of him. Saying nothing, he got up and I could hear him rummaging on his desk. A minute later something sailed across the room with a fluttering sound and landed on me.

"You're lucky I packed it," he said. "I almost didn't. We'll talk about it when you're done."

In the light from the Quad that leaked through the windows I flipped the pages of *Howl*.

"Also a gay man," Wesley said, fluffing his pillow. "Not a rock and roll god — though a bit of a rockstar in his own right."

***

Thus began my education at the University of Massachusetts at Amherst. Classes hadn't even started yet. Before they did, there was a week's worth of University orientation stuff (things like trust falls and RA introductions, I guess), which Wesley called crap. He said we should skip it all in favor of actually learning something. I think I would've gone along with anything he suggested, and for a week we walked around campus and downtown Amherst by ourselves, rode the bus into Northampton, walked down to the banks of the Connecticut River, while I worried that the school wouldn't even know we'd arrived.

Wes had a good sense of things, had an adventurer's spirit, and seemed to know his way around Massachusetts. Although he was from San Francisco he had lived the previous year on Cape Cod with three buddies in an old rented house. He talked about that year a lot. The whole thing seemed intensely romantic to me. I couldn't get enough of his stories of going to laundromats in blizzards and of making lattes at the little shop in East Dennis where he barista'd; of sitting his own coffee cups in snowbanks to cool them on mornings when he had nothing to do but sit on some steps and watch the snow. He'd taken classes at Cape Cod Community that year and so now was technically a sophomore at UMass. To me he seemed even older, a world-wise soul I always wanted to impress.

Picture him scoffing, in the dining hall kitchen where we were walking with our trays one day, "You don't drink *coffee*?" He was appalled by this in a way he never was when I didn't know a book or a band.

"I guess I never really thought about it before," I said. "My parents do."

"Think about it now," he said. "It's the stuff of life."

He set his tray down and got some for himself. Poured it, creamed it, added sugar, stirred. In the reflection of the big silver coffee machine while the steaming brown liquid dribbled into my first cup, I could see myself grinning.

Mine was over-sweetened, had too much milk, was lukewarm — was somehow delicious. I nursed it, leaning back in the dining-hall chair with the front legs lifting off the floor. I was dreamily thinking of coffee cups in snowbanks, like in Wes's stories.

"What's it been like being gay?" he said suddenly. He was drawing shapes in spilled sugar with his finger.

"What's it — like?" I stammered.

We hadn't mentioned my gayness since the first night, and once the news was out I suppose I fell back into my closety groove — it was so much more habitual than an out groove. I may have even forgotten I'd told him.

He added, "When did you come out?"

"Like, last Sunday. My dad confronted me in a boat." I lifted my coffee to my lips and was probably using it to hide my face. There were a lot of people in the dining hall. "Can you, maybe, ask me again tonight? I don't know if I can talk about it here, like —"

"Oh. OK. Yeah."

We had moved on to other topics and I was sipping the brown sugary grinds from the bottom of my cup when I started to feel like I could've talked about it. I wanted to talk about it, I had just been surprised.

After we turned out the lights that night, he said, "I'm supposed to ask you to tell me about being gay." Maybe he sensed I could talk about it better in the dark, or maybe he just liked to talk in the dark.

"Like what about it?"

"I don't know. How was it?"

I laughed. *"How was it?* That's what waiters ask you when you're done with your steak."

"How was your homosexual youth, sir? *Oh, a little chewy, I'm afraid!"*

"A little chewy!" I laughed until my pillow case was damp with tears. I'd never imagined being able to joke about this, but with him it felt natural. When I'd calmed down I said, "I guess it was confusing, mostly."

"Homosexual youth: chewy and confusing."

"I've never put it into words before." I looked up in the dark, where the faint outline of posters glowed. "When I was starting to realize I definitely *was*—and that was a long time ago—I got really afraid it would be obvious to anyone who looked at me. I thought I'd give myself away in every situation. Like, there was this school dance and it was just *fucked*. I guess I tried to get away from any situation where I'd have to play a straight kid because I knew I'd bomb at it. Which basically means you end up acting invisible your whole life because *every* situation is a straight situation."

"Interesting. I suppose you're right."

"And when you have a secret it makes you suspicious that other people have secrets, too."

"I bet."

"In my case you wonder who else is like you. Sometimes you think maybe you've found another one. I had this friend. His name was Boyd. And I was desperate to know, but that means you have to put *yourself* out there. Risk him knowing about you and then finding out he isn't, and meanwhile you're there flapping in the breeze with your secrets hanging out. You know? So you resort to tricks, to cover your ass. It's really terrible actually. We're not friends anymore."

"Wow. Was he? Boyd."

"I don't know."

"Huh."

"The weirdest thing? It's that you exist in kind of a perpetual present or something. There's no future for you. The things people tell you about your so-called wedding day and your kids and your white picket fence or whatever, you know it doesn't apply to you. I'm not going to get to have kids, I'm just not, that's not going to happen for me. And meanwhile you have to sit there living with that knowledge while people blab their fairy tales. They *are* like fairy tales, only the people telling them believe them and you know they'll never be true. There's no version of *your* story. Am I going to have a *life partner* or whatever? What does that look like? Nobody tells me those stories. It's just— I don't know."

"You know, where I grew up, there are a lot of gay people. I saw them all the time. Couples holding hands and stuff. Some even have kids."

"I can't even imagine that. It seems like another planet."

"It isn't."

"I guess, like, with *you*, I can see myself having a place of my own, or sharing a place with someone. Maybe I won't ever find a boyfriend or a quote-unquote *life partner* or whatever. But I can find friends who know the real me and like me anyway, and that's a thing that I can have. It's weird. It feels like having a *future*."

Wesley was quiet for a long time. Lights came in through the window and played on the walls. Finally he said, "Well that's nice of you to say, Ollie." But I think by then I was falling asleep.

***

Picture him friendly but shy. He was quiet in groups, though in some weird way they revolved around him, the way a courtroom revolves around a judge whether she's speaking or not. It must've been because he had the best stories, or because he was exotic (the rest of our hallmates were Mass-holes like me, and as a San Franciscan he may as well have been an alien), or because he had a way (with his curtains, with his music) of making a hallway cohere into a home.

Ours was composed of half of the third floor of Johnson Hall, Northeast Campus. In a double on the other side of the lounge were the two freshman girls we met our first day, Kaitlyn and Amy. Next door to them was a senior, Harriet, who had a room of her own. She was pretty with red hair, dressed Mod, planned to be a playwright. Across from her was Bruno, an oafish junior who wasn't often around, but when he was he loved to tell us the kind of stories nobody is ever interested to listen to—drinking stories, driving-around stories. Beside him was Shelley, a pixie of a girl with curly black hair that bounced when she walked. She was authoritative and competed with Harriet for the role of hallway matriarch even though Shelley was only a sophomore.

One night during the second week when it was too stormy to venture outside, we all sat in the lounge and demonstrated our secret talents. Amy said she could stand on her head without using her hands, and proved it after Shelley ran off to get a pillow. Harriet could name the presidents in eighteen seconds. Kaitlyn could tap dance. Bruno could belch "Stairway to Heaven."

While I watched them I wondered what my talent

could be. You could say that in high school I'd had a talent for acting, playing someone other than who I really was. But at this point I hadn't mentioned that side of myself to my hallmates. It seemed easier to coast on the Wesley success for a while before letting new people in on it.

When my turn came I performed the lightning-fast lyrics of R.E.M.'s "It's the End of the World as We Know It (And I Feel Fine)." The lyrics rattled across my tongue like feet across a crumbling rope bridge while I watched my hallmates watching me. I felt like I might stumble, but each word bought me enough time to remember the next one. Word by word I got through. I ended it slowly, no longer as freaked out by all of them looking at me, and I dragged out the last line, *"It's the end of the world as we knoooow iiiit...."* Breathless but grinning (because who was this boy who had just been so visible?), I collapsed onto the sofa beside Harriet.

"And do you feel fine, Ollie?" Kaitlyn said.

"I do!"

Wes was golf-clapping. "Maybe both a gay guy and a rock and roll god after all," he said.

Everyone suddenly went quiet, as if he'd unplugged a radio. They looked from Wes to me, from me to Wes.

Wes whispered, "Oop...."

Then Harriet made a little raise-the-roof gesture that felt to me like the most welcoming thing in the world, and she offered me her bag of Doritos. Shelley was tapping her chin as if considering whether there were signs she had missed. Bruno looked concerned, as he always did when someone else had a good story. Kaitlyn jumped up and hugged me, knocking the Doritos out of my hand. "I always wanted a gay friend!" she sighed. Only Amy looked uncomfortable. (Later Harriet told me

Amy had had a crush on me.)

"My secret talent is outing my roommate, apparently," said Wes, giving an embarrassed cough.

But of course he had done me a favor.

On purpose or by accident, Wesley always seemed to smooth my path for me. I was starting to love him for it, I knew that, but I wasn't *in* love with him, and sometimes I wondered why. The other hallmates recognized him and me as a duo—Ollie and Wes, Wes and Ollie—but it wasn't like how it had been with Boyd. It felt more sustainable, less like it was tumbling toward some sort of explosion. Having no secrets from Wes let me feel something new: contentment. Nothing loomed. We just hung out. We were *friends*.

Our evenings were spent in the lounge with the hallmates but when they started drifting off to bed or to homework and Wesley and I went back to our room, that's when I was happiest.

Using my stereo he played me different songs from his CD collection, songs I'd never heard but should've, apparently—a lot of which I liked, a lot of which I pretended to like. Boards of Canada, Aphex Twin. We'd lie on our beds and listen to the mechanical crunching sounds of the *Richard D. James Album*. Wes was into old stuff too: Neil Young, Simon & Garfunkel, Sinatra, Billie Holiday. He liked to play me songs, to be my human jukebox and my teacher. It seemed so much more important than homework, I couldn't deny it. I'd done homework for years. I'd never done this.

"Try this one," he would say, and he'd play some weird ambient stuff it must've taken nails, water, rocks to create. He'd lie on his bed with the stereo remote on his belly, listening. When the song was over he'd pause the disc and say, "Thoughts?"

I always told him I liked it, even when I didn't think it was anything much, because I wanted him to keep playing me stuff. I'd pick out some detail of the song to show I was paying attention.

Sometimes he tossed me the remote and gave me a turn. I played him R.E.M. songs. I played him "Find the River," and when it was over he didn't say anything, and when I said "Thoughts?" he cleared his voice in such a way that made me know the song had made him cry.

He told me a lot about his year before UMass, the year he spent on Cape Cod living in that rented house with his three friends. He showed me photos he took in those days, black-and-white action photos of late-teenage fun. The stories that went with the photos were simple and almost mundane and yet had an air of excitement I could barely relate to. I think his stories described happiness. He seemed to glow when he was telling me. He seemed a different version of himself in these stories, different from who he was in this room and at this school—a do-er rather than a remember-er. So much so I sometimes wondered, with a touch of foreboding, why he had come to UMass at all and not stayed on Cape Cod. The fancy, cared-for camera he'd used to take all these romantic pictures was sitting on his desk now. He'd only taken a few shots with it here, though he held it in his hands a lot, as if to be ready for something worthwhile.

***

October came, and on the first cold morning I unearthed a fleece from one of the Tupperware crates under my bed. From his own bed, under his quilt, Wesley looked at me putting it on.

"I'm going to have to skip class today," he said. "I didn't bring anything warm. I don't do cold."

I laughed. "You *do* do cold. You lived on the Cape. I've seen pictures of you in the snow — you were loving it. Coffee cups in snowbanks, remember?"

"Yeah. I don't know." Blankets up to his chin, he stared at the window while I loaded my books into my backpack. "After your classes," he said, "would you want to go to this thrift store in Northampton I heard of? Harriet mentioned it."

"Sure, as long as I don't have to buy anything."

"Why?"

"I hate thrift stores. Used clothes give me the heebie jeebies."

I left him lying in bed. After suffering through two classes and stopping at the dining hall with Shelley for a grilled cheese, I met him back at our room. He had the directions to the thrift store, a place called Garment Alley, written out on a Post-It. He was sitting on his bed looking through his photo album. It was clear he hadn't gone to class.

We walked across the Quad and waited for a Northampton bus at the edge of campus. Picture him wearing a thin sweater, his hands stuffed deep in the pockets of his jeans. Around us the trees were starting to turn. Time was flying; I'd already been at UMass six weeks. I could barely remember anything before it, and almost never tried.

"I should've brought my car to school," I mused. "I didn't expect to leave campus so much."

"Why didn't you?"

"Well, it's kind of a shitbox. I hit a telephone pole junior year and it was never the same after that. I think

I'll sell it next summer and buy a bike."

"A motorcycle?"

"Oh. No. A bicycle."

"On the Cape," he said, "me and the guys shared this old diesel Jetta. It was a shitbox too but I loved it. When we all moved out we drew straws for the car."

"Who won?"

"Not me."

"I want a Jeep someday, I think." I stepped to the curb to look for the bus.

"Like MacGuyver?"

"My friend Boyd had one. I liked it."

"Boyd, Boyd, Boyd."

"Boyd, Boyd, Boyd. Where are your friends now?"

He looked off down the street. A bus was approaching but it wasn't bound for Northampton, and he shivered. "Jim is back in San Francisco, Harley is in Montana, and Scoop is in Mexico City."

"Wow. How'd you end up here in Amherst?"

He sighed. "My parents thought it would be good for me to get back on track. They said one *gap year* is enough."

The bus to Northampton arrived. As we rode Wes was telling me about Jack Kerouac and the Beats, people for whom writing and travel was everything, was life itself. "Imagine being that passionate about anything?" he said. I couldn't.

He stopped talking as the bus crossed the bridge over the Connecticut River. I watched him look out at the water, that wide blue space that cut Massachusetts in half and gave a border to New Hampshire and Vermont. "I miss the ocean," he said quietly, to himself. On the other side he started talking about Kerouac again, as if the little interlude had never happened.

Garment Alley was a big, attic-smelling warehouse with dim lights and green floors. Wesley seemed to think it was heaven, but it skeeved me out. I imagined everything as full of lice and stiff with pit-stains.

Wesley chose a few Seventies-era t-shirts, flopping them over his thin forearm. Then we browsed the coats.

"This one's very cool," he said, pulling an olive Army jacket off the rack. There were a few blue chevrons embroidered on one sleeve. He checked to make sure all the green buttons were still there and then he held it against himself. "Hold these?" He handed me his t-shirts and put the jacket on.

"A little baggy," I said. We walked to a mirror so he could see for himself.

"Yeah," he said, "in the shoulders. It might fit you, though."

"Should I?"

"Go ahead."

Reluctantly I tried it on, mostly to make him happy. It was warm from his body, and yes, it looked better on me; my muscles filled it better (though these days they weren't what they'd been; I still did pushups and situps but I had stopped lifting weights).

"You should buy it," Wes said. "It's only—" He found the tag. "—five dollars!"

"But do you think it's *me*?"

"The only you is the you you choose to be."

"Sure, Captain Fortune Cookie."

He laughed. I bought it.

On the ride back to the dorm he was quiet the whole way. He kept zipping and unzipping the jacket he'd bought, a puffy blue thing. He looked anxious.

"Do you not like your coat?" I said.

"I like it, I'm just— I really shouldn't have skipped classes today. I've skipped too many. I'm getting behind."

"Well now that you can stay warm you won't have to skip any more."

I liked when Wesley skipped—we had fun when we skipped—but there was always a price, for both of us, to our skipping. For me it meant a little extra effort the next day, tracking down homework assignments or whatever. For Wes it always caused regret and a new focus (usually brief) on his classes and his education, which he pronounced as though it had a capital *E*. He always swore he would never skip again. On evenings of days we'd skipped he would hole up at his desk with his books while I chilled in the lounge with Shelley and Harriet. Shelley called these post-skipping nights Wes's "hooky sulks."

During one hooky sulk in mid-October when we were doing homework, our phone rang. The phone jack was located behind my desk and so our phone sat near my laptop, making me feel like the gatekeeper.

"Can you get it?" Wes said from his bed, where he was surrounded by books. That day we'd skipped classes and gone to buy a new lens for his camera. The lens cost him sixty dollars; the skipping cost him six hours in a frenzy about French class.

I picked up the phone. It was Wes's parents. I told him and he sighed and came over.

While he talked to them he sat on the edge of my desk with the phone cord wound up in his lap. I put my reading aside and played a game called Snood on my laptop, glancing occasionally at the freckles on Wes's thin arm. I had come to hate his parents. They didn't call often but their calls always left him upset. Their conversations (or at least Wesley's side of them) would seem to be pleasantries at first, stuff about their dog and his sister. But before long Wesley would be yelling— about his grades, his classes, eventually his capital-*E* education. That was how it went this time, too. My desk started to rattle beneath him. Soon the back of his neck was flushed and he was wiping his eyes. "But Mom," he was saying, "I *am* fucking thinking about the future!"

He was inches away from me but untouchable, and I didn't know what to do.

I closed my laptop and crept out of the room. Shelley was in the lounge peeling an orange. The scent of it filled the air and was a surprising change from the eucalyptus spritz.

"Wesley is having another weird convo with his parents," I said, sitting down beside her. "I had to get out of there."

"The same shit?" She handed me a wedge of orange.

"I don't really like oranges," I said.

"Eat it, it's good for you." Shelley was very mom-ish. I put it in my mouth.

"Yeah, the same shit," I said, chewing. "They put so much pressure on him. This time he was *crying*."

"Yikes."

"I don't like to see him cry, Shel."

Later when I went back to the room the lights were off. Wesley was already in bed. I didn't know how he could be sleeping already, but he was at least pretending. I didn't say anything. It was the first night we didn't talk ourselves to sleep.

***

A day in late October was marked on my calendar with two letters: *UP*.

"I'm almost too psyched to go to class," I told Wes that morning as I was tying my shoes.

He was still in bed, his head resting in the crook of his elbow and his paisley quilt pulled tight to his chin. This seemed like a day he probably wouldn't go to class.

"This is their first album release of my R.E.M. fandom," I went on. "Their last album came out a few months before I got into them, so I missed the spectacle of the launch."

"This is a big deal for you then," he said. He scratched his nose with the quilt. "What time do we need to leave?"

"Well Strawberries reopens at midnight for the release, but I don't know— I want to be in line early, I don't want the CDs to sell out before I get mine. Eleven, I guess? We can take the bus."

"Sounds good."

I went to class, and when I got back that afternoon he was still in bed, lying with his arms folded behind his head, looking at the ceiling. It was probably a hooky sulk. I was afraid he wouldn't want to come to Strawberries, and after he declined to join Kaitlyn and me for dinner it sure seemed to be going that way. But when I got home from dinner he was up and about.

It rained that night and we stood in the rain, with raincoats and wet sneakers, in line with a bunch of other people, some of them R.E.M. fans, some of them fans of other bands releasing albums that day, waiting for the record store to open. It was a cold rain that foreshadowed winter but I was too excited to feel it. Wesley was quiet, stood looking down at his sneakers while water ran off his hood.

At midnight the pink neon Strawberries sign blinked on and a tired employee opened the door. The dripping line worked itself inside, snaking through the aisles, ending at the checkout counter, behind which the day's new releases were still packed like shrink-wrapped gems in their shipping boxes.

"Does it look like a lot of people are buying *Up*?" I said nervously to Wes, standing on my toes trying to see. "What's that guy buying?"

Wes tilted out of line. "Looks like Jets to Brazil. You're safe."

As we got closer to the front of the line I said to Wes, "I'm getting *nerv*ous."

But soon I was there, and one of the *Up* CDs, with its shiny checkerboard cover, was placed in my damp hand. I handed over a twenty with the other. Casually I slipped the CD into my raincoat pocket—it felt like a treasure some desperate person might try to steal.

Outside we waited at a covered bus stop for a ride back to the dorm. Water sluiced off the leaves-covered Plexiglas roof, making it feel like we were behind a waterfall. I held my palm flat against the CD in my pocket.

"When will this bus come?" I complained, bouncing on my toes. "I need to listen!"

Wes pulled a Discman and a pair of headphones out of his coat pocket, held them out to me and said, "Brought this for you. Go for it."

It was the most thoughtful thing I think anyone had ever done for me. Still, I wanted to wait to get back to the dorm so we could listen together, so I could share my band with him the way he'd shared so much with me. And that's how we did it. We lay in our beds and listened to the new songs, warm and dry, and they were amazing.

I wanted that night and all the nights like it to last forever. Somehow I really thought they would, too.

***

After Wesley was gone I wondered often about when exactly he made the decision to leave. I wanted to know which of our fun times he spent knowing he was going. I wanted to know which one of them wasn't quite fun enough to change his mind.

Did he know, on the night of *Up*, that in a month he'd no longer be at UMass? Did he know when we were trying on clothes at the thrift store?

I think he knew on the day he told me he was out of eucalyptus oil. Picture him sitting at his desk, holding the little glass vial up to his eye, looking through it like a jeweler through a lens.

"Oh," I said, maybe sensing somewhere deep that this was a sort of finale. "You can get more, right?"

He let the vial roll back and forth on his palm. "I don't know where I'd find some around here. I guess I could look."

"You should look, I've gotten used to it! It's the trademark of our room!"

He held the little empty vial over our wastebasket, then dropped it in. "So long, eucalyptus," he said.

If he knew then that he was leaving, it was still a few weeks before he told me. When he told me I was confused, as confused as I'd ever been. But could it really have been a surprise? He had all but stopped going to class, and I often saw him in the morning when I was getting ready, sitting in the lounge by himself with open textbooks on the couch, looking out the window, a million miles away already.

He had said something to me that sounded like, "I'm leaving UMass." I looked at him as seconds ticked by. Finally he said something else; this time it sounded like, "I'm going back to California."

I said, "Next year?"

He said, "Next Tuesday."

"You're—? Tuesday?" That was one week away. "But— *Wow*."

I felt as if everything had slowed down but my mind, and I could take the time to examine each little detail of the world as it was and as I was afraid it would become with him gone. The sound of kids playing frisbee on the Quad / the emptiness of the room after next Tuesday. The wood of the desk against my arm / who would play music for me?

I could feel my eyes welling up. "The semester's over in a month," I said. "You aren't going to stick it out?"

"I don't see the point," he said, shrugging his thin shoulders like an old man, his freckles suddenly looking like liver spots. "None of my credits would probably transfer."

"So this is something you're thinking about, or—?"

"It's done. I went to Student Affairs today."

"Oh. OK."

"Yeah. So...." He stood up and went over to the stereo, opened the CD tray and then closed it without putting anything in. "I just need to not be here, Ollie." Again he opened the tray, and closed it. "I mean, you'll probably have your own room. That's cool, right?"

After a minute of silence he left the room, and as soon as I was alone I started to cry. I had a million thoughts running through my head. Who would I talk to? Who would I tell everything to? Who would ask about my classes? Who would I make fun of people with? Joke with? Laugh in the dark with? Who would tell me stories about their adventures? Who would be my best friend?

I pressed my fists against my eyes. I was remembering now what it felt like to be afraid all those years. I was a little boy again with no idea what my future looked like.

***

Wes didn't want the hallmates to know he was leaving and asked me not to tell. He said he wanted to slip away without any fanfare. So I was alone with the knowledge while the hallmates remained in what seemed to me a blissful ignorance. But it was hard to keep secrets in quarters that close. On Thursday of that last week Shelley stopped by our room while Wesley was packing a box.

"Getting ready for the end of the semester?" she said, but I could tell she was suspicious.

"Actually," Wes said, "I'm going home." He smirked uncomfortably.

"What do you mean?" she said.

My muscles tensed. I didn't want to hear him say it again.

"I'm dropping out!" he yelled, as though she'd asked him fifty times instead of just once.

"Explain this to me," she said calmly. She crossed her arms and leaned in our doorway. She didn't tip-toe around things like I did.

"I don't know. I need to not be here."

"It's the end of the semester. You're going to throw away a whole semester?"

"It doesn't matter."

"Why doesn't it matter?" she demanded.

Wes just shrugged and resumed his packing.

Shelley sighed. "Ollie, I'm going to dinner if you want to come."

I looked at Wesley. I looked at Shelley. "OK," I said, and grabbed my Army jacket.

Later that same day Harriet found out secondhand from our RA, Travis, who had asked if she was bummed about Wes. She opened our door without knocking.

"I heard a rumor today," she said, her hand still squeezing the knob, "and someone needs to tell me it's not true." But she was already looking around at the missing belongings and packed boxes.

Wesley just looked at her. Harriet rolled her eyes and stomped up the hall to her room. I got up and followed.

"I'm sorry I didn't tell you," I said. "Wesley didn't want me to tell anyone."

"It's his responsibility, not yours. I just think it's lame I had to find out through Travis." She sighed and turned on her TV. "Whatever. So it goes." She waved her hand and said, "*Pffft.*"

I watched her watching VH1. "You don't seem very upset," I said curiously.

"I knew this was coming, Ollie," she said. And maybe she had, maybe the signs were there; of course the signs were there. But sadness doesn't depend on surprise to be sadness, does it?

"Even if you knew," I said, "aren't you sad you won't see him anymore?" I couldn't understand her nonchalance. Of all our friends, Harriet was almost as close to him as I was.

She looked at me and said, "Who knows what can happen in five years, Ollie, or two years, or sixteen months." She said it like an adage, as if it were the answer to all the world's pain. I didn't get it. Then she added, "This is college. It's the same as life. People leave. Get used to it."

She changed the channel.

***

After my first and only class on the Tuesday before Thanksgiving break I went to the bus station to see Wesley off. The dings and chimes and staticky loudspeaker announcements echoing off the gray walls of that place called to mind the sounds of an intensive-care unit. While I looked for Wes part of me wondered if he'd lied to me about the time of his bus so he could slip away unseen, but soon I found him sitting on a bench in the terminal wearing his puffy blue jacket. Picture him sitting with his suitcase at his feet, the suitcase that once looked like it fell from the sky and then spent three dusty months stashed under a bed.

"How was class?" he said as I sat down.

"Boring," I replied. I looked up at the Departures board's clacking numbers. After he departed, who would ask me how class was? "Is your bus on time?"

"Looks like it," he said. "Fifteen minutes. I think that's mine," he added, pointing beyond the big windows to a Greyhound parked curbside.

He was taking the bus to Worcester Airport, then a plane to Philadelphia, another plane to San Francisco. It seemed like so much work to leave; it hurt me that he was willing to do all that work to leave when it would take no effort to stay.

"I'm not going to cry," I told him, "so don't worry."

"You can cry, Ollie."

"I know you don't want people to make a big deal of you leaving."

"Yeah. Well. Maybe I'm just a little embarrassed." He sighed.

"Don't be embarrassed. I guess I understand, sort of."

"All the same, I know it's hard."

Minutes crept by. People with tickets in hand started lining up near the doors, too close to the doors, which kept automatically opening and closing, letting in gusts of cold air.

"Ever been to California?" he said.

"No, never."

"You'll have to come visit," he said, but he said it wistfully, with the tone people use to soften long goodbyes. I think he knew he wouldn't stay in California for long.

For my own goodbye I had written him a letter during class that morning. I'd written everything I wanted him to know about what these past three months meant to me, about what I would remember about them, about how they changed me. It reminded me of the letter I wrote to my parents, the one I'd planned to read to them on the drive to college but never did. And this one, too— When the time came, I didn't give it to him, didn't hold it out for him when they called his bus and we stood up and looked at each other, roommates, former roommates, because the point of that letter was easy to say, the important part was easy to get at. The rest was just clutter.

"I love you, Wes," I said as I pressed my cheek against the shoulder of his puffy blue jacket.

It wasn't the same kind of love I had felt for Boyd Wren, or the kind I would feel for other boys in the future—but if Wesley thought it was, that was OK, I didn't mind. Three months had done that for me, just three after a lifetime, thanks to him.

He rubbed my back gently, then went to his bus.

***

On my way out of the terminal I spotted a familiar face by the sliding doors. She saw me before I saw her.

"Shelley Cantos," I said, smiling big even though I still had tears running down my cheeks, "are you waiting for *me?*"

She told me she'd had an awkward goodbye with Wes before I got there but had wanted to stick around to make sure I was OK after he left. We walked back to campus together and she put her arm around my waist because she was too short to reach my shoulders.

When I got back to the room I noticed two things standing out in the shocking half-emptiness: On my bed was Wesley's camera, with a note. *"Find things to take pictures of. W."* And I saw that his bare mattress had a cut in the fireproof vinyl near the foot of the bed, with a bump of foam sticking out; that he must've chosen the bad bed on the day I arrived early to get the good one. I picked up the camera and took a photo of his bare mattress. Then I put on *Up* and lay down on his bed, for the first time ever.

After that it was different, it was always different after that. I returned after Thanksgiving break to a place I had to struggle to make my own. I had to find comfort in myself, by myself, with no leads to follow. At first it was terrible. The nights seemed to throb without his voice in the dark. I spent a lot of hours in the lounge because I didn't want to be in my room. I felt like I was on the edge of sinking into something.

A couple of days after break, Bruno sat down on the couch in the lounge.

"Where's Wesley?" he said. "I don't think I've seen him since before Thanksgiving."

I'd been standing near the window watching a snowblower clear new snow in the Quad, but now I went and sat on the other end of the couch. "He's in California," I said.

"Still?"

"Yeah, still."

"Like, for good?"

"He dropped out."

"Huh," he said. "He was kind of weird, right?"

He started talking about something then, one of his dumb Bruno stories, but I wasn't paying attention. People say that when you die your whole life flashes before your eyes — and why not? Sometimes it happened to me when I wasn't even dying. While Bruno talked I remembered every detail of my short, infinite semester with Wesley. Wesley who could've easily been Bruno, or *a* Bruno, but who wasn't, who was Wesley; it felt like the biggest stroke of luck in my life. I remembered it all in a flash, and every detail of that fall semester smelled like eucalyptus, and sounded like laughing and Aphex Twin and R.E.M. Every one tasted like pastrami, and every one, every one, felt like hot coffee cups sitting in snowbanks. It must mean something that the first thing that comes to mind when I think about Wesley, my most vivid memory of Wesley, is one of *his* memories, told to me in the dark, made real with a whisper, brought to life in a hush.

What I think happened is that Wesley had a happy year on Cape Cod, adventuring in the snow with his adventurous friends, plunking away at a community college but doing his thing, peacefully watching his breath unroll into winter air. And his parents, for whatever reason, decided that wasn't good enough, and talked him into structure, into the blazing mainstreamness of a place like UMass. And maybe it caught up with him, faster than he expected. That's what I think, but who knows. I know he didn't stay in San Francisco for long. He spent some time near Big Sur, went up into Washington; later he wrote to me from Montana. After a while the letters dwindled; by spring break we lost touch. Harriet was right: This was college, and people left. Who knew what could happen in two years, or in five? In the meantime I had Wesley's camera, and I had lots of pictures to take.

The First Time

Lying on my back on the bare mattress, I pressed my feet against the wall and pushed. The bed slid away from the wall a foot or two, scraping across the stiff brown carpet. I pushed again until my legs were straight and my heels slipped down along the wall and my feet fell onto the dusty rectangle of carpet that had long been covered by the bed.

No one from Student Affairs had contacted me after Wesley left, and for weeks afterward I'd had the constant nerve-wracking expectation that at any moment my phone would ring and they would spring a new roommate on me.

In January after I'd settled in from winter break, still no word had come. My hallmates agreed that if I hadn't been assigned a new roommate by then, the vacancy had probably slipped under the radar somehow, and I was probably safe for the rest of the year. Probably. But I was confident enough now to start a slow sprawl into Wesley's former space. I started using his bed to put my stuff on—my Army jacket, my books. I started using his chair as a footrest when I worked at my desk. Now it was February and I'd decided to push the two beds together as a final embrace of being alone.

The bed scraped the carpet as I pushed it the last foot, and the two metal frames met with a clang. Laying my eggcrate across the gap between the mattresses, I turned the two twins into a double. It was a makeshift setup because my sheets didn't fit, but when I was done my hallmates came by to admire it.

"So luxurious," Kaitlyn swooned, making a snow-angel motion on the bed and rumpling up the sheets. "So spacious!"

"Enjoy it, dude," Harriet said, "because this like *never* happens."

Bruno came by later and stood in the doorway eating an apple. He had a single of his own but the singles were glorified closets and I could tell he was jealous of my vast space, of my gigantic bed.

"You're single in a single," he observed while chewing loudly. "You got your own sex palace here, man."

That night I lay sprawled on the bed with the phrase *sex palace* throbbing in my mind. It seemed weird of Bruno to mention sex because it was strange to me to think of him ever having it, though I was sure he'd probably done it at least once. It was just as strange to think of myself doing it, and I never had, not even once, though of course I wanted to. And Bruno's comment, and the *bow-chicka-wow* tone he said it with, watered a seed Wesley himself had planted the first day I knew him: that I was free to bring a guy home. In the dark I looked across the empty space, and if I squinted my eyes it was possible to imagine that the shadow of the pillow was a boy lying there, slick and sweaty from being with me. I was eighteen, newly out, single in a single, and maybe I was ready to see what that would be like, having a boy lying there.

But I wondered if Wesley and Bruno, these straight guys who seemed to take it for granted that I would get laid, could've explained to me how. They were probably not thinking outside of themselves. Everyone knew how straight guys got laid, but how did gay guys get laid? I had a vague awareness of parks and truckstops as options for meeting gay men, but what if you wanted more than a blowjob? What if you wanted a boyfriend?

It seemed an exotic thing to me, a boyfriend — an idea I could barely wrap my mind around. The closest I had ever come to getting one had been a disaster. It may even have been all in my head. I hadn't thought much since then about trying again. I didn't know how I would chase a boyfriend down — but I'd have to try. It's not like one was going to show up at my door.

Or maybe one would?

With a sense of fierce liberation I stuck a rainbow sticker on my door and left the door open to hallway traffic when I was home. The sticker was four inches square but to me it felt as big as a billboard. It was half a proud announcement of a part of myself I used to think I'd rather die than have people know, and half plain old boy-bait for a lonely virgin.

With the sticker seeming to glow on my door I would sit in the middle of my giant bed, ostensibly doing homework or watching TV or listening to R.E.M., but really watching people walk by. People came and went — visitors, friends, guys from other floors — and eventually one of them had to be gay. He would see the sticker and stop, and fall for me.

At least that's what I hoped. But it wasn't working.

"Harriet," I said one day when she and I were alone in the lounge, "where do you think I could meet other guys like me?" Harriet was older, a senior, and I thought she might know, from having been around campus for so long.

"Gay boys?"

"Um. Yeah."

"There's a gay student group," she said, thinking, "but they're sort of really *really* gay, if you know what I mean."

"Oh," I said, "yeah," though I didn't, really.

"Like aggressively gay," she added.

"Oh."

"You could always just try the gym," she said. "There's probably gay boys there, right?"

"I used to lift. I could start up again." I squeezed a bicep that had shrunk during the time I'd spent busy with Wes.

"It'd be good," she said. "It would get you out of your room a little."

"Yeah."

"Yeah." She smiled.

I started going to the UMass gym after classes every day. Muscles that had deflated from lack of use during the Wesley-focused semester popped back to what seemed like full strength after two weeks of lifting, as if they'd just gone on vacation until I called them back. But I wasn't meeting any guys at the gym. If there were gay ones there I couldn't tell who they were, and I was afraid of chatting up the wrong one. Instead I started sitting on my sex-palace bed wearing tank-tops and sleeveless tees, showing off my legs with shorts in March. I watched the hallway, waiting for a boy to see the rainbow sticker and enter, and become my boyfriend, and take me. But, you know, none did.

***

Then fate broke a water pipe, or at least it seemed that way. Two days after spring break a pipe burst between the third and fourth floors of the dorm, flooding out the room where our RA Travis lived, five doors down from mine. I heard about this at lunch from Kaitlyn, who had witnessed him early that morning frantically dragging his computer equipment into the hallway, dripping and wearing nothing at all, she claimed, except soaking wet boxers.

"Oh," I said, my pastrami sandwich hovering forgotten near my lips. "Just boxers? What, uh— What color were the boxers?"

She looked at me for a moment and then grinned, as if finally fully believing I was a boy who liked boys. "He *is* sort of hot, isn't he," she said. "Plaid, I think. Blue and gray plaid."

"Plaid."

"The poor guy," she said. "I wonder if they'll get him a hotel?"

I wondered it too. But when I got home from class that day Travis was not at a hotel, he was in my room, fully clothed now, setting up his computer on Wesley's old desk. Soggy clothes hung drying on the headboard rails of my sex-palace bed, and rumpled textbooks were airing out on the floor. A pile of his stuff lay against the armoire. I was very confused; at first I even thought I was in the wrong room. But here was all my stuff too, and there on the door was my rainbow sticker. For some reason it hadn't occurred to either Kaitlyn or me that Travis might get moved into my room—as if my decision to claim both beds had removed the room from the purview of Student Affairs.

"Oliver, hi," Travis said. He was wearing jeans and a stretched-out polo, which showed some reddish chest hair near the buttons. He was looking at my giant bed, standing with his hands on his hips. "We'll need to push these back apart," he said. "It's illegal for me to sleep with my residents." He laughed, but I still felt confused. "Did you hear about my flood?"

"Oh. Yeah, I did, yeah. That sucks."

"So I'll be living in here for a while, until my ceiling gets repaired."

"Oh. Yeah, sure. Um. Welcome!"

I cast a sideways glance at the sticker on the door. I would've peeled it off if I'd known he was coming.

My hallmates started giving me crap about rooming with the RA. They took turns that night in the lounge roasting me about the perks of such a situation, the things I could get away with, who I could have killed if they crossed me—as if an RA were a mafioso I now had an *in* with. "The RA's pet," Bruno called me with a smirk. I sat there and took it, smirking back, happy just to have their company and an excuse not to go in my room. It felt funny being in there. My room, I was discovering, wasn't really mine and never had been. The comfort I felt there with Wesley was about atmosphere, not ownership. Claiming both beds didn't make it mine. Travis or anyone else Student Affairs decided to stick there had every right to be in the room, to come and go, to play music, have friends over, control the TV. And right from the start I wanted him gone.

"It's getting late," Bruno teased, "you better go give the RA his foot-rub."

"Yeah yeah yeah." I rolled my eyes.

And I wondered, *How long will it take to fix a ceiling?*

"Hey, Oliver," Travis said, looking over as I entered the room after the last of my hallmates had drifted out of the lounge.

"Hey, man," I said, straightly.

Something poppy-punk was playing from his computer speakers. He was sitting at the desk typing a paper or something in naught but his boxers—the plaid Kaitlyn had gossiped about—even though it was barely spring and the room was winter-chilly.

Averting my eyes and sidling toward my desk, I opened my laptop.

Travis had been attractive at a distance—worth imagining in the underwear I was seeing now—but got intimidating when he was five feet away. Outside of the bathroom and the locker room, both of which were eyes-to-yourself, I'd never been so close to a guy wearing so little. I'd certainly never had to talk to one. Travis, with all his skin, seemed like a planet I was orbiting; every move I made around the room was in relation to his body. I puttered on my laptop for a while and then got into bed, from which I discreetly watched his smooth back, not muscled but fit enough, and his legs, crossed at the ankles under his desk.

Travis was very different from Wesley already. Wesley's brand of straightness was a gentle, almost feminine straightness—a straightness easy for a gay boy to be comfortable around. He'd slept in a t-shirt and sweatpants, even in early September when it was still hot. I never once saw Wesley shirtless. Travis was, I think Harriet would've said, aggressively straight. Even just sitting there typing, he exuded a masculine sexuality I had no practice at being around and didn't know how to respond to. Travis was all kinds of shirtless and I couldn't stop stealing glances. After a little bit I got up and went to the bathroom to masturbate in one of the stalls.

The next night I went to the gym after dinner and stayed until it closed at 11:00. It was exhausting but I would've stayed even longer if I could've. I hoped Travis would be in bed by the time I got home. In the hallway I saw a crack of light under my door. I stopped and jingled my keys against the doorknob before going in. He was in bed but not asleep. He was reading. He had no shirt on.

"Hey, Oliver," he said.

"Hey, man," I said.

Maybe because I could see his arms and I could see they were smaller than mine, I felt a surge of boldness. I took off my shirt and dropped it in my laundry bag. Not wearing a shirt seemed to be normal but with mine off I felt funny, as if I was performing. And I wondered if he would notice me. Guys always notice other guys' muscles, and tonight, after killing all that time in the gym, mine felt extra big.

Putting my wallet and keys in my desk drawer, I caught sight of Travis in the mirror. He was looking at me. He looked for a second and then went back to his reading.

Quickly I gathered up my towel and toiletries and went to shower. I grew confident under the water, massaging my overworked muscles with my soapy hands. I returned to the room in my underwear with the towel wrapped around me.

Travis had moved to his desk and was looking at some papers in a folder. Seeing him, my confidence evaporated again. I may have been bigger but I felt exposed and silly, trying to be someone I wasn't, this cavalier bro who could walk around shirtless. I dropped my bucket of toiletries onto my dresser, yanked the towel off me, and jumped into bed with the covers pulled high—all before he turned around.

"Wayne and Paul upstairs are fighting," he said, closing the folder and laying it on the desk. He turned in the chair and stretched out his legs, cracked the knuckles of his toes.

"Yeah? Like, punching?"

"No. Wayne says Paul is being insensitive with the lights."

"Oh. Yeah? Insensitive?"

"Who knows." He yawned. "I may have to move one of them. Be nice to me or I'll put one in here with you after I leave. Ha."

"Oh."

"Don't worry, I'm kidding. Though, really, I might have to."

He stood up and walked over to his bed, flopped onto the mattress and clicked his reading lamp on. He looked really attractive lit by the little lamp. The light brought out the blond in his reddish hair, and by shading his muscles made them look more defined than they probably were. I was getting hard under the sheet. I wished I'd jerked off in the shower.

"So have you got a boyfriend, Oliver?" Travis said, turning and looking at me, his hand cupping his cheek, his elbow pressed into his pillow.

"A boyfr—? No. I mean— No. I guess I didn't know you knew I was the type to have one."

"I'm the RA, I know everything about all my residents."

"Oh. Yeah."

He laughed. "Plus, that sign on your door."

"Sign? Oh. Yeah." The rainbow sticker; but of course it *had* been a sign, too. A sign implied an advertisement, and that's just what it was.

"That's too bad, no boyfriend," Travis said, casually but with a growing coyness when he added, "Or who knows—maybe it could be lucky, right? For both of us?"

In my surprise, in my unwillingness to believe, I tried imagining what else he could possibly mean by that, and I really had to scrape. *Lucky for both of us* because he didn't want me to bring a boyfriend here, or something? No—I knew what he meant. I knew where this was suddenly and unexpectedly going. I knew what was probably about to happen. By the tone of his voice, by the way he was looking at my shoulders. It made me excited, but sad too. It was a sad discovery to realize that when it's going to happen it'll be this obvious and happen this easily. How many nighttime drives had I taken with Boyd Wren where I had wallowed in the purgatory of *maybe*, analyzing little comments and gestures when, if it's going to happen, you can know from a look?

The look Travis was giving me.

"So I—," I began. "So do you— Do you think you'll be able to find a room for those guys? Wayne and—"

"Probably, Oliver," Travis said, "but to be honest, right now I'm more interested in you." It was flirty but a weird type of flirty. Not a cutesy kind; it was authoritative, almost stern, almost dismissive, like a boss, like a principal. Like I was in trouble. "Should I come over there?"

I didn't reply but felt half aware that I was licking my lips, which on some level I must've meant to be an invitation. Regardless, he took it as one. He got up. What I had taken for aggressive straightness must simply have been aggressiveness. His skin and body and maleness came over to my bed like a conquering armada and I was shivering, wanting it, afraid of it. He sat down on my bed. His mouth tasted like toothpaste and his stubble was sharp. Whatever he was, I was kissing a boy.

We only kissed for a minute before his hands found my erection and pulled my underwear down. They felt hot and smooth on it. He leaned down and bounced it against his face, and sighed. I tensed when the head grazed his stubble. I watched as if it were happening to someone else, as if this were a porno, but when he took my penis into his mouth I came back to myself and it felt as though all of me was in his mouth, rolling back and forth across his tongue. It was exciting and scary and I felt— I didn't know what I felt.

He only had me in his mouth a few seconds before I said, "Travis, I'm gonna come." I was afraid of shooting in his mouth; I didn't know the etiquette, I didn't know if that's what real people did or if only pornstars did that. He didn't acknowledge me, though he had to have heard me—his ears were only inches from my mouth. "Travis, I'm getting close—" But rather than stopping he sped up. I didn't want to come in his mouth; it was about more than etiquette, I just didn't want to. I put my hand against his head. "Travis—" He didn't stop. "Trav—" And then I came. It was fast, like a lightning strike, not the rumbling, almost-itchy things I had mastered the art of giving to myself. It seemed to slip out of me, out of the hotness of me into the hotness of him, moving from one to another as if we were all one thing. I had never come into anything my own temperature before. I gasped. I could feel him swallowing around me, his tongue and throat working. His eyes were closed. I felt embarrassed. I didn't know what to say. He took my penis out of his mouth and licked up the strings of spit and sperm that had dribbled into the hair. Then he smiled and pulled up my underwear and patted my softening dick through it, the way you pat the head of a good dog.

"I needed that," he said. Then he slid back on my bed and pulled out his own erection, the first I'd ever seen in person. His penis was bigger than mine, and veiny, and the head was shining. I didn't know what he wanted me to do for him now—he seemed to not really know I was still here. He was stroking himself and licking his lips and I, because I had to do something, reached out and rubbed his chest.

"You came so hard," he said. And for some reason I wanted to say I had barely come at all, that I'd hardly felt anything. I wanted it to be over. I wanted him to come and go back to his side of the room.

But while I watched him jerk himself I started to feel turned on again. I moved my hand lower on his belly and laced my fingers through the hair around his dick. It was stiffer than mine, and that surprised me—I must've thought, stupidly, that boys were boys, that I could know about them by exploring myself. Travis felt different from me. Even his come, when it landed on the back of my hand, was different—thinner and more watery than mine. It ran across my knuckles and dripped on the bed.

He lay there breathing heavy for a minute. Then he lifted his head and looked around.

"Hand me a Kleenex?" he said, pointing to my desk with a glistening finger. I got up and got the box, pulling out a few for myself before handing it to him. He yanked out three or four and held them to his belly and said,

"*Wooo*."

He stood up and hiked up his plaid boxers, then dropped the tissues into my wastebasket on his way back to bed.

"Thanks, that was really cool," he said as he clicked off his lamp.

In the darkness I touched myself through my underwear, felt the wetness that was proof of—what? I wondered if I was still a virgin. If that had counted as sex. If I wanted it to count.

Soon I heard him get up and eat a cookie.

"There's the RA's pet," Bruno said to me the next morning as I was heading to class. He clapped me on the shoulder.

In the gym that day I lifted for twice as long as usual, until I was out of breath and my muscles ached. Two days in a row of pushing hard. I looked at myself in the mirror and saw I was not someone to be trifled with. But I met Harriet and Shelley in the dining hall for dinner and didn't hear much of what they were saying. My mind was stuck on yesterday.

That night I lay awake wondering if Travis would come to my bed again, but he didn't, he kept to his normal greetings and homework and reading. Same on the second and third nights. It was like the sex hadn't happened, which made me worry that I'd been bad at it, that I'd tasted bad or smelled funny, that I hadn't said the right things afterward or been too awkward or not helped enough to get him off. I wanted to ask Harriet or Shelley what they thought but I didn't want either of them to know, or anyone to know, and risk getting Travis in trouble. He was, after all, our RA. The rules were clear.

By the fourth night, when we shut off the lights, I was confident in the routine. Small-talk, then quiet, sleep, no chit-chat. The pre-sleep quiet was a starker contrast from Wesley than the shirtlessness had been, than even the blowjob had been, but I was getting used to it.

I was in the first stage of sleep when Travis's voice snapped me awake. He'd said my name. It sounded loud and he added, "Did you like it when I sucked you off the other night? That was pretty hot, right?"

My own voice, fumbling to find itself, sounded loud too. "It was pretty hot, yeah."

"Only *pretty hot?* I bet you're probably getting hard thinking of it."

My mouth was dry. I shifted under the blankets. "I'm — getting a little — a little hard." And I cursed myself for stammering.

I heard him chuckle, then he went quiet. I started to think he was just ramping me up for fun. Then he added, "Maybe I should come over there and help you out again."

I swallowed and took a breath but didn't say anything.

He turned on his reading lamp, aimed it at the wall so it lit the room in a diffuse yellow glow, a little more atmospheric than the first time when it'd been shining right at my bed like a spotlight. He swung his legs out of bed and stood up. His plaid boxers preceded him by the six or seven inches of his erection as he came toward my bed.

I felt clumsy kissing him and I wondered if I was doing it right. Most other people had had practice by this age. I guess maybe I was doing it wrong because this time too he only kissed me for a few seconds. His mouth had other places to be.

He sloppily kissed my shoulders and biceps, leaving cool spots on them with his tongue. Pushing me against the pillow he kissed down my stomach. He reached up into my underwear through the leg holes and hooked his fingers over the waistband, and pulled my underwear down over my thighs and over my knees, past my ankles and off. I had been basically naked with him the first time but this time I felt even more naked. I looked up at him, feeling a little silly, not sure what to say. He told me to roll onto my stomach, so I did. The bed creaked with our weight. My face lay on the pillow and my legs were stretched to the end of the mattress. After kicking off his own underwear he sat with my legs between his thighs; I could feel his balls on the backs of my knees. He kissed down my spine, down and down, and I thought surely he'd stop before my bum, but he didn't. With his palms he spread my cheeks and made a little noise, a small coo, the way someone might at the sight of a puppy. I was pretty sure I knew what he was going to do—I'd looked at enough porn—but I had no expectation of what it would feel like. My body went rigid with the anticipation, and I squeezed my eyes shut. The warmth was surprising, the softness, the slickness of his tongue. It felt good but not a sexy good; it felt like a private good and I didn't like feeling it with him here.

"Travis, I might not be clean—"

"You're clean," he said, stopping just long enough to say it. "You taste amazing."

Which confused me, because if I was clean, what was there to taste? Did I have a natural taste there? How could it be amazing? He continued for a minute or two while I stared into the pillowcase, my mind racing and my heart thumping to keep up. He kissed up around my butt cheek and bared his teeth against my skin.

"Have you ever gotten fucked, Oliver?" he whispered.

"Yes," I lied quickly.

"Did you like it? Of course you did. It feels amazing, right?"

"Yeah," I lied. What could I do after lying once, except double down?

"How much do you want me to fuck you right now, Oliver?"

How much? What kind of question was that? There was no answer for it, or there were many. The truth is I did want him to fuck me, a lot, now that I'd been awakened by his tongue. I wanted him to fuck me the way fucking worked in my imagination, though—with the sweetness and the effortless glide it had in my imagination. I had no idea how that would translate into real life, into real feeling or real pain. I was afraid. And so the second, equal truth is that I didn't want him to fuck me, not at all. But the third truth: I knew he was going to.

What's strange is that I also knew that, if I wanted to, I could push him off me and throw him across the room, back to his own bed. So why did I feel like he was holding me down with the weight of his tongue?

Before I told him anything he got off my bed and hopped naked to his side of the room, where he rummaged in a duffel bag he had not unpacked. I heard the rip of foil and when he turned around again he was putting on a condom.

I was excited. I was terrified. Would it hurt? Would I be able to do it? Would he know from my body language that I had lied?

I rolled onto my back, because I liked it best in porn when the guys looked into each other's eyes.

"Oh, lube," he whispered, returning to the duffel and pulling out a bottle. "Lube lube lube. We'll use a lot."

As he approached my bed I spread my legs. My penis was barely erect, flopped against my belly.

"This body, Oliver," Travis murmured, running his fingers across my abs.

"Go slow, OK?" I think I heard my voice crack, or maybe it was just that my throat was so dry.

"Don't worry, we'll take our time." He kneeled on the bed beside me. "Here," he said, tapping my hip with the back of his hand, "roll over back onto your belly again. It's better that way."

I did what he said because although I had wanted to face him, being on my belly hid my softness.

He kneeled in the space between my spread thighs, which he spread wider with his knees, and repeated what he'd done earlier—kissed my neck, my traps, my spine, worked his way down to my butt. Again he held my cheeks open and swirled his tongue. I liked it better this time because I knew what to expect. I was getting hard against the mattress and I thought that this could be good, this would be all we needed to do. If I let him know I was enjoying this maybe he wouldn't stop, maybe he could make me come this way, maybe if I came I could roll over and show him the dark spot on the sheet and say, "Sorry, maybe next time?" And maybe his ceiling would be fixed before there was a next time.

I sighed into the pillow and moaned pornographically, "That feels really good. Please don't stop." I started rubbing my pelvis against the mattress to make myself come. An orgasm could be my escape hatch.

After a moment he did stop, though. I heard him sniffle a laugh as he wiped his forearm across his mouth. "I don't want to accidentally finish you off before we get to the fun part."

And again, because it had been feeling good, I was excited, but I also didn't stop rubbing against the mattress, and I didn't stop trying to come. I was stuck bewilderingly between wanting and not wanting.

I heard the click of the lube bottle and then felt the frigid touch of his wet fingers. True to his word, he used a lot, and he worked it inside me with his fingertips. I had touched myself this way before and knew I didn't like it, and I liked it even less when someone else was doing it. I heard the click of the bottle again, heard the squicking sound of the latex being lubed. He wiped the excess off his hands against my butt and my upper thighs and the small of my back.

"You're shining like marble," he said. There was haunting wonder in his voice and it made me nervous, made me afraid to tell him to stop or slow down. Wonder like that would mean repercussions if it was stymied.

"Like marble?"

"You have the nicest body I've ever been with. It's, like, *crazy.*"

"I do?"

He leaned forward and put his palms on the mattress near my armpits, and pressed his body on top of me. I could feel his erection against my bum and it was OK there, and I thought how much better this would be if it stayed there, outside. His weight ground my own erection harder against the mattress and I focused on coming, knew I had a small window left to come.

His lubricated dick slipped around against me while

he sucked my earlobe. Then he leaned onto one hand and used the other to guide his penis. I felt him find the spot with the tip of his finger and then press his penis there. My heart was pounding like a machine gun against the mattress. I could feel my bum muscles shaking. The whole bed was rattling.

"Relax," Travis said, kissing my shoulder, "relax a little. I know you're hungry for it but you need to relax a little."

I could feel lube squish between his groin and my bum and run down my hip in cold stripes. How many minutes of slow, steady, overwhelming pressure ("You're so tight, aren't you?"), and then the tip was in. *The tip is in*, I thought, and I started to feel relief and even exhilaration. *A boy's penis is inside me.* This was happening and it was OK. But could the tip be enough? Would that be OK?

"There we go," Travis whispered, "*finally*. Now just relax because I've got more for you."

The *more* was the difficult part, the part that felt like a smooth hot sharp poop that was stuck. The part I wanted to be over. Like with the rimming at first, this was a feeling I didn't think I should be feeling with another person here.

"How great does that feel?" he whispered, pressing steadily inward. "Yeah, yeah."

He adjusted his angle a little and some muscle inside me surrendered to him and he slipped in the rest of the way. I gasped and felt the jersey-cotton pillowcase dry out my tongue. He moved out and then in again and suddenly inside me I felt nerve endings connect like perfect circuits, as if a new part of me was coming online for the first time. It was explosively good, and where was it coming from? What secret place inside? Then he moved out again and the goodness faded. Leaning forward over me he slipped his arms underneath me so that his inner elbows fused with my armpits. I was locked to him; it was almost a headlock. His forehead was pressed into the pillow beside me. Our cheeks touched.

Full of him, I *felt* full of him, and I felt like I was coming but I had no erection and now I could feel tears in my eyes. Or was that sweat on my cheeks? I was sweating. *Was* I sweating?

He began to rock his pelvis against me, moving his erection in and out, slowly at first. It made a squishing sound.

"I love that freshman twink ass," he sighed. Leaning up, he spit between my shoulder blades and then licked it off.

I was starting to feel nauseous, which brought a flare of panic. What if I threw up? His thrusting got faster and I said, "Slow, slow," because I didn't have any choice but to say it. And he replied, "You like it nice and slow, huh?"

And I did like it better nice and slow — the steadiness of the rhythm took the scary anticipation out of wondering if the next thrust would hurt. I started to feel confident that what I was feeling was all I would feel. And it wasn't awesome but it wasn't bad, and maybe it was nice. I was OK. He kept the rhythm steady, steady as a drummer, like I had asked, and I told myself he was doing what I had asked, he was obeying my rules, he respected them, I had the power here, I was in control, I could tell him anything because I had the power, and this was OK. This was OK. This was mutual, I told myself, this was something we both wanted because he was doing what I asked, we were connected, and he was a good person, he was a beautiful person, and maybe I loved him, and this was OK. This was OK. But I had tears in my eyes and he started going faster.

I came with no erection and hardly an orgasm; I wouldn't have noticed except for the hotness spreading on the sheet against my belly. For a horrible moment I wondered if I had peed, if his thrusting had pushed pee out of me. Immediately after I came my body started trying to push him out. I could feel my muscles tensing, and he had to fight my bum to stay inside it. He slid a hand under my stomach and pulled me up against him. But it only took another minute, and then it was done.

***

Afterward I lay in my bed, stiff with drying sweat, sperm, lube, while Travis went to shower. Although the bathroom had multiple stalls he had asked me to wait in our room because it would look suspicious if an RA and a resident who lived together were showering at the same time, at this hour. I could hear him out in the hallway talking to someone after he closed our door, and I wondered if that person could sense that Travis had just fucked Ollie. Was it Kaitlyn? Would she know? Was it Shelley? Did she know what his body had just done?

I curled into a ball under the covers and touched my bum to make sure everything was OK. It felt normal to my fingers but it was sore. When Travis came back to the room smelling of soap and shampoo I pretended to be asleep. Not long afterward in the moonlight I noticed that one of my R.E.M. posters was crooked and I thought about the crookedness all night long.

I was confused. I had liked it and hated it and I

didn't know which one to feel bad about.

***

The next day between classes I met Harriet for lunch in the dining hall. She looked tired; her eyes were framed with dark circles behind her square glasses. She looked like how I felt. She was working on a new play for her writing class and it'd been taking up all of her time lately. Normally it's what she would've been talking about now—stage directions, character stuff—but today she was only poking at her fries.

"Have you heard from Wesley lately?" she said absently.

It was a name from another lifetime and it caught me off-guard. "Not since before spring break," I said. We were quiet for a while after that, looking at the big-screen TV against the wall across the dining hall, past the silhouettes of other kids' heads.

"Ollie," she laughed, "will you quit sliding around in that chair? It's like your butt is on wheels today."

"Oh, ha, no, I'm just antsy, I guess." The truth was, my bum was sore. It felt OK on the outside but I imagined the inside as swollen and red. I didn't know if it was supposed to feel this way the day after. I didn't know if Harriet would be able to tell me but I thought maybe she'd know, and suddenly I was saying, "Hey. So. Travis and me." I said it low, almost a whisper, and then stopped.

The TV went to a commercial but she kept watching it anyway. "Travis and you?"

"We've— So we've been having sex."

Now she looked at me and her eyes seemed much more awake. "You're having sex with Travis?"

I reached for my ginger ale and gulped. "Twice."

"I didn't know he was gay."

"I guess he is?"

"OK," she said, dragging out the word incredulously, like, *Oookaaay*. "You don't look very happy about this."

"I don't know what I am." Suddenly I felt embarrassed, pathetic. "I mean I liked it, it was really fun. But—"

"But what? Have you had sex before? Or was this your first time, with him?"

"... My first time."

"Oh Ollie."

"It was fine, Harriet, really."

"Your first time shouldn't just be *fine*. Do you like him?"

I shrugged.

"Did you even *want* to have sex with him, Ollie, or did he push it on you?"

"Why would you think he would push it on me?" I resented the idea that I could be pushed.

"Because he's older than you. Because— Because you have tears in your eyes, Oliver!" She covered her mouth with her hand.

I slapped at my eyes with the backs of mine.

"What kind of sex was it?" she said.

"*Harriet.* Well, I was the—the receiver."

A flare of pink lit her cheeks. "Did he hurt you?"

"No. No. I mean it hurt. But it always hurts the first time, right? That's normal, right?"

"There's a difference between it being sore and you getting hurt. And I don't just mean physically."

"I could've thrown him across the room if I wanted, Harriet," I said dismissively. "I can bench the guy's body weight."

"Just because you're physically stronger than him doesn't mean he can't still take advantage of you. He's older than you. He's an RA."

"I know."

"RAs aren't *allowed* to date their residents. It's against the rules. He would know that."

"He does. He told me we should keep it a secret. And we're not dating."

"Ollie."

"He didn't force me, Harriet. It wasn't like that."

She looked away from me, aggressively rubbing her tongue over her teeth in a half snarl, like a mother wolf. "But you don't feel good about it."

"I guess not."

She was quiet for a long time. She leaned back in the booth and threw a fry at her plate. "Honestly, I don't know what I'm supposed to do now."

"Why are you supposed to do anything? I'm just telling you, Harriet. I don't want to make a thing about it."

"Well clearly you're uncomfortable with what happened. —He wore a condom, right?"

"Of course."

She took a breath. "I mean, am I supposed to let you go back to your room with him there?"

"Of course, Harriet. Harriet, I can throw him out the window if he pressures me."

"But you wouldn't." We were quiet for a while. Then she said, "Do you want to keep having sex with him?"

"I don't know. I think I might? It just happened so fast. And it's my fault because I told him I'd done it before."

"It's absolutely not your fault, Ollie, but you

should've been honest."

"I think I might want to do it again. Is that bad?"

"It's not bad, Ollie. Just— Please don't let him pressure you into anything you don't want to do."

"I know."

"Just take some time."

"I know. I will."

"Sleep in my room for a couple nights if you want; I have the air mattress. If you need space."

I felt a surge of relief, such a surge it embarrassed me. "I could? You wouldn't mind?"

"No."

"Cool. Thank you."

She picked up the fry again but didn't eat it. "I have some advice for you."

"Advice?"

"I don't know if you realize it, but you are really good looking."

"Harriet."

"And frankly the gym has made it worse. I watched you walk from the kitchen to this booth and I saw no fewer than three girls with their eyes locked on you — and look around, it's not even that crowded in here. And most girls will just whisper and giggle and go back to their lunch. But you're not into girls, you're into men, and men are going to be more aggressive, Ollie. Especially when they're older, like Travis. And especially when they have some authority. Like Travis. You're cute, and they're going to want things. And you just— You just have to be pretty assertive, is all I'm saying. I hope you have all the sex you want. But if you're crying afterward, Ollie, that's not good."

She was right—I couldn't deny there were tears in

my eyes when I was telling her about Travis. I guess I didn't really know why they were there. In most moments, I wanted to do it again. I had even jerked off to the memory of it that morning. Equally and separately, I hated him. I didn't know how to reconcile those two things at all.

***

Harriet's room was cluttered as hell with a senior's accumulation of stuff, but she moved things around and stacked things against walls so she could blow up the air mattress on the floor beside her bed. I sat on it and we laughed at how it bobbed me around.

We watched *Say Anything* on her little TV. Later in the dark in the glow of her pink lava lamp when we were in our pajamas she told me about her play, her characters, her writer's block, but I was only hearing bits and pieces of it, and I had only paid attention to bits and pieces of the movie. I was comfortable here with her but I was feeling stupid for wanting to be here, for maybe even needing to be here. It felt cowardly. My room for months with Wesley had been my perfect home, my comfort zone, and now I'd been displaced by the very thing I'd wanted and craved and advertised for. The big s-e-x. I hated Travis and I wanted him. I imagined going down the hall to my room—to *my* room—and waking him up and fucking him, not asking him, just pushing him face-down on the bed and ripping his plaid boxers off. If I even could. If I could even get hard.

Harriet went to sleep with the lava lamp on and finally I reached up and clicked it off, sending the room into darkness.

***

In the morning while Harriet showered I sat on her bed and looked out the window, down at the Quad. It was busy with kids on their way to breakfast and classes. When I spotted Travis heading away from the dorm with his backpack, with his hands in his pockets and white breath poofing out in front of him, I went to my room.

His bed was unmade. I took off my clothes and got into it and jerked off holding a pair of his underwear against my face. When I was done it occurred to me to roll over and rub the come off my belly against his sheets, but when I couldn't even do that I started to cry.

I kept busy that day, hung out in the dining hall and library between classes, lifted late at the gym, and when I got back to the dorm that night I went directly to Harriet's room. My own door was closed and I didn't know if Travis was in there yet, though I assumed he was. I'd been carrying my toothbrush and a change of clothes around with me since morning.

"You don't mind this, do you Harriet?" I asked, while the humming little motor blew up the air mattress again.

"I don't," she said, "I like our slumber parties." But she continued, "We need to get this worked out somehow for your sake, though."

"I think I'll talk to him tomorrow," I said, "yeah."

But in the dark, tomorrow seemed like too long to wait. I didn't want to talk to him, anyway. I wanted to fuck him. Maybe I even wanted to get fucked by him. I worked myself into silent rage made all the more confusing by the growing hardness in my sweatpants.

For a while I listened to Harriet's breathing, and when I was sure she was asleep, I rolled off the air mattress onto the floor. I felt for my keys in the pocket of my backpack. Slowly I unlocked her door and slipped into the hallway, blinking in the fluorescent light. The lounge was empty. Bruno's door was ajar and some music was playing in there. My own door was closed. I touched the knob and gave it a timid turn, but it didn't move. I raised my key to the lock. Then I stopped and turned and leaned against the wall. I was shaking and I could feel the wetness of precome in my underwear.

I took a breath, fitted the key in the lock, and opened the door. It was dark. I flipped on the light.

"Travis, I want—"

All of his things were gone. That half of the room was as empty as the day Wesley left. I felt a sort of whiplash of loss. For a minute I sat on the bare mattress, and then I paced the room for what felt like a long time. On the whiteboard above my desk, near the mirror where I'd first seen him looking at me, was a note. *My room is done. Thanks!* It wasn't signed.

Thanks! That was it. *Thanks!*

There was a knock at the door and I jumped.

I stood up straight and puffed out my chest. I wondered what I would say if it was Travis. I wondered if anything would happen if it was Travis.

Shivering a little, I opened the door. It was Bruno. He had on a *Beavis & Butthead* t-shirt.

"Hey," he said, "I heard you come in. Can you do me a huge favor?"

"Oh. OK."

"Can I borrow your camera? That nice one?"

"Wesley's?"

He nodded. "I'm supposed to do this photo project

for Media, and I didn't get to the equipment dispensary in time and all I own is a Polaroid and— Hey." He had noticed the half-empty room behind me. "The RA is gone, huh?"

"He left today." Letting the door swing slowly open, I went over to my desk and picked up my camera. I checked the film roll. There were still a few pictures left but I popped it out anyway and put the roll on my desk.

"So you're single in a single again, huh?" Bruno said with that *bow-chicka-wow* tone. "You must be glad to get your sex palace back."

"I guess." I handed him the camera. "Be careful with it. It was my roommate's."

The Six Months Between
Then & Now

NOW

I was the opposite of expecting to get dumped—though I guess that's what everyone says. Maybe every story about getting dumped is cliché. The same surprise, the same denial, the same obviousness in hindsight. In my case even the name is cliché: Johnny. Who hasn't been dumped by a Johnny?

The end began with me waiting for him in the parking lot of a shopping plaza outside campus. A bookstore. Lots of glass, colorful signage lighting the early dark. It was November, my junior year at UMass; the leaves had turned. I was nervous and it was that exciting kind of nervous, the way you feel about a boyfriend you've only been with three weeks. I was sitting on a curb, my bike leaning against a trash barrel beside me, yellow-leaved trees rustling behind me. Shoppers rushed this way and that, and cars crawled by looking to park. I watched through them, my hands clasped between my knees to keep warm. I watched the bookstore's revolving door. It was a Roulette wheel and my number was Johnny.

Before it slung him out I spotted him inside; a flash of familiarity had made me focus beyond the glass. He was letting someone exit ahead of him, then another person, then another. He was either very patient or too timid to seize his turn, I didn't know yet, I was still learning. Soon he slipped into an open wedge and with a spin emerged onto the sidewalk. I could feel myself smiling. I'd never had an actual boyfriend before.

He looked around, not seeing me yet. He pushed up his sleeve and checked his watch, exposing a flash of pale skin. He was in his work clothes, khakis crisp, gray fleece jacket over his blue button-down. He tucked a flat shopping bag under his arm and zipped up.

When he looked again he spotted me. I waved, a quick rainbow motion, but I didn't stand up. Sitting, I thought, made me seem casual and cool. I wanted to seem that. I had to earn his being here—we were still too new for obligations. He smiled as he walked toward me. His teeth were crooked and white.

"Buy anything fun?" I asked, stretching out my leg and touching a sneaker to his shiny black loafer.

"*Justice League, Flash, Wonder Woman* this week," he said, looking down at me. "My one indulgence." His speech had a touch of South Carolina in it. He handed me the bag so I could see. "Were you waiting long? You should've come inside."

"I have my bike," I said. I pulled the comics out of the bag and glanced at their covers; I didn't know anything about comic books but I liked the bright colors. I handed them back. "And it's never a wait when I'm waiting for you," I added cheesily, blowing my cool. I stood up, wiped mulch off the back of my jeans and then reached for my bike, bounced the front wheel over the curb.

Johnny rolled his eyes, as if he couldn't believe I could find him worth waiting for, but then he smiled and closed them; he tended to close his eyes when he smiled. I liked that because it gave me a second to have his face to myself. The clarity of his fair skin, which looked like it had never known a zit. The line where his light-brown hair met his forehead and temples. I knew all the parts of him now—I knew he had a birthmark shaped like a seahorse in a soft place his underwear covered—but his face was my favorite. His face was the part of him that looked back at me and knew how I felt, even if he seemed not to believe it, and that was the novelty of Johnny for me.

"I'm hungry," he said. "You hungry?"

"Starving. Should we walk or drive?"

"Let's drive," he said. "Do your bike."

Our codes, our slang; we already had them. *Do your bike.* We'd discovered a week earlier that if I took off my bike's front wheel it fit perfectly in the back seat of his Hyundai. It felt exciting, this discovery—a sign that we fit.

THEN

Before Johnny I hadn't been fitting, not with any of the flash-flood of guys I dated sophomore year. That thing with Travis—whatever else it was, it was a gateway drug to boys. It made me want more and it made me bolder about finding them. No longer was I content to leave my door open and wait. I went out with a guy on the floor below mine, then with an off-campus student named Daryl. I dated a guy Kaitlyn set me up with, and even one Bruno set me up with ("I know another gay guy," he had heroically).

None of the guys became more than flings, though—a few dates and a fadeaway, that was how it worked. Although I fit in their beds I found it too hard to fit in their lives.

My problem was their context—their details and dramas and complexities. Every guy had a life that never included me before and now would have to make room. Meet-cutes and first dates inevitably butted against the existence of their friends, exes, family, work. Context built up and overwhelmed me. I didn't want to hang out with their friends; I had friends. I didn't want to meet their parents; I had parents. After all my struggle to acknowledge to myself and others that I wanted these guys' attention, why did I now have to compete for it? I'd waited too long to have to compete.

I had mostly been meeting these guys through friends, and that was the worst because it brought context immediately: from the start he's not quite yours, you're sharing him with that mutual friend. So I decided to try my own luck online, with personal ads—tiny thumbnail photos, cursors manifesting text. Context seemed avoidable there. Which was stupid; they were the same guys. But that was easy to ignore when you were supplied with dozens of faces with no context. These guys seemed like nothing more than what they could be for me. Names, ages, likes and dislikes—these faces had lives small enough to fit in your pocket. I saw a face named Johnny I thought would fit perfectly in mine.

We IMed for a week before deciding to meet. I was optimistic, but cautiously. There'd been little talk of context while we were IMing but I knew that even if you can hold if off, context eventually rushes in like cold air with a winter guest. To my relief, he didn't invite me to a friend's party or on a double date or to a brother's basketball game. He invited me to Friendly's for ice cream, just us.

He got to the restaurant first and was in a booth sipping from a sweating glass of ice water when I arrived. His hand was cold from the glass when we shook, but then his other, warmer hand clasped the back of mine.

"I'm Johnny," he said.

"I know," I laughed as I slid into the booth and wriggled out of my jacket.

We perused the glossy menus in nervous silence for a while, and then ordered sundaes. While we waited he tried on my bike helmet and said, "How do I look?"

"Cute," I said, watching the blue buckles swing beneath his smooth chin.

"You rode your bike here?" he said.

"I ride pretty much everywhere. I used to have a car but it was too cumbersome to keep it on campus."

"Tell me about your school," he said, handing me back the helmet and smoothing his hair with his palm. He knew from IMing that I went to UMass. He asked about my dorm, my classes, my photography minor. I told him everything, most of it for the second time, though it was nice this time to see his face instead of a screen reflecting my own.

Soon the sundaes were set in front of us. He began carving whipped cream delicately with the tip of his long-handled silver spoon. "I would love to go to school," he said wistfully.

"Yeah," I said, "so you don't? Why's that?"

"You're dripping," he said, catching a bead of peanut butter running down the back of my dish.

"Thanks," I said softly.

He put the spoon in his mouth and licked my peanut butter. He didn't seem to mean for it to be erotic, but good god.

"Yeah, I don't go to school," he continued. "I was supposed to. I would like to. Someday." He smirked. He'd said it the way people say *someday* about owning a Ferrari, about backpacking through Europe. For him an education seemed something to aspire to, and I wondered why; for me, I was privileged enough to see it as a dutiful slog.

I said, "What do you mean, you were *supposed* to?"

It took him a few seconds to answer. "Just decided to go in a different direction."

"You said you work for a vet? That must be cool. No exams!"

"A receptionist for a vet," he corrected, scrunching his face. "I make teeth-cleaning appointments for cats." He leaned forward, a little conspiratorially. "There's so many lesbians around here, and they're very up on dental hygiene for their pets."

"Wouldn't your parents help, though?" I said, still too curious to laugh. "If you did want to go to school?"

He shook his head and then focused on his sundae. He tipped the dish and showed me the secret cluster of M&Ms he'd uncovered at the bottom. And from this he seemed to be telling me to drop the school talk. I did, and reminded myself to be glad of no context.

With him, context turned out to be easy to avoid. He had an apartment in Amherst but didn't talk much about it, except to say his roommate was an older black man named Will. He didn't say anything more about his job at the vet. Instead he told me all the ways to slay a dragon. He talked about being the first human on Mars.

About what he would do if he won the lottery, about buying a copy of *Action Comics* #1. He seemed not to have any past but talked for an hour about his fantastical future, like a book with nothing on its pages but the promise of an amazing sequel. I noticed, at some point, two things: how pretty his amber eyes were, and that they hadn't left my own face. Not to scan the booths for people he knew. Not to check his cellphone for missed calls; he didn't even have a cellphone. When our ice cream dishes were empty and sitting in rings of melt on the table, we ordered food, to make it last.

After almost three hours chilling in that Friendly's booth my veins felt full of coffee and I wanted to run through the parking lot wagging my arms, but I contained myself. We walked to his car. He had a white Hyundai with rust rimming the wheel wells.

"I feel like a villain making you pedal back to your dorm," he said. "But I don't think your bike can fit in my car...."

"It's cool," I said, eyeing his small back seat and agreeing that my bike probably wouldn't fit. "Biking keeps my muscles hard. I used to lift weights, and I was pretty big, but I kind of, I dunno, I stopped."

He blushed and looked down at my tires or my sneakers or the ground I was standing on. I wanted to kiss him — would've tried, except we were in public.

"I wish I didn't have work in the morning," he said, "so this could go... longer?"

I told him we'd do it again, the sooner the better, and he made me promise, and I promised. Then I buckled my helmet with the straps that had hugged his chin, and rode away.

Soon after I got home Shelley came by my room. She had moved out of Johnson Hall for her senior year and lived in the building next door, but the prospect of news of my date enticed her to make a trek across the Quad.

"You look happy!" she said, sitting down on my bed and fitting one of my pillows behind her. She let me blabber for a few minutes about my date and then asked to see Johnny's photo again. I brought it up on my computer, the little thumbnail from his ad.

"Oh," she said, "he's cute."

"I hadn't noticed."

She laughed. "So what's his story?"

"Shelley, I don't even know. I don't think he *has* one."

"Oh." She frowned. "But that's bad, right? He's boring?"

"No, no, it's good. That's why I'm happy. He's not boring. He's a blank page. I *love* it."

When Johnny and I met up again three long nights later I imagined pulling our dates together like pieces of string and tying them into one seamless evening, omitting the hours we'd spent apart.

This time I invited him to the UMass dining hall for dinner after he got off work. I was short on money and I could feed him for free there.

"Pick a table," I told him as we entered amid the clatter of voices and silverware, and he said, "Any table?"

"Fill your plate," I told him as we wandered the buffet, and he said, "With whatever I want?"

He seemed to feel out of place and he looked it too, in his ironed work clothes surrounded by kids in t-shirts and slippers and unimpressed glares. But he grinned mysteriously while we ate.

"Imagine if I went to UMass too?" he said — whispered, actually, as though he were afraid of someone nearby laughing at him. "We could have lunch every single—" He paused, suddenly bashful.

"Minute?" I offered hopefully, and he looked surprised.

It was enough to tell each other that this was mutual. It was enough for me to know to bring him back to my room.

We crossed the Quad in the chilly evening. I had my own room that year, and as I closed the door behind us I asked gently what he wanted to do. I had my nice underwear on under my jeans but was feeling comfortable enough and secure enough to not be disappointed when he asked if I had cable.

"Of course," I said. "We get all the channels."

He took off his shoes and sat cross-legged beside me on my bed, so our knees were just touching. He was wearing those thin black office socks, and they looked funny near the toes of my puffy white Hanes. We watched something on MTV, crept higher to E!, crept higher to Showtime. He put his hand on my thigh and I started to get hard, but when he didn't move it any more I understood the touch was an ends, not a means.

The TV flickered and droned. Johnny surfed higher, to HBO. It was after 10:00 when I started to fixate on the clock by my bed. I hoped some magical deadline of lateness would compel him to sleep over. Close to midnight, when I thought I was safely past that deadline, I yawned and stretched my legs.

"Oh," he said, pulling his hand from my thigh and glancing around for the clock, almost bewildered, as if he'd just woken up, "it's late."

Softly, because our faces were close, I said, "You can just— If you want to— You're welcome to stay over." He leaned away from me and I could see he was considering doing the *Oh I couldn't really* thing, but that only meant he wanted to stay. "We don't have to do anything," I added. "But I'd be happy if you stayed."

"Let's not, uh, rule anything out," he said, and then he raised his eyes toward the ceiling and let out a short whistle.

I picked out some of my shorts and a t-shirt for him so he could change out of his work clothes. Then I went to the bathroom and scrubbed my teeth and tongue to minty freshness while pacing past the shower stalls and willing my heartbeat to slow. *Let's not rule anything out*, he had said, which meant I was going to get laid. By *him*, by Johnny, slayer of dragons.

When I got back to my room he was wearing my clothes. I felt a wave of quiet comfort come over me. I guess for a person like me, a person wary of context, there was no better image than the one I was seeing: a guy with so little of his own context that he was dressed in my clothes.

He was taller than I was, and the shorts, which were knee-length on me, hit him mid-thigh, showing off his long, lean bare legs, dusted with wiry brown hairs.

"Could I borrow some mouthwash or something?" he asked, idly touching the faded UMass logo on his t-shirt.

I lent him my bucket of toiletries. While he was in the bathroom I carefully folded the pants he'd left balled up on my floor—29x36 was the size—and smoothed them over a hanger along with his red-and-blue gingham shirt. I hung his clothes in my armoire and lined up his shoes in front of it, with his socks draped over them to air out.

After what seemed like a long time he returned smelling of Icy Mint Blast.

I was standing beside the bed but lacked the boldness to get into it. I was used to being on some sort of horny autopilot in these situations but around Johnny I felt hyper aware of everything. Casually, leaning against the dresser with one hand in the pocket of my shorts to camouflage my erection, I told him I'd hung up his clothes.

He surprised me by looking surprised. "You—hung them up?"

"Well I mean— I didn't want them to get wrinkled."

Touching one hand to his cheek, he stood looking at me as though I were a puzzle, as though something about me didn't make sense to him and needed figuring out. Finally he looked down, smoothing my t-shirt against his flat belly. "I need to set an alarm for work tomorrow," he said. "Can I use your clock?"

While he was programming it I hopped into bed. Then from under the covers I watched him poke around my room. I watched him trace his thin fingers down the spines of my tapes and CDs, look at photos pinned to the wall of me and my friends, and pick up the cameras that had taken them. He seemed to be stalling, too. I rolled over and faced the wall to give him some privacy.

It was only a minute later that he climbed under the covers carefully, quietly, as if I were already asleep and he didn't want to disturb me—though of course I wasn't asleep and would not sleep. I reached up and shut off the reading lamp clamped to the headboard.

"Enough room?" I whispered.

He said yes, though he was probably hanging over the edge. We lay side by side, him on his back, me on my side, stiff as strangers in an elevator. It was the kind of awkwardness you can appreciate, though, and savor, because you know it'll only feel this way once, and as soon as the first kiss happens it'll be over and it'll never come back, this all-consuming moment of *will-we-or-won't-we*. Soon it did end: he turned his head and kissed my ear. Then he rolled over and yanked the jersey-cotton sheet over his head. "That was so lame of me!" he laughed from beneath.

Spooning against him, because *will-we-or-won't-we* had become *we-are*, I told him it wasn't lame at all. His bare legs were like fuzzy silk, and his back was so warm. I scrubbed my nose against his hair. He squeezed my feet between his feet.

"This is nice," I said, feeling him inside my own clothes.

"This *is* nice," he replied.

We stayed that way for a little bit and then he moved his bum back and forth against me, noticing or confirming my hardness. He stopped and was quiet.

"There's something I want you to know about me, Ollie," he whispered, "before we go any further. OK?"

"Oh," I said, "OK," and I got scared. It wasn't his words so much as his tone, and the implication that even though he was in bed with someone this whatever-it-was still had a grip on his thoughts. My boner softened as my mind went to AIDS, herpes, cancer. He wanted to tell me he saw ghosts. He was a Communist, a vampire. He was molested. He molested. He did time. He had a boyfriend. Oh no, did he have a boyfriend?

Finally he said, "I'm sort of... on my own."

"You're on your own?"

I didn't know what he could mean. I was holding him.

NOW

With his comic books and my rattling bike stowed in the back seat behind us, he drove out of the bookstore parking lot. Our agenda was food.

"What're you in the mood for?" he said, fiddling with a loose knob on his dashboard. Cold air started pouring against my shins.

"We could do that Irish place in Northampton?"

"OK."

We headed that way, but it was rush hour and the traffic on Route 9 was thick, so instead of going all the way to Northampton we detoured to a pizza place in Hadley that Shelley and I went to a lot. In the booth while we waited for our pizza he cupped his hand under his chin and looked at me thoughtfully, with what I would later decide was regret. It made me uncomfortable.

"So how was— How was work today?" I said.

He leaned back and folded his hands on the table. He looked tired. "The phones rang so much. Never-ending pussycat dental issues." Sighing, he went on. "People are crazy, Ollie, aren't they? The cruel things they'll do to other people, and in the next breath they'll make a *dentist* appointment for a *cat*."

"Probably not the same people," I laughed.

"No, Ollie. The same people."

Our waiter approached our table with a pizza but it was a false alarm; it was for the people beside us.

"I talked to my sister today," he said after a minute of what seemed like contemplation, a time during which

I felt unsure what to say.

"How's she doing?"

"She's concerned about what I'm doing for Thanksgiving. The holidays get hard for me."

"I'm sure they do. It's OK. I just assumed you would come to my family's."

He sniffed hard, as if I was being silly. "Ollie, I can't do that. You can't just take me in."

"Of course. Why wouldn't we?"

"We've only been dating a few weeks. It's too — fast."

"So? They love you. They *will* take you in. My mom is probably relieved that I have someone as amazing as you. They can be your new family."

"*Ollie*," he said. He looked down at his hands.

THEN

Johnny's story, the story he told me as he lay in my bed wearing my clothes, went like this, like something out of a sad pop-up book: Two years earlier, when Johnny was seventeen years and six months old, Johnny's parents found out that Johnny was gay. He wasn't sure how they found out, what evidence they uncovered, but he knew the moment he came home from school one day that they knew. They didn't say anything but he could tell. His house fell into a three-day silence — his mother seemed perpetually away with his little sister, and his father seemed to leave the garage only to get food from the kitchen.

On the third day, Johnny told me, his parents came into his bedroom and asked him if it was true that he was *that way*. It was his father who asked, but it was a statement, not a question — they had already decided. Johnny said yes, it was true. His father started to yell.

His mother didn't say anything, just lowered her eyes as the life drained out of her face.

On the fourth day, Johnny's parents told Johnny that when he turned eighteen, on his eighteenth birthday, they wanted him to leave the family and not speak to them or his little sister again. After delivering this news with eyes hard in spite of tears, they left, shutting Johnny's door quietly behind them.

While he was telling me this his body felt stiff against mine. I imagined I could feel goosebumps on him. But when he spoke there was no emotion in his voice.

"It was a pretty tough six months," he said, and laughed stiffly, "believe me."

I didn't know what to say. That story from that voice, from this boy— I was shaking. He must've felt it because he reached back and squeezed my shoulder and told me it was OK.

"Luckily I had time to graduate," he continued, "but college was out; I had no money for it. On my birthday they told me to take my car and they gave me three thousand dollars. They said goodbye. It was almost like a little ceremony." And he went on, "I'd heard there are a lot of gay people in this part of the country. It seemed as good a place as any."

"But— I— Wasn't there someone in South Carolina you could've stayed with? Like, other family? Friends?"

"You don't really want to stick around after something like that," he said, shaking his head against the pillow.

I squeezed him tighter because I thought he needed it, or because I needed it, and I felt more angry than I'd ever felt. I wanted to find his parents and kill them—*kill* them, that's the honest truth. They deserved execution. I wanted to rescue his sister from them, put her up for adoption. I didn't know how they could do that to him. But what was most confusing to me was that he didn't seem to hate them.

"They just don't understand," he whispered.

"What about your sister?" I asked, leaning up on one elbow. Light from my screensaver lit the side of his face and I looked for tears but didn't see any. "Have you talked to her?"

"Officially she's not allowed to talk to me. But sometimes I chat online with her at work when she's at her friend Lisa's house."

"Jesus, Johnny."

I wanted him to cry. I sent telepathic pleas for him to break down and cry. I would've known what to do with that. Crying would've been something to be resolved, a surmountable distance to *better*. But he wasn't crying. And I didn't think he was going to. So instead, because I didn't know what else to do, I asked him a question I'm proud of asking, because even though it sounds a little strange, a little like I was taking advantage, I know that in that moment it was the right thing to say.

He smiled at me and said that yes, we could, and we took off our clothes.

NOW

We split the big pizza and ended up talking about music. Thanksgiving was off the table for now, though I knew I would try again soon. He told me that Whitney Houston's album *I'm Your Baby Tonight* was underappreciated. I told him she would never hold a candle to R.E.M. Because he seemed sadder tonight than usual, and because the holidays loomed, I also told him I loved him. I thought it would make him feel better and safer to know it. A magical fix, and it had the virtue of being true. But when I said it he winced, as though I'd slipped a knife into his side.

THEN

In the morning he pulled his arm out from under me, banged his hand around beside the bed, and shut off the beeping alarm clock. I felt groggily sad that he needed to leave. I turned my head on the pillow we were sharing and pressed my lips against his smooth shoulder. They lingered there until he pulled away and the blanket flopped back on top of me. Through half-open eyes I watched him being naked in my room, moving around in front of the blue-lit window, his thin limbs lanky as he reached for something.

I heard some beeps. A moment later I heard him say he wasn't feeling well. I heard the clack of my phone returning to its cradle. The blankets lifted up in a puff of cold air, then an instant warmth as he settled against me.

"Oh," I said happily, my eyes closing again.

At 10:00, after sleeping for three hours more, we emerged naked from the jersey-cotton sheets. Sitting on my bed, we ate everything I had in my room: a box of animal crackers, a Snickers, half a bottle of flat Mountain Dew. Around 11:00 we had sex again, happy this time, no tears, and he laughed when I blew raspberries against his neck after we had come. At noon we watched Oprah. At 1:00 I asked him to be my boyfriend. He got out of bed and stood looking out the window for a while, then he turned to me and said yes.

He was beautiful, funny, playful, sexy, smart, strong, vulnerable—Johnny was the dictionary. But his complexity seemed to begin and end within himself. His story, tragic as it was, meant that he was free of other context, and because of that I saw how easily he would fit in my life. His parents were monsters and what they had done to him made me furious, but I felt uniquely suited to work with it. I wanted to be needed and he would need me in a way other guys with other contexts never would. Short of a few coworkers and a nine-to-five, I was all Johnny had in the world.

I brought him around campus and introduced him to my friends — to Shelley, to Kaitlyn, to Bruno. I even had him meet my parents. I showed him my context, all of it. I saw him as someone who could wear my whole life the way he'd worn my clothes. I didn't realize that it was too much, that I was becoming what I'd avoided in other guys. I was overwhelming him. I was making middle-school dating mistakes when I was twenty, with a guy who really mattered. I was still learning, and I was screwing up when it mattered. This was the tragedy of growing up a closeted gay boy: you've had no practice when it matters.

NOW

Piece by piece our pizza disappeared like a countdown around the dented platter. By the time the check came Johnny was all but silent. I knew I'd screwed up by telling him I was in love with him, I just didn't know why it was bad.

"I didn't mean to put pressure on you," I said as I counted bills from my wallet.

"No," he said, "it's fine, it's something everyone wants to hear. It's a nice thing, Ollie."

"You don't seem like you wanted to hear it, Johnny."

"I guess I've just been in a petulant mood all day," he said. "It's not your fault. Thank you for getting the pizza."

"You're cute even when you're petulant."

He smiled weakly.

We pulled on our jackets and left the restaurant. Outside the wind blew orange and yellow leaves around the parking lot, which the pizza place shared with a dry cleaner and a hot-tub store that isn't there anymore. I stuck my hands in my pockets and walked close enough to him so that our elbows touched.

"Wanna go back to my dorm and make out?" I said. "That'll make you un-petulant."

"I don't know," he said, though I could tell he didn't want to, he was just stalling. "Let's sit down over there, OK?" He motioned with his chin to a low brick retaining wall at the edge of the lot.

"But your car is over there." I pointed away from where he was heading.

"I know, just—"

We sat down on the brick wall, and Johnny broke up with me there. He did it so quickly and gently, like a magician yanking a tablecloth without disturbing the china, that I wasn't aware at first that it had even happened.

When I did realize, though, I stared at the ground, watching leaves roll across the tops of my sneakers. "Did I do something wrong?"

"No," he said quietly. "No, Ollie, of course not." He crossed his arms and leaned forward, away from me.

"I do love you," I said, "I wasn't just saying it to try to make you feel better. It's true." My nose was running and I wiped it with my glove. "I can be everything you lost. There's enough room in my life to hold you."

Once it was said, that too didn't seem like the right thing to say. When he didn't respond I started tumbling over promises and pleas, trying to find whatever would fix things. "I'll give you all the space you need, if that's what you need," I promised. "Please don't end this when it's just starting. I don't want to lose you."

He closed his eyes but this time he wasn't smiling. If the best things I could think of were hurting him, what could I do? Should I have told him I hated him? Should I have hit him?

"You don't have to be on your own anymore, Johnny," I said. "You don't."

"I wasn't looking for a relationship," he said, more businesslike after clearing his voice. "I was just online for a hookup. I didn't mean for this to get like this."

"Like this what? Serious? But it doesn't have to be serious." That sounded good, at least to my ears, and I repeated it like a great idea, like a discovery—like our salvation. "It doesn't have to be serious, right! We can just hang out. Then we can be together."

He looked at me but by that point it was as though he were looking through glass. Like a person looking through a pet-store window at a puppy he knows better than to bring home.

"Let's go undo your bike," he said.

Halfway to his car I stopped and pretended to have to fix my shoelace. I was afraid that if we got any closer to his getaway, I really would lose him.

"I think we should test out being friends," I said. "Give it a try."

"Ollie—"

"Friend Johnny, would you like to go hang out at my dorm?" I bounced my eyebrows, trying to keep it light but feeling like I was cracking in half. "We could play some *Mario Kart*!"

"Ollie, I think—" He was looking down at the pavement. "You deserve someone less damaged than me."

"You're not damaged. It's not your fault your parents are awful." It didn't get a reaction and I swung to a different tact: "I'm damaged too! Have I told you about my crooked lines? I have obsessions. I call them my ticks!"

He was walking again. I followed. He unlocked his car and pulled out my front wheel, handed it to me. I took it. Then he pulled out the rest of my bike, and when I wouldn't take it he laid it on the ground. My helmet rocked in the sand and a pedal spun slowly.

"Thank you for everything, Ollie. You're very sweet and I had fun."

"That's not fair. You can't just say thank you and say you're too damaged and all this stuff and then break up with me."

"If life was fair I'd be in South Carolina right now, Ollie, and we never would've met at all." His voice made it sound like the most obvious thing in the world, and maybe it was. He opened his door and started to get in. "It's best if you just forget about me." Then he looked up, his face a sort of blank surprise, as if he couldn't believe he'd done it. "That's all. Goodbye."

When my hands stopped being as useless as my voice I reassembled my bike as fast as I could and rode after him, my front wheel rattling dangerously. I could see his car a little way down Route 9, in a line of traffic caught by a red light.

I sped out of the parking lot and across the street. I

almost got hit. Two cars honked and one guy yelled. I caught up with Johnny at the light. I didn't say anything; he just looked at me through the glass and said, "I can't."

The cars in front of him were starting to move now. My mouth was dry and my hands were hanging limply on the handlebars. My heart was pounding. With my bike cutting across the yellow lines, I watched his taillights shrink down the street as traffic moved by on both sides of me, honking. A car went by dragging its muffler.

That was the last time I saw Johnny. He blocked my IMs later that same night, did not respond to my emails. He was ignoring me, and it hurt, and I truly began to understand that the worst thing you can do to a person is to ignore them. To treat them like they don't even exist. Johnny should've known that. Maybe he did. I knew it now, too. And I knew that just because a guy's family doesn't interrupt your dinner doesn't mean they're not all sitting in your booth. Sometimes no context is the biggest context of all.

For a long time—through the rest of junior year and through senior year and even after I graduated from UMass—I saw his face in random faces. I smelled his smell when I passed certain basement windows puffing air sweetened with a certain fabric softener. For a long time I waited for the call or the email or the IM that would say he was wrong, he was sorry for abandoning me, for cutting me off and leaving me on my own. But it didn't happen. The fact that I was still waiting to be taken back was proof, to me, that he was still waiting, too.

Honeymoon for Knights

Two princesses sat in the waiting area. I guessed they were about seven and five. The older one, decked in frilly pink nylon and a tall, conical hat with pink ribbons streaming from the point, was swinging her legs and wore a shit-eating grin. The younger, in yellow, was spread out on the bench, pressing her face into the coat sleeve of a gray-haired woman who sat between the two girls; she was pounding the woman's thigh with a little fist.

The woman told the yellow princess to settle down and the pink one smiled harder, swung her legs harder beneath the bench.

A cowboy, leather chaps tight across his college-jock thighs, had emerged from one of the costume rooms and now sat down on the bench near the younger princess. Both girls looked up. He tipped his pinto-patterned hat at them and they smiled. The older one blushed, too. Who could blame her?

I reached in my pocket for my appointment list, unfolded it and gave it a look. The two girls were my 1:00 but there were no single boys on the list. He could be a walk-in, but people never did this type of thing by themselves; they needed goading. And sure enough, a helmeted astronaut soon sauntered over to the smiling cowboy, did a fashion-show twirl and swung its bulky hips. I got excited—was this a gay couple? Then the astronaut removed its helmet and shook out its hair and revealed itself to be a girl. I felt disappointed, stupid, a little embarrassed for assuming.

The astronaut sat down beside the cowboy. Beyond them outside the store, mall shoppers passed back and forth at a steady pace, as though the shiny beige floor were a moving sidewalk. They carried bags and drinks, pushed strollers. The light from the orange Orange Julius sign blended with the pink from the Spencer's Gifts sign and cast everything in a pallid, funereal glow. Muzak played. It was February vacation and the weather was shitty; everyone in the world had come to the Holyoke Mall. Three teenagers stood in line for pretzels and watched an unattended three-year-old run around screaming.

I could see it all through an open doorway from where I sat in back-of-house of Fantasy Foto. I ate a curly fry from Arby's—my lunch. Beside me my coworker Patrice dropped an empty yogurt container into the trash and picked up a camera. She breathed on the lens and wiped it with a microfiber cloth.

"I'll trade you the princesses for those other two," I said out of the corner of my mouth.

"No chance, Wade," Patrice said, not even looking at them. "I already earned my wings today after that dog pissed on my tripod. Anyway, you're good with the little kids."

"I was just hoping to pose the cowboy with his shirt off."

Now she looked out into the waiting area. "Ooh."

"This job has few perks, Patrice. I take 'em where I

can get 'em." I put the appointment list back in my pocket and ate another fry. "Well, if you won't trade, you need to let me shoot at your station. The princesses are going to want the castle, and mine is ripped." In my other pocket my cellphone started vibrating. I pulled it out. "It's my mom. Weird."

"Maybe she sensed you eating french fries as your lunch again." She held the camera lens up to the light to check for smudges. "Be nice to her and I'll pose Cowboy shirtless for you. Just don't leer from across the studio."

"I've never leered in my life."

I answered the phone.

"Fries," I said. My mom had asked what I was eating for lunch, a question which had followed other mothery pleasantries. "I can't talk long, Mom. I'm getting low on my minutes. Was there a reason you called?"

"Would you get a real phone, Oliver, please? You obsess about those minutes. I just bought you some more at Christmas, didn't I?"

"They disappear; I'm popular. Anyway, if I had a real phone you wouldn't be able to call me at work."

She sighed. In the waiting area the older princess got up and did a cartwheel that knocked off her conical hat. I figured she was trying to impress the cowboy.

"I need to go, Mom. My next glamtastic supremes are getting restless out there."

"Oliver, before you go— Did you hear about Dwight?"

"Dwight who?" I dropped my empty fries bag into the trash.

"Dwight Macklin, your old friend from when you were little. The one who stopped talking."

"No. What about him?"

"He was in an accident," she said, and she sighed. And now I knew why she had called. "Did he ever start talking again?"

"I don't know. He must have, that was like ten years ago. You know I don't keep in touch with anyone from high school. What kind of accident?"

"Car. A drunk ran a stop sign and hit him. Very sad."

"Wow. That's terrible."

"I wanted to let you know in case you want to go to the calling hours."

"Calling hours? Wait, he's *dead?*" Patrice looked up looking concerned.

"Oh. Yes, Ollie. On impact, they say."

"Jesus."

"I don't like to think about it." She sighed again. I could imagine her nervously winding the phone cord around her fingers, turning the tips of them blue. "Lois Branch told me about it in the market this afternoon. All I could picture was you in that car, Ollie. I'm sorry, I guess I just wanted to hear your voice."

"Wow. Dwight is dead. Huh." I watched the older princess turn another cartwheel. The astronaut clapped.

"It's very sad," my mother continued. "I'll send you the obituary. It's on a website. I'll email you the thing, the link. It has the information. I think you should probably go to the calling hours. These things are important."

"Yeah, thanks."

"Do you think you'll go?"

"I don't know, Mom, I'll think about it."

When I got back to work I was glad for the princesses and I didn't think of the cowboy again much.

***

Since graduating from UMass I had lived in an apartment in Amherst with two guys I never knew very well. Straight guys. I had answered an ad. I had my own room in the apartment and they shared the second bedroom. Though they were jockish, intimidating, I thought at first their bunk beds were a cover for a secret romance. But they weren't gay, the guys only needed the money and so had bought the bunks and sublet one of their rooms. Often enough I saw one or the other of them sexiled on the living-room couch.

One of them, Corey, I didn't talk to much at all. He treated me like a neighbor you wave to each morning but never make an effort to get to know. The other, Theo, was a mechanic who seemed grateful and relieved to discover that I'd worked in an auto-body shop during high school—he latched on to that fact and with Theo I talked about cars. He had fat hands and a burly laugh and he seemed not to know what to make of me, of my gayness, of the fact that I sometimes brought guys home, but he did what he could. Still, I understood that if they'd known I was gay before they rented to me, they would not have rented to me.

It was a crowded apartment but I often felt isolated there. At night I could hear them talking and laughing in their bunks like college boys, and it felt strange to be in another room apart from them. Often their voices made me think of my former roommates and hallmates, made me want to live a life where I could live with them again. But on that night, after my mom called about Dwight, I wasn't thinking of college, I was thinking back farther.

I'd told my mom I would think about it but really at first I had no intention of going to Dwight's funeral. I didn't see the point. Dwight was dead and I hadn't even seen the guy since before I started shaving. In the dark I lay with my arms behind my head, looking up at the ceiling at my R.E.M. posters, battered now, and wrinkled, but still some sort of guide. Next door Corey and Theo were laughing hysterically about something.

You don't go to funerals for the dead, though. It's not like they'll know. It's not like they'll look back at you from the plush confines of the casket and check your name off a list. You go to funerals for the living. If I went, it might be so his parents in their time of tragedy could believe their son had made an impression throughout his short life, that he had had friends, that he would be remembered and missed. And if they were going to be made to feel that way, there weren't many people from Dwight's youth who could make them feel it. Because the truth was, back when I knew him, Dwight had not made an impression. He had not really had friends, and when he moved away he had not really been missed. It was up to me—and, I suspected, maybe one other person from Lee. A person who, for all I knew, wasn't even still alive himself.

In the end, if I'm honest, that one other person is the only reason I decided to go.

I made plans to leave work early on the day of the funeral—Patrice agreed to cover my shift in exchange for me doing all of her animal shoots for the next month. On my way home I stopped for a haircut—a haircut for a funeral. At home I shaved and cleaned up my eyebrows, feeling a bit like a douche but wanting to be prepared. I had already picked out my clothes, an outfit that could do double duty as mournful and hip.

After I showered I stood in front of the hallway mirror putting on my tie. Corey, the one I hardly ever talked to, who was home for some reason, saw it and said, "Job interview?"

"Funeral for a friend," I said.

"Oh," he said, "sorry." There was a long pause. "Young guy?"

"Yeah."

He bit at his lip. "Was it—? Never mind, sorry."

"Car accident," I said, but I knew he'd been thinking of AIDS.

I left my tie loose. I had a two-hour drive—Dwight's service was in Newton, just outside Boston, through which I'd once traveled on a rainbow subway. Today it was gray and cloudy, would probably rain. February was a shit month. I drove along the Mass Pike, a wet black ribbon, from Amherst to Newton. I was starting to feel like my life would be easier if I lived in Boston. R.E.M. on the stereo, of course—the *Out of Time* album. I was thinking about him. Not Dwight.

Newton was a clusterfuck of rotaries but I found my way to the funeral home eventually and was still way early. The calling hours were from 4:00 to 7:00; it was only 3:20. After sitting in the parking lot for a while with the windshield wipers switching back and forth, I decided it was awkward to be sitting there so long. So I drove across the street to a Dunkin' Donuts, whose sign had been glowing-up the raindrops on my passenger window.

I ran from my Jeep into the Dunkins, careful not to let my fresh haircut get wet. Inside I ordered a coffee, drank it slowly, looked out at the funeral home through the big steamy windows. I wondered if I would recognize him when I finally laid eyes on him. It had been so long with no word. Or would I be too startled? Would it feel too odd? With all the apparatus of the funeral around us. With the coffin. With Dwight lying there dead. Would his face have anything in common with the one I fell in love with?

Across the street two cars pulled into the funeral home lot from the same direction. The passengers got out and stood looking at each other vacantly in the drizzle for a minute before putting their arms around each other and heading toward the entrance. They had to turn on a ramp and briefly faced my direction before going inside. I recognized Dwight's parents—older, grayer—among them.

A few minutes later another car arrived and I watched the people go inside. This Dunkin' Donuts was a good spot to see everyone who entered the funeral home. If he came I'd be able to see him from here. I ordered a second coffee and returned quickly to the window, focusing past my own reflection, sipping more slowly this time—I couldn't keep drinking coffee for three hours or my heart would explode when I saw him.

By 4:30 the parking lot was half full with a steady turnover of comings and goings. People were entering and leaving the funeral home in groups that sometimes got jumbled and I began to feel nervous that I might miss him. I pitched the near-empty coffee in the trash and pulled out my keys, and drove back across the street. I parked near the back and sat, saw a place open up right near the entrance ramp and moved there to take it. It was almost 5:00 now. I waited in my car until 6:00, then I went inside.

It was busier now that the workday was over. I stood in a line that moved slowly down a long hallway wallpapered with flowers. I could see everyone in front of me up to a corner that turned, and from time to time I'd look back to see what new people had gotten in line. Very few were around my age; it was mostly people who looked like friends of Dwight's parents. Self-righteously I told myself it was good I had come.

After turning the corner I could see into the main room, where Dwight's family was arranged in a receiving line that stemmed away from the casket — his parents, probably an uncle and aunt, a grandmother and grandfather. I'd been worried the image of Dwight lying in his casket would conjure one of my last memories of him — the moment I was sitting on him on his bed, his sweatshirt clenched in my fists, bashing him against the mattress so hard his glasses fell off. But the casket was closed.

"Oh," I said in surprise, and my voice cracked. And I actually gulped. A hot rock of spit thudded into my stomach. I must've been imagining old-people funerals — peaceful sleeping corpses — but this wasn't one of those. Dwight was my age, and people my age didn't pass away sweetly in their sleep. Dwight had been mangled by metal and glass so completely that he had died. What had been left of him? Had the bespectacled boy I once knew ended up in pieces? I reached for the back of a chair, feeling delirious with shame. I had gotten a haircut? I had cleaned up my eyebrows?

The casket was dark wood and seeing it closed had put tears in my eyes. I walked quickly past it and went through the receiving line in a blur and was coughed out at the end of it with my palm wet from tear-stained handshakes.

"So nice to see one of Dwight's old friends from Lee," his mother had said sedately when I told her who I was. So I guessed I was the first, or the only, but I didn't care anymore. It was only 6:30 but I wanted out. I felt so stupid. I walked quickly back along the line, around the corner. Ahead was the door opening to the rainy evening. Then a hand sprung out of the line and grabbed my arm.

"Ollie? Ollie Wade!" A loud whisper, loud as the speaker dared in such a place.

I turned. Looked at the hand on my arm. Looked up at the face. He was my age still, though now he looked like a man. We had gone to school together once, had been great friends once, but were not anymore, and hadn't been even the last time we saw each other. But he wasn't who I had come for. He wasn't *Boyd*.

"I thought it was you!" he said. He put his hands on his chest. "Mike Alonzo, remember!"

"Itchy Chin Mike! I'm sorry I walked right past you. It was kind of brutal in there."

"I bet," he said. "I'm thankful for that corner." He seemed to debate it for a second and then hugged me. He smelled good and was wearing a nice crisp suit, and it was clear to me at a glance that when he'd become popular in high school, it had stuck. "How are you, man? Wow! Ollie Wade!"

"All things considered, OK."

"Yeah it's really terrible," he said. "So sad, man."

"How are you, Mike Alonzo? It's been a long time."

"It has. I'm good. I'm working. Things are good."

"That sounds good." I paused awkwardly. "Had you kept in touch with...?" I tipped my head in the direction the line was facing.

"No, not really, no." He said it guiltily.

"I know."

"Yeah. You know, you just never think— Well, you

lose track, I guess." He shrugged.

"I didn't keep in touch either. Not with any of you."

He nodded. "Are you sticking around? Or are you heading— Where's home?"

"Amherst," I said. "And I was. But I can hang out and shoot the shit for a while if you're not in a hurry. Would you want to get a burger or something?"

"Cool, cool. That would be cool. Let me just, you know, do this. Where will you be?"

"I'll be in my car. I'm the black Jeep, near the front."

I sat in the car wondering why I'd said it, about shooting the shit. I didn't want to shoot the shit. I didn't know what we would possibly shoot the shit about. I wanted to go home. I thought about driving away. I would have, but there was still fifteen minutes left, and now that I'd seen Mike Alonzo there seemed an even better chance that I might see *him*, so I watched the door.

In the last ten minutes no new people arrived, but still I waited, and at 7:05 Mike emerged from the funeral home and stood at the bottom of the ramp, looking at the lot. He spotted my Jeep and jogged over through the drizzle glistening in the yellow floodlights. He opened the passenger door and leaned in.

"There's a pub place a few blocks down," he said. "You up for that?"

"Sounds good. I can drive if you want."

He got in, and I was angry it was him getting in, only him. The ease and naturalness with which this was happening was being wasted by him not being Boyd.

"You were right about it being brutal, man. Jesus." He pointed. "Turn left. It's just up the street."

The hostess sat us at a booth near the back, under dim lighting; it was almost romantic and again it seemed like an insult that Mike was the wrong guy. We looked at the menu, made comments to serve as small-talk, ordered beers and burgers and fries.

"So what made you come?" I asked, taking one of the rolls the waiter had supplied, and buttering it slowly.

"Guilt." He laughed and reached for a roll. "Jesus, these are like iron," he said, banging the roll on the table. "Guilt, maybe gratitude. Dwight's parents are good people. They did a lot for me when I was a kid."

"I remember you spending a lot of time at his house."

"We lived next door," he continued. "My parents were not the most... parental people in the world. Dwight's parents covered for them a lot. Which is weird, I guess, since Dwight and I were never real close. Maybe we were like brothers who had the same parents but weren't actually close ourselves. I dunno. It was weird seeing them today, they look so much older. I guess so do we. —How about you? What made you come?"

"Same as you, I guess: guilt. Or shame, maybe. I don't know. It was all a long time ago. But I do remember the last time I saw Dwight, and I wasn't very nice to him. Pretty awful actually. And I've always felt bad about that. I guess I thought I'd at least say goodbye."

"When did you see him? I don't think I saw him after his family moved out this way. When was that? Sophomore year?"

"Just before sophomore year. That summer. That's when he'd stopped talking. Do you remember that? This giant mystery, no one knew why."

He shut his eyes, almost winced. "I do remember.

His parents asked me to come try to cheer him up or whatever, get him to talk. And I said no." He looked into his beer bottle. "God, I was such a fucking shitbag."

"They asked me too, and I went to see him."

"Yeah."

"It was fucking weird, man."

"He didn't talk?"

"He didn't talk and I just got so frustrated with him that I ended up beating the shit out of him in his bedroom."

He'd been about to take a bite of his roll but his hand dropped away from his mouth. "Really?"

"I mean I didn't really *beat the shit* out of him, I think I just pushed him around a little. His glasses flew off, I remember that. But I've always felt bad about it."

"Guilt tends to make people remember themselves as bigger douches than they probably actually were," Mike said monkishly.

Our food came and for a minute we ate without talking. Mike's mouth made funny smacking sounds as he chewed. Although it was easy to see why he'd gotten popular, it was still easy to see why he'd been a geek, too.

"If it's true what you said about guilt and memory," I said after a minute, "then in ten years or so I'll feel pretty douchey about today."

"How so?"

"My motives for coming today weren't exactly pure." I took a sip of beer. "Want to know why I came?"

"Hit me."

"I was hoping to run into Boyd Wren."

"Boyd Wren. Now there's a name I haven't thought of in a long time."

"Yup."

"I guess I'm surprised you would even need to run into him."

"Oh yeah?"

"I remember you guys had some kind of falling-out or something, right?"

"We did. Junior year."

"Yeah. I dunno, I guess I figured you would've patched things up pretty quick."

"We never did. That was the end of us."

"That's surprising. You guys were like two peas in a fucking pod."

"You thought so, huh? I like that you'd think so."

"To be honest, Ollie, you two were impenetrable."

"Impenetrable?"

"I guess when it was the five of us I didn't notice it as much. But then Tyson went off to St. Mark's after eighth grade, and then Dwight's family moved away, and it was just the three of us. And dude I felt so fucking lonely around you two. You had your thing and it was the Ollie and Boyd Show every day. And I felt like there was no room for me at all in that."

"You did? Really?" I put down my burger.

"Dude, it sucked being the third wheel like that. I had to go get other friends. I felt like such a poser at first when I joined the baseball team but it was better than being lonely. And then I kind of fell in with a different group of people."

"Weird. I never saw it that way at all."

"What'd you think, that I just ditched you for the cool kids?"

"Yes. Exactly that."

He shook his head. "Impenetrable, man. Truly."

"I didn't mean to be, Mike. I'm sorry if we pushed you out. We didn't mean to. *I* didn't mean to."

"Don't sweat it, Ollie, I ended up prom king." He winked. "Anyway, kids never mean anything, even when they're mean. Kids are just acted on by life. Dwight— I don't know, I think that kid probably never had a say in any goddamn thing. The only time he probably had a say was when he decided to stop talking."

My burger was gone. I wiped my hands on a napkin and then dragged a cluster of fries through some ketchup.

"So can I tell you something, Mike? It's something that, I don't know if it's going to make you uncomfortable."

"I'm hard to rattle," he said.

"If I seemed like I was pushing you out back then, it wasn't because of you. It was because I was in love with Boyd."

He paused, touched his beer bottle to his lips, and seemed to be thinking. I didn't know if he was pondering the revelation that I was gay, or if he was just reexamining the past in light of this new information.

"In love with him, like, in a gay type of way?"

"Yeah, I'm a gay guy."

"Huh." He put down the beer. "OK. And you knew it way back then, huh?"

"I knew way before then, Mike."

He frowned; I didn't know why. "And Boyd? Was he into you, too?"

"Mike, I wish I knew, man. To this day that's a question that keeps me up at night sometimes."

He leaned back in his seat. He lifted his hand and touched the heel of it to his chin and rubbed. After all this time he was still Itchy Chin Mike. "Yeah, I guess it kind of makes sense now," he said. "I know every time

I've been in love it's like the rest of the world didn't even need to exist. I guess now I see I was the rest of your world that didn't need to exist."

"I'm sorry, Mike, it sounds terrible when you say it like that."

"Nah, it's cool, Ollie, don't worry about it. Everything worked out fine for me. But... You really don't know about Boyd?"

The way he said it made me think he had inside information, some tidbit of high-school lore passed through a cool-kid grapevine I never knew anything about. "Do *you*?" I said.

"Me? No," he said quickly. "No."

"OK. Well yeah, I don't know if he loved me back. I don't know if he's gay or straight. I don't even know if he still exists."

"Have you tried looking him up on the Internet? Maybe that Friendster thing?"

"There's nothing. If he's alive he must be in the Witness Protection Program or something. But I'm sure he's alive. My mother would've heard if he died." I smirked.

"He went to college out west, I think."

"Yeah. Oregon, as far as I know."

Mike touched his bottle to his lips again. "I wouldn't be surprised if he went all that way to get away from his dad. Guy was a *major* douche, a drunk. Remember that?"

I didn't. "I guess I remember Boyd stealing beers from him...."

"Just a mega dick. On Boyd's ass for everything. But I mean, I don't know if that impacted anything, really."

And of course I didn't either. I had learned it was dangerous to ascribe motives to Boyd. "So. Anyway," I went on, "I came today because I thought he might be at the funeral."

Mike was quiet for a minute. "I'm trying to think of who I could ask," he said. "I'm in touch with some people from Lee but I don't think any of them would know about Boyd. Not a lot of people knew you guys."

"I guess, yeah."

The waiter cleared our plates. Mike asked for a dessert menu.

"So how about *you*, Mike," I said, and he laughed. "I didn't mean for this to be all about me."

He laughed again. "Well there's nothing I can say that'll top your thing."

We ate bread pudding and he told me about his life, about his fiancée Bianca, about his job testing blood samples for drugs at a diagnostic facility in Waltham. He was looking into getting a dog, a pug or a Boston terrier; it was a tough choice. He seemed like an unburdened guy. I wondered if that was because he was straight or because he was just lucky.

"So I have a question," he said when we were splitting the bill.

"Shoot."

"What caused your falling-out with Boyd? You said you were in love with him. What happened?"

"I wimped out, Mike. That's the short answer. I wimped out."

I drove Mike back to his car in the funeral home lot. The only other car still there was the one Dwight's parents had arrived in. I imagined them inside standing at the casket alone. The sky had cleared and the moon and the signs made the rain puddles glow.

"It was good running into you, Ollie," Mike said. "I'm sorry I wasn't Boyd."

"It's fine, Mike. You know, I'm not really as— I mean, it was a long time ago. I've had other loves. I'm not completely pathetic. I just figured I'd try."

"No, I get it. The first one's hard to let go of."

We pressed each other's numbers into our cellphones and then he opened the door and got out. As he looked about to shut it he said, "Do you want to know what I really meant when I said you guys were impenetrable?"

"Yes."

He stood with one hand on the door; the other hung in his pocket. "When I was alone with you, Ollie, when we were hanging out, you only ever talked about Boyd. Boyd this, Boyd that, what you guys had done, what you were going to do, where he was now, when he was getting back."

I understood where he was going with this. I wasn't sure I wanted to hear it out loud. Maybe he sensed that, because he waited for me to prompt him for the rest. "Mike?"

"Yeah?"

"And how about when you were alone with Boyd?"

"Same, Ollie. Same exact thing."

***

Two knights sat in the waiting area. They were side by side on the bench, their armored legs sticking out stiffly in front of them. I could see the colorful soles of their sneakers under the flaps of toe metal. Red and yellow— Nike knights. They sat with their helmets in their laps. One knight was idly plucking the bristly red brush that ran like a mohawk along the crown of his helmet. That knight was a redhead, the other was blond; they had the same ducktail haircuts. With their bodies covered in bulky armor it was hard to tell how old they were, but their faces looked boyish, young enough to need a ride to the mall. It was the last day of February vacation.

I slipped my appointment list back in my pocket. The knights were whispering to each other when I said, "You dudes ready?" And I gestured for them to come around back to the studio.

The metal velcroed to their arms and legs clanged loudly as they got up and followed me.

"I'm guessing you guys want the castle backdrop? My castle is ripped, so we'll need to steal hers." I pointed at Patrice, who was shooting an elderly couple dressed as ancient Egyptians.

"Actually," the redheaded knight said, "we want the tropical beach one?" He looked to the blond, who nodded.

"Ah, OK," I laughed. "I guess even knights need to go on vacation once in a while, right?"

"Not vacation," the same one said. He let it hang for a second while some kind of boldness built inside him, then he added, "They're on their honeymoon."

The blond knight reached out and pressed the back of his gloved hand against the redhead's hip, uncomfortably, as if to hold him back and keep him from saying anything more.

I stared at them much longer than I should've, long enough to make me worry they would think I was like other people who stared. I couldn't help it.

"How— How old are you guys?"

"Fifteen," the redhead said. "Well Colin will be fifteen next month." Colin, the blond, was looking down at his armored feet.

Fourteen. This boy, this Colin, this hero of mine, was *fourteen*. Dwight's death had reminded me that we can be snuffed out at any moment, that life was short. And sometimes I was afraid that I waited too long to start living mine, that I missed things because of it that I'll never get back. Things these boys had. Was it only time, only my place in history's progressing march, that had kept me from being like these two boys? Or did they have some greater bravery, some greater willingness to be who they were, that it took me much longer to muster?

"So OK, the beach, the beach. Let's find you guys the beach." I pulled down a few backdrops looking for it— the space station, the laser maze, the rainforest, the Eiffel Tower, the torn castle. I found the beach, pulled it all the way down to the floor, to the colorful soles of their sneakers. "Of course knights would honeymoon at the beach. That's really sweet. You guys are adorable."

Colin looked at me and I saw a wall come down a little behind his eyes.

"You dudes decide how you want to stand for the pictures. Let me get a sunlight gel in this light here so we can make it look really real, like a real beach. Like a sunny day."

They decided they wanted to stand side by side with their helmets on, with their faceplates down, nothing fancy. I took a few shots that way but it seemed funny to me that their faces weren't showing.

"Dude who's not Colin—" I pointed.

"Robbie."

"Robbie, turn a little to your left for me, your armor is giving me lens flares."

He did, and then he said, "Smile, boy," from inside his helmet, touching Colin's glove. It took me a second to understand—at first I thought he'd said *"Smile, Boyd."* I ran my hand over my hair and took a deep breath before snapping another few pictures.

"I'm good," I said then, and the knights started to step away from the backdrop. "Wait— Do you want to do one with your helmets off? Don't you want to see your faces?"

The redhead, Robbie, flipped up his faceplate. "We're doing it like this so Colin can have the picture beside his bed, like in his room, and no one will know who it is. But he'll know. Like, you know, for secret."

"For secret. I hear you," I said. "My parents had a hard time with it too." It wasn't exactly the truth but maybe I wished it was. Maybe it would've explained why I waited so much longer than Robbie and Colin.

"I'll tell you what," I said. "It's not part of the package you picked, but if you want to do one with your helmets off I'll throw in a couple wallet-size photos and you can keep them just for secret. I think someday you're going to want to see how happy you were together."

After a second Colin spoke. "Yeah, that would be cool," he said. He had a cute, little voice for a boy so brave.

They took off their helmets and held them at their sides.

"OK, smile on three, ready...." I did a countdown but I didn't even need to. Those boys were already smiling.

Abbey's Mohawk

In the dawn, in the dark, I put down my phone and whispered, half to myself, "I'm having a baby."

Even whispered, some things are loud enough to make a person thrash awake and sit up. The guy in my bed beside me did. The sheet bunched around his naked lap. His hair was askew. He blurted, croaky from sleep, "I used a condom!"

I looked at him. I was pretty sure his name was Dylan. "What?"

In the low light he looked back at me, squinted his eyes, reached for the eyeglasses perched on a stack of photo albums by my bed, put them on, looked at me again. "Oh," he said. "*Phew*. You're a guy."

I said again, laughing a little this time, "What?"

He sighed. "I'm bi. It's a consideration." He flopped back down on the pillow and shivered. "You know, pregnancy. I got nervous there for a second."

"Don't worry." I patted his arm. "I'm not the one pregnant. And you're not the father."

"Who is?"

"I am."

Dylan—that was indeed his name, I discovered after

tentatively trying it out while he hurriedly dressed — hopped out of my apartment with his sneakers untied and his t-shirt on backward. I suspected that if for some reason the door hadn't opened for him he would've put a Dylan-shaped hole in it. I stood looking at it for a minute after it swung closed behind him.

"I'm not even going to ask," said Corey, my roommate, as I entered the kitchen, where he was pouring a measured amount of whey powder into the blender. The gallon tub of whey sat on the counter alongside an ice tray and an array of diced fruit. I plucked a chunk of banana off the cutting board.

Since our other roommate Theo moved out to live with his girlfriend last year it'd just been the two of us here. We weren't exactly friends and we had no special dynamic, like the Odd Couple or something, but Corey, never very welcoming when he'd had a fellow straightboy around to keep up appearances for, had loosened up a little around me lately. He no longer seemed quite as put off by my gayness, and sometimes even asked questions when he smelled a story. Other times, like now, he only fished.

"My kid was born this morning," I said, leaning against the sink. "I think that guy wanted to blast out of here before I could make him a step-father."

"So you're a dad?"

"I'm a father." I ate the chunk of banana. "I've reproduced, isn't that wild?" Corey, a manly man, had not reproduced, and I got a certain satisfaction out of rubbing in the fact that the homo had done it first. Corey didn't even have a girlfriend. "It's a girl."

"Wow. Congratulations."

"Thanks."

He dumped some ice and the cut-up fruit into the

blender and then switched it on. We stood there watching it puree, saying nothing.

***

It was an important distinction: I was a father and not a dad. That was the arrangement. I'd known it going in, agreed to it—it sounded fine.

The conception of the idea, if not the actual baby, happened on a bench outside the Chocolate Emporium in Northampton, where my old college pal Harriet and I were eating obscenely big ice cream sundaes. It was September, a blistering Indian summer day, and ice cream kept dribbling down the sides of our dishes and splattering in our laps, which we'd covered with napkins to keep our shorts clean.

Four years older than me, Harriet had lived in Spain for a few years after graduating from UMass, and there she'd met a fellow expat named Trudy. It shocked me when Harriet first told me they were in love, since I'd never known she could find that in a woman, though in hindsight it seemed fitting. In college she had earnestly labeled me *cute* without an ounce of seeming to feel it herself. I'd told myself it was because I was gay, that she wasn't wasting any time pursuing me. It turned out it was because she was, too.

She and Trudy came back to America, to Amherst, when same-sex marriage was legalized in Massachusetts that spring. Harriet was twenty-eight by then, Trudy a few years older, and they were ready for "the next step." In my mind that meant marriage. Our new right, unimaginable even a few years earlier, seemed both exotic and fragile, something to sign up for quickly and then hang on to for dear life. It hadn't occurred to me at that point that you could get married and then need another step.

"We've been looking at donors," Harriet said, however, sucking a lump of gleaming fudge off her red plastic spoon.

"Donors?" I said. "You mean like blood donors?"

"Blood donors, Ollie, really?" She turned and looked at me, her eyes wide with amusement behind her Mod glasses. She laughed. "*Sperm* donors, silly."

"I was kidding, Harriet, obviously." I hadn't been kidding. "So you want to have a kid?"

"Believe me, Oliver, that's the only thing Trudy and I want with sperm."

"What does looking for donors entail?"

"Well, it—"

"Is it fun? I feel like I could get into it, if you need help."

"God, you need a boyfriend," she said, rolling her eyes. "We went to an agency. There's a book of profiles. We've got it narrowed down to a couple guys. It's so hard to choose."

"So it's all going to be anonymous, then?"

"We think it's the best way. I'm not totally sold on the idea of the kid not knowing who her father is—or who *his* father is—but Trudy and I want to be the parents. Exclusively, you know?"

"That makes sense. So who'll get preggo?"

"Me."

"Ah." I ate a bite of ice cream.

"I hate that word," she laughed. "*Preggo.*"

"*With child.* Is that better?"

"It'll do."

We were quiet for a few minutes, and my mind wandered back to when I was a little freshman with a pushy RA, and Harriet had taken care of me, given me a place to stay. When our spoons were starting to scratch at the bottom of our styrofoam dishes I said, "You'll be a good mom, Harriet."

"Thank you. I think I will. I think I'm ready."

We tossed our trash and walked up Main Street. We walked up through the campus grounds of girls-only Smith College, where I reminded Harriet to be wary of roving bands of horny lesbians.

"They'll be able to tell you want a baby," I said, "by your pheromones."

She started laughing, and she laughed so hard she had to sit down right there in the grass, even though my joke was barely funny. I think the talk of a baby had made her happy, giddy. It did seem to lighten everything somehow. Even I was happy to be thinking of something I'd always believed would be closed to me because I was gay.

There's a lake on the Smith campus at the bottom of a steep, grassy embankment, and we sat on the grass watching girls paddle canoes.

I lay back beside Harriet with my arms behind my head and my eyes closed, and I listened to her tell about the two donors she and Trudy were trying to choose between. I tried to picture the donors and couldn't. Anonymous men had no faces no matter what else you knew about them. A faceless lawyer, a faceless teacher. A *cum laude* graduate, but faceless. A triathlete, but faceless. I didn't like either of them. I probably didn't realize it at the time, but I think I was jealous that a faceless man would step in and do for my friend what I was capable of doing too.

"Well," Harriet said finally, when the sun was

starting to go down behind the green hills, "I suppose I should be getting home."

"I'd do it for you, Harriet, if you want," I said. Although I hadn't thought about ever saying such a thing until a few minutes earlier, I can't say it surprised me. Maybe it was something I'd been thinking about for years without noticing.

Harriet, now standing, turned her head very slowly and looked down at me where I lay in the grass. "Do what, Oliver?"

I laughed and felt my face get a little red. I sat up. "If all you want is for someone to put sperm in a cup, I can do that for you."

She sat down again in the grass with a heavy *oomph*, as though I'd pulled the ground out from under her. The continued blankness on her face instinctually made me start trying to persuade her.

"I mean, you know me better than any of those guys in some dumb book," I said. "I'm smart-ish, I'm decently attractive (you said so yourself, once), and I've always been healthy. I'm a little twitchy in the brain but it's never really held me back. I mean, I'd do it for you, is what I'm saying."

Her blank expression broke and she laughed. "Ollie, don't be silly."

"What's silly about it? I'm not being silly."

She looked out at the girls in the canoes as though they were holding all of her attention, but I think she just didn't know where to look. "You're—really serious?"

I *felt* serious, I really did. "Why not?"

Still she was looking vaguely at the lake, or past it at the hills, or beyond those at the future. She was quiet.

"Harriet?"

"Why would you want to do that, Ollie? You're

twenty-three years old."

"I'm twenty-four last month."

She huffed. "The point is, you're too young."

"Too young to squirt in a cup? The key thing, Harriet, is that I'm not at a point where I want more than to squirt in a cup. You told me you're not looking for the donor to be a dad. Would you want me to be a dad?"

"... We're not looking for a dad."

"So." I held up my hands. "I'm just putting it out there, lady."

"I think—" And then she stopped. And then she began again, after putting her hand on my knee. "I think everyone will need to take a lot of time to think about this."

But around the edges of her lips she was smiling.

***

I have a daughter, so you know what we decided. I got together with Harriet and Trudy four times over the next few weeks to hash things out, to get everyone clear on expectations. They wanted the kid, if there turned out to be a kid, to know I was the father but my role in his or her life would be more like that of an uncle or a family friend—I could have a relationship but no say in the raising. They couldn't promise to stay in Amherst or even Massachusetts after the kid was born, if a kid was ever born. The kid, if there ever was a kid, wouldn't have my last name.

I agreed to it all. Even the idea that they might move away didn't much phase me. I imagined that if I had a kid and rarely saw her it wouldn't be much different from not having one at all. And they looked so happy.

A whirlwind began, of blood tests, of legal

documents signed and of rights released, of masturbating in little rooms under harsh lighting into little plastic cups. Harriet got pregnant in November, after two tries. She told me the news over the phone while I was photographing some pilgrims at Fantasy Foto and my first thought was, *I work*. It was the same thought I had when I lost my virginity, when my inner nerves fired into wakefulness. *I work*, I thought, *my body works*.

***

I told my parents in January, after Harriet said she was far enough along to tell. It was a Sunday; I was visiting them in Lee for the afternoon. Big puffy snowflakes blew around in the air without falling, and the center of town, in its smallness, felt like the inside of a snowglobe. We were out for a late lunch at the Italian place beside the bank, across the street from the auto-body shop where I worked in high school. Through the steamed windows of the restaurant I saw a guy I'd worked with standing in the auto-body lot, wearing blue coveralls with a rag hanging out of his pocket. It surprised me that he would still work there after all this time—but of course *all this time* had only been six years. Six years, and look, I was going to be a father.

If every six years were as big for me as these last six, who would I possibly be in twelve? In twenty-four? I would have a grown-up child in twenty-four.

I told my parents this after we ordered. I hadn't needed to write anything down for a speech. The news came out easily, almost skipped out, as if on a giddy breeze.

My mother just stared at me, her forehead wrinkles

smoothing as her brows slowly sank. My father calmly put his bread down beside a buttery knife. He said, "You think you're prepared to raise a kid?"

"That's— Dad—" I probably had let my excitement get ahead of the details. I should've led with the arrangements, the contract, the waivers. "I'm not going to raise him," I explained. "This will be Harriet and Trudy's kid, I'm just supplying the—you know. Making it possible for them to make a family."

"Of course you're going to help raise him," my mother said. "This will be your baby, too. It'll be *ours*."

"No, I signed papers," I said, looking back and forth between my parents. I felt like this was going off the rails and I didn't know how to get it back. "I'm— He's going to be Harriet's and Trudy's. Exclusively."

Disbelief and quiet rage were blooming in my father's eyes, and he looked at me as though I was the stupidest person he'd ever seen. "You signed—? What kind of papers did you sign, Oliver?"

I took a gulp of water. "I read them carefully, they weren't long. It's fine. I'm basically an anonymous donor even though it's not anonymous. They'll be the parents. I'll just be Ollie."

My mother took a deep breath. My father rubbed his face. "*You'll just be Ollie?* What the hell does that mean?" My mother put her hand on his arm because his voice was getting loud.

"I don't know, that I have no parental rights to the—"

"No rights?" My father laughed in a disbelief that was morphing into denial. "Jesus Christ, Oliver. You need to get them back. We need to talk to a lawyer."

"Dad. No, see— It's done."

He looked down at the red-and-white checkered tablecloth and traced one of the white squares with his thumbnail, leaving dents in the fabric. Without looking at me he said, "Please tell us you're kidding. Please tell us this is just some joke. Did they move April Fools?"

"It's the truth. I'm happy about it. I thought *you'd* be happy."

"*Happy?* That we're going to have a grandchild you've signed over to other people like goddamn real estate? People we've never met? Are we ever going to meet *him?*"

"We don't know it's a him, I'm just—"

"Ollie, Jesus, it's irrelevant. Him, her, it's irrelevant. Are we ever going to meet our own grandchild?"

"Probably, I guess. Dad—"

"Oh Jesus, Oliver."

"Why would you *do* a thing like this?" my mother said. She had tears in her eyes now.

Seeing her, it was the first time I wondered if I'd made a mistake, if I'd been too rash and not thought this through. In fact I *hadn't* thought it through, it had been one of the most spontaneous things I'd ever done. It had felt right, though. Up until today it always felt right, not the kind of thing that needed second thoughts or second guessing. You don't weigh pros and cons when you're giving a gift. But now, seeing my parents—

Under the table my knee started to shake, and anger came swooping in and bolstered me and overwhelmed my sudden doubts. Just then the waiter arrived with our food. We smiled, said thank you; he went away.

In front of me spaghetti steamed and I spoke as calmly as I could. "In case you two forgot, I'm a homo. How many more opportunities in life do you think I'm ever going to get to have a kid? This might be it for me." My face was getting flushed and it was starting to feel hot in the restaurant. The steaming windows were dripping. It felt like a hothouse, a sauna. "Harriet is a good person. I'm sure Trudy is, too."

"*You're sure?*" my mother gasped. "Have you even *met* this person?"

"Of course I've met her. A bunch of times."

"Oliver," my father said.

"I'm spreading your genes, Dad! I thought you'd be happy that for once I wasn't dumping them into assholes!"

"Oliver!" my mother cried.

My eyes were bugging. Had I ever been this angry? And part of it, I was sure, was because by now I was afraid they might be right.

But my dad seemed chastened, and I knew then that he had not taken my outburst as a wild insult or as an outrageous accusation but as some kind of bitter truth.

A silence fell over our table and the restaurant's ambient sounds filled the gaps. Orders being mumbled, the chime of silverware against plates.

Finally my mother pushed her untouched meal away from herself. "I don't feel hungry," she said. My father did the same, then got up and went outside. It was hard to tell but I think he was crying. I paid the check and drove back to Amherst.

***

My parents and I didn't speak for three months after that. It was the longest I'd ever gone without talking to them. Eventually there was a thaw, though, because after each milestone in Harriet's pregnancy I understood more and more why they had freaked out. Harriet and Trudy were drifting away from me on a course that seemed natural and that also had been documented and prepared for and agreed to in pages of legal jargon. This was their journey; they told me about it but I wasn't on it with them. Harriet excitedly showed me her sonogram photos but didn't invite me to be there for their taking. She told me the baby names she and Trudy were considering but didn't ask for my opinions. Each milestone left me with less. Not less than I expected, but less, it turned out, than I wanted. I had thought of fathering the baby for them as a gift but now I was realizing that in order to give a gift you have to give something away.

My parents had understood that right away. Maybe only parents understand it.

I went home to see my mother one day in April when my father was out of town. I showed her the sonogram photo. Her eyes welled up and she laughed and put her hand over her mouth. "She's beautiful," my mom said.

"I miss her already and she's not even here yet, Mom."

"Oh Ollie," she said, pulling or letting me push my face into her shoulder. "That just means you're a parent. To be a parent is to miss your kid. Take it from me, kiddo."

It made me remember: Back when I was going off to college my dad had mentioned the existence of mother miles, and I thought back then that if there are mother miles there must be father miles too—maybe not as long, like cat years to dog years, but still there. What would the father miles be for a father like me?

"What do I do?" I said.

She was rubbing my back and she took a long time to answer, and the answer was honest but tinged with regret. "I think you be what Harriet and Trudy need you to be, when they need you to be it. And I think for now that means you let them be."

***

Harriet and the baby were in UMass Memorial, in Worcester. I didn't rush. I wanted to give her and Trudy time. I drove there after I got off work at the mall. It was hot out; my daughter was a summer baby like me, and in fact had missed my birthday by less than a week—a near miss. I would've liked to have shared the day with her.

In the visitor lot I parked my Jeep and sat for a while wondering what I would say. I'd never been near an infant before, let alone my own. Would she look like me? Would it be better if she didn't?

I got out of the Jeep and took off my Fantasy Foto t-shirt and replaced it with the ironed button-down I'd hung up in the back to keep it from getting wrinkled. I hadn't known what to wear to meet my kid but I thought an ironed button-down would be OK.

As I entered the hospital I saw a giftshop and went in and bought a cluster of shiny balloons, one of which said *Congratulations!*, and another, *It's a girl!*

"Well that's happy news," said the woman at the register, pointing up at the balloons with one hand while she rang up the sale with the other. "Who's the lucky parents?" she said. "Family? Friends of yours?"

I looked at her and felt confused in a way I'd never felt before and yet would feel often in the days and years to come, and ultimately I said not much of anything. "Yeah," I told her, and handed her my credit card. By then she was already waving to someone else who'd come into the store.

On the elevator I held the balloons low, my fingers up near their tied-off foil nubs, and the colorful strings swirled around my sneakers on the blue linoleum floor.

"Ollie, hi!" a voice behind me called as I was walking down the pink hallway of the maternity ward. "Hi! Ollie!"

I turned. It was Trudy.

"Were you sleepwalking?" she laughed as she jogged over to me. She looked a crazy mixture of exhausted and deliriously happy, as though she might collapse right here in front of me with a smile on her face. Her shoulder-length brown hair was tied back in a ponytail. She had on a yellow t-shirt with a wet spot, probably baby spit, on the shoulder. She hugged me. I put one arm around her and held the balloons away from us with the other.

"Oh Ollie, she's just beautiful. She looks so much like Harriet, it's crazy."

I smiled. I found I didn't know what to say. "Everyone's good?" I asked. "Healthy?"

"So good."

"Good."

"Ollie, I'm a mother!" Her eyes brimmed with tears and she laughed and rubbed them away. "I need to run back to Amherst to get some things. Harriet will be happy to see you. Some people were here earlier but right now it's just her and the baby."

"Is her room —? I think I might be heading the wrong way."

"You came from the elevators?"

"Yeah."

"You went past it, silly. It's back this way. I'll show you."

Harriet was sitting in a rocking chair near the window

with a pink-blanketed bundle in her arms.

"Visitor, hon," Trudy said, and then after casting a longing gaze at Harriet she left us.

My fingers released the balloons and they bumped against the ceiling tiles, forgotten in the presence of this better, brighter thing.

"Hi, Mama," I said.

"Ollie," she said, in a you-devil-you way. "Nice shirt, dude."

I approached her slowly, and the balloon strings danced ahead of me and then out of my way.

"Oliver Wade, this is Abbey," she said, turning to show me the perfect little face, red with a newborn's rash. She was wearing a little yellow hat.

"That's her name?"

"Abbey," Harriet repeated, delighting in the sound. "Not Abigail, just Abbey. With an e-y. Like Abbey Road."

"Abbey Road?"

"The Beatles. You know?"

"The Beatles?"

"Ollie, the Beatles!" she laughed. And only then did I notice the sound of John Lennon singing softly from an iPod speaker dock by the bed. Everything Beatles.

"Oh. Of course," I said. "Yeah. I've always been more of an R.E.M. guy."

"Look at her hair," Harriet said, peeling off the little yellow hat. "Isn't this the cutest thing ever?"

The baby had what could only be called a mohawk, a crest of thick brown hair running down the middle of her otherwise bald head.

"She's a little punk," I laughed. I stroked the baby's mohawk with my thumb. The hair was as silky and fine as the thread inchworms use to repel out of trees.

"Get a chair, Ollie," Harriet said, gesturing to one against the other wall. "Just throw Trudy's stuff on the bed."

Among the clothes on the chair was a camera, and I remembered I'd forgotten to bring mine. I'd been so worried about the shirt, I'd forgotten myself.

"She's been taking a billion pictures," Harriet added, seeing me looking at the camera. "We'll do some of you before you leave."

I pulled the chair over next to hers and sat down. With my elbows on my knees and my chin in my hands, I stared at the baby and her little mohawk. And I thought again, with pride, *I work.*

"Did you ever think, Harriet— When you met me, when I was a dorky freshman sleeping on your floor, did you ever think that I was the guy who was going to be your baby's father someday?"

"I definitely didn't, Ollie. But, you know, if some time traveler had come and told me, I would've been glad."

That made me feel nice. "When Wesley left and I was freaking out," I said, "I remember you telling me something about how there's no way to tell what can happen in a year or two years or whatever. And at the time I didn't know what you meant. I mean it was obvious but I was so wrecked I didn't know what you were getting at."

She smiled. "I guess I just meant that you can't get too bent out of shape about anything, because you never know how things will turn out. The worst thing can lead to the best thing. The shit is the shit that flowers grow out of."

"Yeah. Yeah, that's what I think you meant, too."

For a long time Harriet and I watched the baby's

face. It was the most interesting thing in the world for us, the way the mouth opened and closed, the little nose, the hint of eyebrows.

"My parents are going to want to meet her at some point," I said.

"I know. I know they are. That's fine. They should. But for now—maybe a picture will do? Just until we get settled?"

"Of course. There are so many grandparents."

"So many."

"Are Trudy's parents coming out from Seattle?"

"They might. But I don't know. We might be there soon, so it really depends on what kind of flights they can get, if it's even worth it for them to come right away."

"You'll be where soon? In Seattle?"

"I didn't tell you? Trudy had a second interview the other day. By phone this time, thank god. If she gets the job, we're going to go."

"But you guys won't be married there."

"I know, it's a huge drawback, but we think it's worth it to have her family close."

"Oh. Yeah. That'll be really helpful, to have her parents nearby to help, and stuff. Yeah." I went quiet again, thinking, and then I said, "Can I hold her?"

"Of course," Harriet replied, blushing. "I'm so sorry, I should've offered. Of course you can. It's so hard to let her go! Be careful of her head. Her neck isn't strong enough to hold it up, so you have to hold it, see?"

She passed the baby to me slowly, from her arms to mine. The little bundle was light but delicate; in a weird way, light enough to drop easily. I almost wanted a cake pan or something to put her in. "Am I doing it right?"

"I think so." She laughed. No, she giggled, like a girl.

"I'm still figuring it out too." She picked Trudy's camera up off the bed and told me to smile. She took a few for good luck. "I'll have Trudy email them to you," she said. She watched me hold the baby for a little while. I can't say for sure how long. It wasn't a time for noticing time.

"Do you want to hang out with her a while, just the two of you?" she said finally. "I'd love to go take a walk, stretch my legs. Trudy's been a regular Nurse Ratchett, not letting me leave the bed."

"Sure, OK."

She looked from the baby to me, and put her hand on my shoulder. "I'll love you my whole life for this, Oliver Wade."

I smiled. "No problem, Harriet."

When I looked up a minute later I noticed she was gone. The aloneness, just me and Abbey, felt heavy with importance, but I didn't know what to do or how to make use of it in a worthy way. Carefully I freed a hand and turned off the Beatles music and held the baby in silence. I tugged off her little hat to see her hair again.

"Lookit you," I said, "you do have a little mohawk, a little baby mohawk." We stood and I rocked her and we looked out the window together. I could see our reflections in the glass. Calmly I whispered to her, "Don't be like me, little girl. Belong. Belong better than me. OK?" I rocked her and looked at us in the glass.

***

By the time I got home the late-setting summer sun was gone.

Corey was on the couch in the living room playing *Grand Theft Auto.*

"Did you see your kid?" he asked over the squeal of

tires.

"Yup."

"Ten fingers, ten toes?"

"She's perfect."

"Nice."

He didn't ask to see a photo but if he had I wouldn't have had one to show him. I hoped Trudy would email one to me soon. I was afraid of forgetting what Abbey looked like. I seemed to have so little of her.

"I'm hitting the sack," I told Corey, but he didn't reply.

I went to my room and undressed and lay in bed for a while. The sheets still smelled like that Dylan guy. Now the cologne that had smelled so intoxicating last night when I needed a distraction from Harriet's labor smelled sour and sad. I got up and walked to the bathroom. There in the pinkish light from the row of bare bulbs over the sink I looked at myself in the mirror. I was a father now. I had a daughter now. Abbey. Abbey with the mohawk hair.

I squatted down and searched under the sink, found the box with the hair clippers, unwound the cord and plugged them in. I clicked the trimmer guide down to its shortest setting. I looked at myself. Holding the buzzing clippers, I tilted my head side to side. I raised the clippers to my head. I took a breath. Hair dropped into the sink, big brown tufts of it. When I was done the sides of my head were reduced to short bristles, and down the middle I was left with a thick crest of hair.

"Abbey," I said to myself. It was a good name.

(Age 25)

Lumberjack Slams
& Hurricane Swirls

It was the ass-crack of a Tuesday dawn in early July and I was on my way to meet my old friend Shelley in Boston. We were going apartment hunting together. I was ready to get out of Amherst, ready to stop living with straightboys and shuck off the lingering tentacles of college. Meanwhile the rent on Shelley's South End studio was going up in September, so it was a good time for us both to get moving. She'd picked out a bunch of apartments she wanted us to look at—two-bedrooms strewn across the city—and set up a bunch of appointments that day for us to see them. The first appointment was at 8:30. I got to her building at 7:33 and parked on the street. She buzzed me in.

"Two things," she said when I entered her cramped but neat fourth-floor apartment. She was very concise, had always been very organized. She liked lists. "One, there's an emergency at work and I have to go in."

This news relieved me somewhat. I could take a nap. Standing on my toes I spotted her mattress in the loft. It looked soft. "No problem. Um. For how long?"

"The morning," she said. "Possibly the whole day.

I'm sorry—"

I dropped back on my heels. "Shelley! The whole day! I drove all that way! I got up at 4:30 in the morning!"

She held up her hand with her palm facing my face and I stopped. "I know you did. Which is why: Two, my cousin Angel is in the city and he's going with you instead."

"To look at the apartments? Why would your cousin even want to do that?"

"Because he's a dumbass and he's got nothing better to do. I'll let him explain to you." She went in the bathroom, which was about three feet away from where we were standing—which was about three feet away from everything in this studio. I followed her and slouched in the doorway.

"Shelley, I'm going to feel so stupid dragging him around on my errands. He's going to be so bored. — Angel was the soldier, right? Didn't you say he re-enlisted?"

"He's in the process," she said. She held some of her bouncy black curls in place and blasted them with hairspray.

I stepped back from the toxic cloud and pulled my t-shirt over my mouth. "I don't know what I'll possibly talk to a soldier about all day," I complained through the fabric. "Shelley, this'll be weird."

"Talk about the apartments. It'll be good for him." She gave her hair two more blasts. "He came out a few months ago. Gay gay gay. Did I tell you? I was thinking maybe you could—"

"He's gay? The soldier? You did *not* tell me!" My mind started to wander. "I could what?"

"I don't know, talk to him about things." She flicked

off the bathroom light and walked past me into the main room.

"About being gay?" I said.

"Sure, yeah."

"Shelley, I know about being gay working at the Holyoke Mall taking pictures of kids dressed like princesses, I don't know about being gay getting shot at in Afghanistan."

"But he's been working at a lumber yard in Vermont for the past two years. You're not so different. Talk to him." She picked a big envelope up off a dresser that stored, I knew from earlier visits, both underwear and canned soup, and handed it to me. "This has everything you'll need for the apartments today. The listings, et cetera."

I took the envelope from her but ignored it. "I've seen pictures of Angel on your MySpace, Shelley; he's like beautiful. I'll be lucky if I can remember my own name when I'm talking to him."

She laughed. "Oliver, just look at the apartments and find us a good one, OK? He's going back into the Army tomorrow, so just— He's off limits."

Shelley only had one key to her apartment, so when she left for work she locked the door behind us and left me sitting in a small square of grass, curbside, in front of her building. Angel was in a cab somewhere on his way from the airport but, with the morning traffic (which I'd purposely left early to beat), it was taking him forever to get here. In the meantime I perused the papers in the bulging envelope Shelley had given me. They were printouts of apartment listings: pictures, prices, maps; details about first, last, and security; hot water included or not; even little meters hand-drawn in purple ink indicating how friendly the landlords had sounded on the phone. One place in Jamaica Plain looked especially nice. Lots of light. Landlord earned an eight out of ten.

When a cab pulled up I stuffed the papers back in the envelope. The cab idled there double-parked while the passenger paid. A minute later Angel got out dragging a huge green military duffel bag behind him. Pulling the strap up over his thick shoulder, he said thanks to the cabbie and shut the door.

He turned and, squinting in the sun, sort of pointed at me. He was shorter than he looked in the pictures I'd seen, shorter than me, but with a glance you could tell he was built like a tank, which I was also not expecting even though Shelley had told me he spent a lot of time at the gym. He was bigger than I ever was. Biceps like my thighs, a chest like Superman, sturdy calves. He had on khaki shorts and a gray t-shirt with an American flag on the chest.

"Angel!" I said, standing up slowly, cool. I had hoped to make it seem like we already knew each other, like we'd seen each other just yesterday, but I was thrown off my game by his body, his face; he was pretty. His eyebrows were thick and black but ended cleanly on his brown forehead rather than thinning to fine hairs. He smiled. His teeth were straight and white. Friendly dark eyes.

"Ollie? Hi, hey, nice to finally meet you, finally."

"Yeah, so, uh. Yeah! You too! Hi!"

We looked at each other for an awkward moment. I felt like we were both thinking, of ourselves, *You dumbass*—or at least I was. He rubbed his hair, black in a slightly overgrown military high-and-tight cut. I wondered what he was thinking about me and my decidedly un-military mohawk. Once upon a time I had been told I was cute, but she turned out to be a lesbian.

Finally he bent to put the duffel on the sidewalk and, sue me, but I sneaked a peek of his butt. There was a lot of it.

"You made it," I said.

"Yeah," he said. He held out his hand and I shook it. He had a firm grip. "I guess my cousin has a real estate adventure or something set up for us or something?"

I wondered if he was as nervous as he sounded. But, too, I was practically shaking. "It seems so. She and I are trying to find a place."

"Cool, cool. Moving in together."

"Yeah, yup, moving in."

"Where do you live now?"

"Amherst."

"Oh, sure. Right on 91."

"Basically."

"I'm from Brattleboro. Vermont."

"I know it. We could've carpooled today."

"Ha. Yeah. I took a bus." He put his hands in his pockets; the shorts were kind of tight on him and his hands only went in up to the knuckles. "So all around the city or something?"

"Yeah, all around. Various neighborhoods. But I have my car, don't worry." I pointed to where my Jeep was parked on the street.

He turned and looked. Then he rocked back on his heels boyishly. "Is it OK if I drive?"

"My car?"

"Sometimes I get car-sick when I'm in the passenger seat."

"Oh. Sure. Yeah. That's cool." I paused. "Think you can handle Boston traffic, a Vermont guy like you?"

"I've driven tanks," he said matter-of-factly.

"Are you calling my car a tank?"

I didn't know what I meant by it. My prediction had come true: I could barely remember my name.

It was awkward, as I guess it was bound to be, being driven around in my own car by someone I'd just met. Conversation came in clunky sentences that dropped with a thud and then went nowhere—commentary about pedestrians, other drivers, fast-food joints, the heat. We busied ourselves with Shelley's envelope and the city map she'd included. Numbers written in purple ink on the map coordinated with the printed rental ads.

I commented on all the paperwork and Angel only smiled and said that was Shelley. He seemed quiet in a way that made me worry he wasn't totally into this errand despite Shelley's assurances that he had nothing better to do. I started zoning out wondering what the rest of the day would be like, if it would get easier, if it would drag.

After a few minutes of driving he got a call from someone named Daniel Rodriguez (I could see the caller ID on his phone), and the name in its Latino-ness made me feel like he had his own people and I was not really belonging here even though it was my errand and my car. He talked for a minute while I squiggled my finger around on the map, content not to have to say anything for a while. Then he hung up.

"Sorry about that," he said.

"No problem."

He stopped at a red light and reached for the seat's adjusting lever and pulled the seat closer to the wheel. He was settling in. It was annoying and then endearing, and I felt myself relax a little.

"What time are we supposed to be at this first apartment again?" he said.

"Eight-thirty." It was 8:22 now. "I think we'll make it."

The first apartment was in a big building near a place called Kenmore Square, a busy area near where the Red Sox played. Angel parallel-parked the Jeep skillfully in a space I wouldn't even have tried to fit in. I wondered where a guy from Brattleboro learned to city-park like that, and if he'd really learned it in a tank.

"Look," he said, pointing at the rooftops as we got out of the Jeep, "it's the Citgo sign there. You'd be close to games." He swung an invisible bat; the invisible weight made his visible biceps bulge.

"But the crowds, though," I said. "I'm surprised Shelley put this place on the list."

"It could be good," he added optimistically.

The woman smoking on the front steps turned out to be the building manager. She brought us inside. The apartment itself was OK—I could see why Shelley wanted to see it—spacious with in-unit laundry—but it was between an apartment with a crying baby and another one with a barking dog. This early, it was easy to write off. I told the woman I'd have to think about it. She looked at Angel as if to solicit his opinion, but he didn't say anything, and we left.

"You're not really going to think about it, are you?" Angel said.

"I'm holding out for something better," I replied.

Angel started the car while I looked for the next page of Shelley's itinerary. I'd gotten them all mixed up when I was sitting in her yard.

"Next is in — Brighton," I said. "Nine-fifteen."

He looked at the clock. It was 8:52. "Is Brighton close?"

"Doesn't look too far. But she really spread some of these out."

"It's OK," he said, tapping the dashboard, "we've got plenty of gas."

For a few blocks he silently followed my navigations. Then he said, "Are you making notes?"

"Notes?"

"Your feelings about these apartments. Are you writing them down?"

"I figure I'll know the right one when I see it."

"My cousin is going to want notes," he said confidently.

"Hmm. You're probably right. I don't have a pen."

"Check the glove compartment," he said.

I laughed. "This is *my* car, kiddo." But I did check it, and found a mechanical pencil, and Angel smirked. "Aren't you smart," I added, and clicked out some lead.

I wrote for a minute.

"What are you putting?" he said.

"*Too close to ballpark, barking dog, heat and hot water not included despite ad....*"

"That laundry was nice."

"*Nice laundry,*" I wrote, and figured that would do. I placed the pencil in the cup holder.

He was looking at me. "By the way, I like the hair. Ya punk." He said it matter-of-factly but I felt I could get away with taking it as flirty if I wanted to, and I kind of wanted to.

"Oh. Yeah. Thanks!" I rubbed my mohawk. In an effort to look more presentable to landlords, I hadn't put anything in it today, and it was flopping around in the breeze from the open window. After a while I added, "I did it for my kid."

His thick eyebrows went up. "You've got a kid?"

"A daughter. Abbey. Yup."

"I thought you were a gay guy."

"Oh I am. Big time. *Giant* homo." And I added, "I donated to my lesbian friend Harriet. She went to UMass with Shelley and me."

After a period of what appeared to be intense thought he said, "Cool."

"Yeah." I reached for the stereo. There was a CD already in it. "Mind some R.E.M.? I'm a fan."

"Sure," he said. "They're OK."

"They're my favorite. This album came out last fall. *Around the Sun*. I'm a little obsessed with it. And by a little I mean a lot."

Angel laughed.

"And by a lot I mean completely."

I felt more relaxed now that Michael Stipe was in the car with us, and maybe somehow more so now that Angel had approved of my kid.

"So there's some funny reason you're in the city?" I said. "Shelley said you should tell me."

He sighed. "No big story. I'm flying out tomorrow. I thought it was today. I took a bus, got to the airport at 7:00. Twenty-four hours early. D'oh!"

"Wow, that sucks so much."

"Right?"

"Shelley called you a dumbass."

He smirked. "I was."

"Flying out to where?"

"Fort Hood."

"Where's that?"

"Texas."

"Like, good Texas or bad Texas?"

"Near Austin," he said. "Is that good?"

"I hear Austin is good."

"Good."

"So this is for an Army thing?"

He paused. "Most of my things are Army things." Then he added, "I'm going back in, and that's where they put me."

I laughed. "So you just had the wrong day to go?"

"Yeah. Wrong day. Don't tell the Army." Then he blurted, "Come on, gramps, come on!," and gestured to an old Camry trying to merge.

"Well I'm glad you're here," I said. "I wouldn't want to be doing this all by myself."

"Yeah. So. Am I going the right way still? There's a turn soon I think, you'll have to tell me." He was glancing at the map in my lap.

A few blocks later he said, "What makes you say Austin is good?"

"I guess because there's more gay people around there, so you'll feel at home?"

"Ah. Shelley told you my life story, huh?"

"Not the *whole* story. Just the fun parts. You're just coming out?"

He shook his head; he had cute ears, almost too big. "I came out to a few of my Army buddies during my last assignment. I've been out."

"Even with Don't Ask Don't Tell?"

"I told people I trust; it was an acceptable risk. And I just told most of my family a while ago. I should've told Shelley sooner, but whatever. So the only thing new for me is that they know."

"So you're not exactly an innocent gay virgin boy then?" I laughed a little. You can get away with saying a lot of things if you laugh a little.

He laughed too, maybe blushed, which made me blush. "No," he said, "uh, not exactly."

The second apartment was in a squeezed brownstone, and going up the narrow staircase I could smell Angel in front of me. He had one constant scent, an almost unnoticeable spicy scent, manly and sharp, and it never changed throughout the day, never got more or less noticeable, it was just there. I didn't know if it was his deodorant, his hair stuff, or just his body, but once I noticed it it made me feel comfortable and I wanted to be close to it. The kind of smell you want to lean against. I remembered that thing about how a person can judge another person by pheromones and I thought, *This is a smell that smells new and like home at the same time.* And then I thought, *Jesus Ollie, calm yourself.*

The landlord, a fat man with a wheeze, brought up the rear as we climbed the stairs.

Angel and I waited at the landing in front of the door for the landlord to make his way up. Angel gave me a little smirk that I returned. A key box, locked with one of those spinning barrels of numbers, hung from the doorknob. The landlord arrived and applied the combination, took the key out of the box, and used it to unlock the door. Then he stepped aside.

"After you," he said to Angel. I was noticing that everyone deferred to Angel.

"After you," Angel said to me. My elbow grazed his warm abs in the tight space as I went inside.

It was nice. Points for hardwood, points for newish kitchen, points for in-unit laundry. The bedrooms were vastly different sizes, though, which could make it difficult to decide how to split the rent. The place was already partially furnished: a leather sofa sat in a beam of sunlight, and a pub-style table fit nicely in the kitchen. Points if these items came with the apartment, though I could do without the kitty-cat clock in the kitchen.

The landlord must've noticed me eyeing the furniture because he was quick to point out that the current tenants were returning for the rest of it next week.

"I kind of like this one," Angel said, pushing out his bottom lip to indicate being mildly impressed. He had his hands clasped behind his back. The landlord showed him the bathroom while I checked out the view from the windows.

When we were back in the car Angel said, "What are you writing for this one?"

"*Nice floors, laundry; Angel likes. Different bedrooms; narrow stairs; landlord has difficulty ascending.*"

"*Ascending.* Nice." He crossed his arms over the steering wheel and leaned forward. I thought he was watching for an opening in the traffic, but he pointed to the green sticker on my windshield. "What's this?"

"That would be my employee parking sticker."

"You work at the Holyoke Mall?" He laughed. "What store? Hot Topic?"

"No, not Hot Topic, Angel, for heaven's sake. You know those photography studios where people dress up in costumes and get their pictures taken?"

He laughed. "You work at one of those?"

"I like photography." I shrugged. "It's the best I could do for now."

"It's cool," he said. "You ever do self-portraits?" He leaned back and swung his hand through the small space between my head and the ceiling—the space my mohawk would be occupying if I'd done it up today. It made me duck.

I said, "Don't grab at me like that or I might let you get me."

He laughed. "OK, where to now?" he said.

"Next up is Charlestown. Eleven o'clock."

"Where's Charlestown?"

"Um, way back the other way, I guess. Almost near the airport."

"Ugh, my favorite place. We've got plenty of time, though. Off we go."

He seemed to be getting into this a little now, and I was relieved that I wasn't actually dragging him around. Of course he had nowhere to be, but I was glad he was having fun.

"How old's your kid?" he asked while he drove.

"You're very curious about my child," I laughed.

"Sorry."

"I like it. She turns one at the end of this month."

"Do you see her and stuff?"

"No. I mean I did, for the first few months. But Harriet's wife ended up getting a job in Seattle and they moved last December."

"That's a bummer. Do you miss her?"

"To be a parent is to miss your kid. That's what my mother says." After a second I added, "Want to see a picture?"

"Sure."

I pulled one out of my wallet and held it up. He looked over quick a few times as he drove. "She's cute," he said.

"Yeah, I made a good one."

"Her eyes look like yours."

"Yeah?"

He looked at the photo again, as if to confirm. "Yup."

The Charlestown apartment was a mistake — it had only one bedroom. It was nice though, a ground-floor place with a patio and a deeded parking space. It was near a tall stone tower that looked like a smaller version of the Washington Monument. All were obvious reasons why Shelley probably wanted to see it but certain details must've slipped past her.

"Did this always have just one bedroom?" I asked the landlord, an elderly lesbian in a black Adidas tracksuit. "I mean, we're sort of looking for a place that has two."

"Oh," she said. "Two? No, no, it's always had the one. I just figured you boys were together?"

I laughed out loud but my heart *ka-thumped*. I looked at Angel and his face was unreadable. He started examining the crown molding around the ceiling very intently.

We got back in the car. I wrote, "*Only 1 bedroom, whoops!*"

"That was funny," I said, clicking the mechanical pencil repeatedly until the lead looked like a hypodermic needle, "what she thought. That we were together." I clicked and chuckled. "Wasn't it?"

"Yeah," he said, a little monotone, "that *was* funny." He looked at the pencil. "You're losing your lead."

"Oop." I guided it back in with my fingertip.

He watched me and then shook his head, as if clearing a foggy idea out of his brain, and said, "Where to next?"

"Next is, uh," I flipped some pages, "Jamaica Plain, way back the other way again. I told you Shelley really spread these suckers out. This one looks very promising,

I was reading about it earlier."

"Good. When do we need to be there?"

"Twelve-fifteen."

We drove for a long time this time. For part of it we were on I-93, an eight-lane highway from which all the skyline of Boston was visible. Seeing all of it, all at once, screwed with the notions I had of Boston being a manageable upgrade from quaint Amherst and quainter Lee. I think I suddenly wondered what I was doing, and whether I was ready for this. I looked at Angel. "This is busy, huh?" I said, and gazed again out the window, which I'd rolled up against the wind. "I'm not used to it."

"Busy busy," he said. And he added, "Don't worry, you'll be just fine."

The traffic bunched up a few miles before our exit. You never know how someone new is going to react to traffic, so I let some silence build to give him space. Like Shelley had said, Angel had nowhere to be, and my errand wasn't his errand, but impatience doesn't need a reason when you're staring at brake lights. He didn't seem to mind the slow going, though. He sat quietly with one hand on the wheel and the other in his lap, rubbing a fingernail along the outer seam of his shorts.

"So what's wrong with Brattleboro?" I said.

"What would be wrong with it?"

"You're leaving. There must be something wrong with it."

He shook his head. "There's nothing wrong with it. I'm just ready to get back in the Army."

"So no boyfriend you're running away from?"

"Nah. No. I haven't dated anyone since I decided to re-enlist."

"When was that?"

"Six or seven months ago."

"Wow. Why?"

"Why'd I re-enlist?"

"Why did you stop dating?"

"I don't know, just didn't want to make leaving hard. I need a new beginning, I don't want to have anyone dragging along behind me when I'm trying to start a new life. Clean slate and stuff."

I turned a little in the seat. "That assumes anyone you date would turn into an insta-boyfriend."

"Well no," he said. "But that's what you hope for, right? Otherwise what's the point?"

"I don't know. A nice time?"

"Well, it was a decision I made and it's been for the best."

"No hookups even?" I said incredulously, with a smirk that made my own heart skip.

"I mean," he said, "maybe one or two."

"I thought maybe that guy who called you earlier was your boyfriend."

"Daniel? God no." He laughed. "Daniel is fifty-something and three hundred pounds. And it ain't muscle."

I laughed. "I used to lift, too."

He looked at me, at my arms. "What made you stop?"

"I stopped making time for it, I guess."

He was quiet for a minute. "You should start again."

"Think so?"

"Sure, I bet you'd look good buff."

I didn't know if it was a compliment or if it kind of broke my heart.

The neighborhood we were in when it was time to start watching for house numbers was less dense, and quieter, than the highway had teased. We found the building but couldn't find a place to park, and we were running late, so Angel told me he'd drop me off and circle the block while I checked out the apartment. I jumped out at a corner, found the right building, a three-decker, and buzzed. This was the apartment that had been my favorite when I was perusing the printouts that morning, and I'd assumed it would be the one I would settle on. But, guided by the landlord, I walked the rooms feeling hardly any interest in the place. I missed having Angel with me. It was silly, but this wasn't fun without him, and I was eager to get it over with so we could tour another one together. *Oh man, Ollie*, I thought.

The landlord asked for the second or third time if I had any questions, and coming out of a daze I realized I had quickly come to rely on Angel to ask about price and utilities and stuff. After confirming these details I told the landlord I'd be in touch, and then walked out.

For a minute I stood on the sidewalk, then I spotted my Jeep coming toward me. I waved. Angel pulled over. I got in. The Jeep smelled like him now, that spicy, manly smell. Already it felt natural for him to be driving my car. I hadn't thought twice about leaving him alone with it.

"Any good?" he said.

"Better in the pictures." I jotted some notes, then flipped through the remaining printouts. "Next one's in Cambridge, but not until 2:15." It was 12:38 now. "This must be our lunch break."

"Good," he said, "I'm starving."

We chose to eat at Denny's because chains are

comforting for out-of-towners and because we were both in the mood for breakfast even though it was well after noon. Denny's, that place buried in every American's consciousness even though you hardly ever see them around. When we passed one on our way to the apartment in Cambridge we couldn't not stop.

The host seated us at a booth and Angel, after sliding in across the red vinyl, surprised me by looking short at the table. Maybe when he was standing his width created the illusion that he was taller than he really was, but at the booth I could only see him from his pectorals up. It struck me as super endearing and I tried not to smile too obviously.

For a minute we looked at the menus. I was nervous again, as though now that we were face to face rather than side by side we were meeting all over again, and I had to seem cool. I wondered what it would be cool to order.

"I think I'm gonna go for it," he said finally, clapping his menu shut.

"What are you getting?"

"This," he said, pointing on my menu, "the Lumberjack Slam."

I looked at the picture at the end of his finger (there was a little bit of dirt under his nail, which seemed manly). The Lumberjack Slam consisted of pretty much everything an American human could eat for breakfast: pancakes, eggs, ham, bacon, sausage, French toast, hashbrowns, iced coffee. It was a heart attack waiting to happen and of course I had to join him at it.

"I'll have the same," I told the waitress.

We waited for our food. Conversation jumped from topic to topic, sometimes silly, sometimes serious, never staying on one topic for more than a minute. It was like how we talked in the car, where everything seemed punctuated by traffic lights and stop signs.

"So you're moving to Boston?" he said, though of course he knew I was.

I was balancing a spoon on my knuckles. "Yup. Time to see if I have what it takes to make my way in the big city."

"You should move to Texas," he said, matter-of-factly but looking away across the restaurant, as if not to meet my eyes.

"*You're* moving to Texas," I teased, but I was taking it as, I don't know, a fun coincidence and somehow failing to appreciate what, just maybe, he'd been insinuating.

"Yup," he said.

"Is that everything you're bringing? Out there in your duffel bag, I mean?"

"For now. The Army is moving the rest of my stuff."

"They do it for you?"

"I could've arranged it and they would've paid me back, but I didn't want to, so they're handling the arrangements."

"Sounds fancy."

He shrugged. "It's just how it works."

"Did they do your flight, too?"

"I did the flight. They gave me a time to appear, and I need to get myself there." He ripped his silverware out of its napkin sleeve. "I don't have to report until next week but I wanted to give myself a few days to settle in."

"So I guess we both have big life changes ahead of us."

"You leaving anything behind?" he said. "Anyone?"

I looked at him, at his pretty eyes, and all at once I felt, for a bunch of reasons, a really overwhelming loneliness that felt deeply rooted in my life. It was probably silly, certainly premature, but I was starting to feel like I belonged with Angel, and yet I didn't; I didn't even belong where I belonged.

"Not really," I said. "I, uh— I haven't really been able to carve out much of anything there for myself, to be honest. I've never even really had a boyfriend. I was with a guy for three weeks once."

He nodded, leaned back in the booth. "I'm getting pretty hungry," he said.

His feet came up from under the table and rested on the booth near my thigh. He had on black Nikes with a strip of bright white around the soles. He wore no socks or those invisible socks, and his leg hair was glossy black and looked soft. I wanted to touch his ankles, wedge my thumb into the notch where they met.

Our food came and he pulled them back and sat up.

"Oh man oh man," he said, rubbing his hands. "Look at *this*."

"This is embarrassing," I said, surveying the vastness of our meals, the running syrup, the oozing butter. Barrels of iced coffee sweated on the table. "I'm completely embarrassed."

While he was eating he got a blob of butter on his lip and I thought I might have to wipe it for him, like in a movie. But it was only there for a second before he licked it away.

At that moment he started laughing, I assumed about the butter. I could see chewed-up food in his mouth but it wasn't gross, it was cute. "Oh my god," he said, "look at that kid's shirt. Behind you."

I turned around in the booth and spotted, a few booths back, a boy of about eleven wearing a t-shirt that said *No. 1 Grandpa*.

"That kid is awesome," Angel said, catching his breath. "That kid is my new hero. That's the funniest thing I've ever seen." He didn't seem to be exaggerating.

"That *is* pretty funny," I said, but I was laughing more because Angel was laughing; it was hard not to.

When we were finishing lunch I got up to run to the bathroom and he said, "While you're gone I'm going to spike your drink — roofie your drink." He nodded to my tub of iced coffee. I laughed and thought, but didn't say, that he wouldn't even have to, that I would go willingly wherever he wanted. But his tone hadn't been flirty or coy, it had that same steadiness it always had, that same matter-of-factness, both reassuring and confusing, so I didn't know if he was being flirty or just teasing me.

At the checkout counter Angel debated about buying a Denny's-branded travel mug, and haggled with the cashier, an attractive, squinty-eyed surfer-type guy who looked imported from Southern California, to give him the mug free as a gift. Surfer Guy said he couldn't do it, brah, and Angel asked if he could have one of those Denny's tote-bags free as a gift if he paid for a mug.

"Brah, that doesn't even make any sense, brah, the tote-bag costs more than the mug!" said Surfer Guy.

Angel was being playful and I'm sure Surfer Guy didn't even realize he was being flirted with, that this hulking guy in front of him was a boy who liked boys. But the exchange fascinated me because up to then I hadn't seen Angel interact with any guy other than me. Only because Surfer Guy was so objectively cute did I know Angel must be flirting. *So this is how Angel flirts*, I thought. In light of this I replayed the day in my head and realized there were a number of times Angel had talked to me with the same tone he was using on Surfer

Guy.

As we left the restaurant I teased him about it. "You liked that Denny's guy, huh?"

"He was OK."

I asked him if he got hit on by a lot of soldier-fetish type guys, and if he minded it, and he said yes he did get hit on by those guys, and that it depended on the particular person whether he minded it or not. He wouldn't, for example, have minded it from the Denny's guy.

I thought I'd asked because I was curious, but after he answered I knew I'd asked because I was protective. I guess I didn't like the idea of someone only seeing the uniform, and not knowing that Angel was the kind of guy who reminded you to take notes, who got car-sick, who complimented your kid, who laughed at funny t-shirts, who haggled for tote-bags.

The Cambridge apartment on Shelley's list was near Harvard Square and MIT. Not only were the two guys still living there, they were home, playing video games in their dirty apartment, and they watched warily as the landlord led us around. The bedrooms smelled like pot and dirty sheets and the bathroom mirror was spattered with toothpaste. Clearly the photos in the ad Shelley printed had been taken before these guys moved in. We slunk through the place without asking questions and I felt slightly grimy leaving the building.

"Sorry about that one," I said to Angel as the sunlight hit and refreshed us. The Jeep was parked down the street. "That was so awkward."

"It could be good if they weren't still living in it."

"Yeah, but, just.... No."

He said, "It was like being at a yard sale where you

don't want to buy anything but you feel like you have to because they're all looking at you."

"But I feel like they aren't leaving voluntarily. I smell eviction."

"If you moved in, one day they'd show up again, back!"

As we walked to the car, side by side on the sidewalk, our knuckles brushed together and I felt, clear as anything, but with sudden wondrous surprise, that I would be comfortable holding his hand. Even on this busy street, even among all these people walking by. I had never held a guy's hand in public before. Never with Johnny, not even in Northampton where there are so many gays—it just wasn't something I could do. But I knew I would've done it with Angel. I couldn't have explained it and I didn't know what to make of it. I felt safe with him. Nothing could touch me with him. With Angel I imagined a time when—I don't know—lines would never get crooked, where all my ticks would be muscled away. It was silly. I had known him seven hours.

When we got back to the car and I saw his duffel bag in the back I wondered what he had in there and I wondered if I would ever be alone with it long enough to reach inside and pull something out, whatever I could get, and keep it to remind me of him. Because more and more I wanted something to remember him by.

We were still near Harvard Square when my phone rang. It was Shelley. She wanted to know how the day was going.

"Good places and bad places," I told her. "I've been keeping notes." At this Angel smirked thoughtfully. "But there's a couple good candidates, so we're doing

OK. I'll give you the full report tonight."

"What time is she getting off work?" Angel said. "I need a nap now."

"What time are you getting out of work?" I asked.

She told me probably not until 6:00 or 7:00, she was really sorry, and if we couldn't kill the time, we were welcome to stop by her office and get her apartment key so we could go back to her place.

"We might do that," I told her. "Your cousin is getting cranky. He's been up many hours and needs to sleep."

Angel scrunched his face at me.

"How many places do you still have to see?" Shelley asked.

"Just two," I said. "After that, we'll be in touch."

We were driving to the first of the last two apartments. Somerville, 3:15. Being driven around in my own car was making me happy. Maybe because Angel was driving. I felt like a superhero sidekick in my own car. I held my hand out the window, cupping the hot wind with my palm. I didn't want the day to end, and it was so close to ending.

"Do you have any cowlicks in your beard?" Angel said.

I turned. "Cowlicks?"

"Like little cowlicks in your beard hairs."

"Weird. I don't know, I've never grown out my beard. I don't think so. Why?"

"But you can tell from the stubble, how the hairs go. I have beard-hair cowlicks." He leaned toward me and pressed his finger to his cheek. "See?"

"Oh," I said awkwardly, not knowing quite what to do with having my attention called to his skin. To his body. "I see them." He had a few days' worth of black stubble and on his cheek by his jaw was clearly visible a circular pattern of hairs. "They're like little hurricane swirls."

"Yeah, my hurricane swirls. They're hard to shave." He said it as matter-of-factly as he said everything, and although I now knew this was how he flirted I still couldn't tell whether he was flirting or whether, this many hours into the day, he was really reaching for small-talk topics.

The Somerville apartment would've been a contender but although it was empty and broom-swept clean it reeked of cigarette smoke. Angel didn't ask any questions. Rather than writing any notes on Shelley's printout I drew a cigarette and circled it.

"Next one's the last one," I said to Angel.

"Already?" He leaned back in the seat and closed his eyes. "But we're just starting to get good at this, Ollie the trolley."

When we met this morning I would not have guessed that he'd be playing with my name by the end of the day. I was looking at him now, I knew, the way you look at someone you've already been given the privilege of touching. His eyes being closed made it easier to imagine I had been given it. But I stopped my hand when it was halfway between us, though my fingertips seemed pulled as if by magnets to his brown arm. Before he opened his eyes I leaned back against the headrest and closed mine, too. We had both been up since before dawn.

"All right," he said, and I heard him start the Jeep, "let's do this."

The landlord of the last apartment, a fourth-floor walkup in the South End near where we'd started, made the wheezing landlord at the Brighton brownstone look like an athlete by comparison. Clearly he had no intention of climbing the stairs.

After rummaging in his baggy pockets he handed Angel a key. "Go up, have a look, kick the tires, take your time, I'll be here." He coughed.

Nervous with what felt like freedom and responsibility, I started up the carpeted stairs. I looked back past Angel and saw the rotund landlord pull a magazine out of his pants pocket.

When we got up to the apartment I could think of little except the fact that Angel and I were in it alone together. It was the first time all day that we'd been alone and unobserved. Would something ignite here between us? Would I kiss him? Would he slip his hand down my pants and whisper in my ear? Would he hold my hand?

No. We would look at the bare rooms, we would test the water pressure, we would observe that the garbage disposal was broken. The aloneness made me more reserved. And the emptiness of the apartment was a reminder of what Angel wanted right now: no strings, a clean slate, a new life.

I was turning to leave, and I knew that leaving would mean leaving him and our day and everything, and I couldn't do that so easily. I thought, *Oh fuck it*. Who cared what Angel Cantos thought he wanted? He wanted to start a new life but there's no such thing as a new life, there's only life, and that can be good or bad but it's true either way. Life had been going on when he was in Brattleboro and I was in Amherst and we were a half-hour drive from one another and never knew it, and life would go on when I was here in Boston and he was at Fort Hood. In between those two things, and part of those two things, was today. And the only thing that makes today special is that it's the only part of life you have control over. The rest is memories or imagination. The rest is could'ves or shoulds.

"Angel?"

He was near the living-room window pulling at the blinds, trying to get them to hang straight.

"Sorry," he said, "they were crooked, it was annoying me."

I looked at him and smiled and liked him all over again.

"Angel. So I know you're leaving, and this is a bad time, and you don't date. And— But I would really like to go on a date with you. Tonight. Now, I guess. If you wanted."

I thought I would've been shivering with nervous energy but I wasn't. I felt good. It was because of him.

"Ollie...." He still had the cord from the blinds wrapped around his fist and when he lowered his hand absentmindedly the blinds leapt up. Neither of us looked at them, though.

"I've felt really nice with you today, Angel. I've had a good day. I want you to know that. You make me feel really comfortable, and safe in this new place or whatever, and—"

"I've had a good day, too."

"So—yes?"

"What good is one date, though, Ollie? If it's good— that would be bad."

"Come on. Nothing is better?"

He looked from me to the cord in his hand. "I'm excited about this move, Ollie. I've been looking forward to it for a long time. I don't want to get down to Texas and have my mind be on Boston."

It was a fair point, painfully fair. "I'm moving on, too. I just— I feel like we've connected today, Angel, and I don't want to say goodbye with a handshake. I don't want it to just be *that*."

"How do you *want* to say goodbye?"

"Angel, don't make me blush."

"Ollie, I like you too. I've liked you since Denny's. This has been a fun day. I would be happy that you just asked me out, I just don't think I can do it."

"OK. OK, yeah. I'm sorry. I'm not trying to pressure you, I just wanted to be honest."

"It's cool, we're cool."

I leaned in the living-room doorway and put my hands in my pockets. "I had an experience once," I said, "where I was really into a guy and I didn't make a move and it became too late. I told myself I'd never do that again."

"You're really into me?" He was still standing by the window with the blinds cord in his hand. He pulled it again and they went straight.

"You're right," I laughed, "it's silly. Shelley told me you were off-limits. She'd freak out if I took advantage of you."

I was halfway down the first flight of stairs before I heard him shut and lock the door and follow after me.

In the car, when we were stuck in rush-hour traffic a few blocks from Shelley's, Angel interrupted what had been a deep silence between us by asking if the sun was getting on me. I hadn't noticed, but he was right—a thick, late-afternoon beam of it lay across my arm and thighs, had been for the minutes we'd been sitting here, burning.

He inched the Jeep up a few feet, almost touching the bumper of the sedan in front of us; it was enough to put the sun behind a bank of traffic signs. The shade was cool and I told him, "Thanks."

A few minutes later, after I had pushed the R.E.M. CD back into the stereo, he kissed me. It happened easily: He kind of just leaned toward me, almost as if he was going to check his hair in the rearview, and I noticed, and it happened. There in the sea of brake lights and honking horns.

When it was done I looked ahead smirking. I had been able to feel him smiling against my lips. I savored the feeling of not caring if other drivers saw us. What would they dare do to him, to someone like him, or to me, with someone like him? Then I remembered something and couldn't help grinning and reached for the pencil and pulled out one of the printouts from Shelley's envelope. On the back I made some notes.

"You are *not* writing notes on my kissing," Angel laughed. "Oh my god, what are you writing?"

"Nice lips, nice taste, perfect 10 of a kiss."

"You dork."

"You did kind of set yourself up for it, though."

"I did, I did." He was smiling, shaking his head, playing at being exasperated. "So we're on a date," he said. "You win, I surrender. We're officially on a date."

"Yes! See, isn't it fun?" I slapped his knee playfully.

"I don't know, so far we're just sitting in traffic."

"Jerk," I said, and he laughed.

"Kiss was decent, though. Yep." Like in that one apartment, he stuck out his bottom lip to indicate being mildly impressed.

"I'm gonna wipe that hurricane swirl right off your

jerky face," I warned.

He laughed again. "What do you even mean by that, though?"

"I don't even know."

"OK, so you need to tell me what we're doing on this date. Where are you taking me? I want details."

Suddenly I was deliriously aroused and had butterflies in my stomach.

I said, "What if we say the whole day so far has been the date?"

"Yeah, and—?" I noticed him shift in his seat the way a guy shifts when he's contending with a boner.

I said, "What if we go somewhere we can kiss more?"

We let the question sit there for a minute, sultry, way too sultry, almost to see if that was really how this was going to play out. With that tone. Then we both laughed. "Oh my god, I sounded like we're in a porno," I said.

But he didn't let the thread go, only its cheesy tone. "Shelley's?"

"She might come home."

"We could, um—" He was blushing. "We could get a hotel room?" He looked at me sheepishly. "Or, actually— One of the apartments had its key in a lockbox, I saw him do the code on the lockbox. Eight-seven-six. But— I don't remember which place it was."

I liked the idea of a hotel but I liked this even better. "Would we break in? That would be crazy. What else do you remember? Where were you standing? Think hard." I was shifting in my seat, too.

He stroked his stubble thoughtfully. "We were standing on a landing. Small staircase. Oh! It was the one with the fat landlord. The first fat landlord."

"I remember. Which apartment was that, though?"

"He had difficulty *ascending*. You wrote a note."

I grabbed the envelope and flipped through the printouts scanning my notes. "*Difficulty ascending*. Here it is! Brighton!"

Angel looked at me, perhaps a little bashfully now that this was a real possibility, that we had a destination, that there was a plan. "Now," he said, "aren't you glad I made you take notes?"

I was blushing so hard I couldn't respond.

We didn't touch or kiss again in the car, or even speak other than for navigation, and the silence was full and sexy and exciting. Outside the building in Brighton, we stood for five minutes waiting for someone to go in or out so we could sneak through the locked main door. Still we didn't talk, just looked at each other once every few seconds and traded little smiles. Finally, impatient and fearful that he might change his mind if we didn't get this show on the road, I pressed a button on the intercom by the door. Someone answered. "Hey. Sorry," I said. "This is Jimmy from 4R. I'm an idiot, I locked myself out. Can you buzz me?"

Angel looked at me and mouthed, "Jimmy?"

A second later the door buzzed.

"Did you know a Jimmy lives in 4D?" Angel said, holding open the door.

"I have no idea who lives in 4D. Neither do they, though, apparently."

He cocked his head in appreciation.

As we ran up the narrow stairs our hands bumped together and our fingers entwined. All the walls could've gone invisible and I wouldn't have cared who saw us.

Eight seven six — the passcode was almost like a

countdown. Six-thirty—nine hours since we were here the first time. We locked the door behind us and went to the room with the couch in it. There was no lamp except for the yellowish ceiling light in the kitchen; the light filtered dimly here and washed into the blue, early-evening light from the windows. We stood on the hardwood floor looking at each other, nonchalant, five feet apart, like people who are about to fight. But we weren't going to fight.

Angel's voice was soft and shy. "Don't watch me take off my shoes," he said, lifting a foot and holding the heel of his sneaker but stopping short of pulling it off.

"Why?"

"I'm wearing those invisible socks and they look like ballerina slippers and they look kind of silly. I didn't know that—that this would be happening."

"I won't watch," I told him. But I did; I wouldn't have missed it. I watched him take off his black Nikes and then peel off his invisible socks, which did indeed look like black ballerina slippers and which did indeed look kind of silly. But then he was standing in front of me barefoot on the empty floor and his legs looked like brown granite and his dark eyes gleamed.

We took off our shirts. I had imagined him with tattoos but his skin was clear. His chest hair was thick and black.

"You're handsome," I said.

"You too," he whispered. He was whispering.

We let our shorts fall down, and then our underwear. I was hard and he was hard and we stood looking at each other. My heart was racing and I was happy.

Slowly I walked toward him naked and leaned against him, and smelled the smell I'd wanted to be near, and felt the hardness and smoothness of him, this goofy, thick, cautious guy on the edge of a new life and already in it. He pulled me hard against himself with one hand and with the other he ruffled the back of my mohawk playfully. He whispered, "Punk." I was right about how it would feel to be in his arms. Then I tipped my head and lay my tongue flat against one of his hurricane swirls. And we were off.

Is it enough to say we did everything? Things I'd never done with anyone? Things I'd never wanted to do before he was here to do them to and with? Things that were risky, things we didn't have the proper protection for but did anyway? Maybe we thought that whatever happened that day could be left behind with everything else when we moved on.

We did it all on the couch, and after all the things we did, we finished together just sitting side by side, almost as if we were back in the car. We sat for a long time afterward, close, hands still lying in each other's lap where they'd moved to take over in the final seconds. We glanced at each other from the side of our eyes not knowing quite what to say; maybe we were surprised at the things we had done. When we finally got up the couch gleamed with our sweat and I used one of my socks to wipe it dry, and he told me I was silly, it would dry by itself.

The bathroom had a shower curtain and a watercolor of Boston Harbor on the wall. Using water someone else was paying for, we stood together in the tub and rinsed off silently, probably still speechless. Finally Angel cut the silence by joking that the only thing left for us to do now was to pee on each other.

I stood looking at him, trying to judge if he was serious or just joking around. I didn't know if he was serious but if he was, it seemed a small thing after everything else. And I wanted it all, even the things I didn't necessarily want. Spreading my stance and holding my fists at my hips, I told him to go for it.

"Are you—? Really?" he said. "I've never done it, I've never even really thought about it, I was just—"

"We *are* in the shower," I said. "Go for it."

And he did; or, he started to try. For a while there was nothing, just an embarrassed smirk, then a trickle came, then a stream as his body relaxed or as he became confident that I wasn't going to scream. He targeted my belly button. The stream was clear and hot, hotter than the lukewarm water crashing against my back. There was a serious expression on his face. We watched it spatter against my belly, and after a few seconds it slowed and stopped. Angel said, "That's all I've got."

We looked at each other and laughed.

I shut the shower off and, dripping, he pulled back the curtain and said, "Uh."

My first thought was that there was someone there in the apartment, that we were caught. But the idea caused me no anxiety—I was with Angel, after all.

"No towels," he continued, looking at me with his lips pushed out. "We forgot."

"Oh," I said, "uh oh."

We squeegeed ourselves and each other, head to toe, front and back, with our hands, *thwacking* loose water into the tub. But we were still too wet to put on clothes.

"C'mon, let's stand by the window," he said, "and air dry."

"Air drying in a stranger's apartment," I laughed. "Whose life is this?"

He laughed, hard—not *No. 1 Grandpa* hard, but hard.

I followed his footprints across the hardwood floor of the bedroom that one month from now I'd be living in. We opened the window and stood there side by side, looking out, Angel and me, our shoulders and side-bums touching, our forearms folded on the wide sill. Outside was street, and some rooftops, and beyond that a river, and beyond that Cambridge—a new city, a new chapter much more pronounced now that I was leaving someone behind, and being left behind.

I put my hand on his back, felt the now-familiar ridges of his muscles, and rubbed in little circles. Only after a minute did I realize he was dry.

"I'm hungry now," he said, scratching his fluffy chest hair. It was 8:15.

"We could go back to Denny's," I proposed. "For old time's sake."

"Yeah, let's. Old time's sake."

He got dressed and I watched him while I put on my own clothes, confident that with every article he was putting on, he was covering up something I'd never see again. But that was OK. I got to see it once, and once is a universe away from never.

"You know you have to rent this apartment now," he told me as he was placing the key back in the lockbox.

In my head I had already filled out the paperwork.

I hoped we'd be put in the same booth, and I would've asked for it if we weren't, but I could see a couple of stoned guys sitting there eating pancakes.

Again we ordered Lumberjack Slams, and while we waited for them Angel again stretched his legs beneath the table and rested his feet on the booth beside me— black Nikes that would be exchanged for Army boots again soon. I tapped on the laces with my fingers and then cupped his leg, my hand sliding across the fuzzy ridge of his calf. He smiled, but a moment later he pulled his legs back.

Shelley called while we were eating. She was home. It was late. She had an air mattress and half of her own bed to offer us, and Angel and I went there full of pancakes, groggy as zombies, and slept.

I like to think that what Angel and I had shared that day was obvious and observable, and that Shelley could immediately sense something had happened between him and me, but she didn't seem to notice and if she had any suspicions she never mentioned them to me. I never told her how I chose our apartment either; she never would've let me hear the end of it about Angel and me having unprotected sex. On that score we had been risky and were lucky; in the end all Angel gave me were memories.

It was almost still night when he put his hand on the air mattress, wobbling me awake. He was squatting on the floor beside me, his elbows resting on his thick knees. Beside him on the floor was the olive green hulk of his duffel bag.

"Hey," he whispered, "Ollie, I'm heading to the airport. The cab is here. Just wanted to say see ya."

I leaned up on an elbow, which squished deeply into the softening mattress. "Can I go with you?"

He blinked. "To the Army?"

"To the airport."

"Nah. I got it." It was matter-of-fact.

"You sure?"

"I got it, Ollie." A little less matter-of-fact.

"OK, Angel."

He looked at me for a long time. I thought he might

reach out and touch my hair the way he had last night, but he didn't. He stood up. I reached out and held his ankle.

"Did we make it harder?" I said, looking up at him, dark and kind of unknowable in the shadows of Shelley's dim studio.

"Yes. We did."

"Do you regret that?"

"No. We're tough. Hard is good."

I wanted to pull him down for a kiss, a last kiss to say goodbye, but I didn't. Hard was good, but maybe harder wasn't. You had to know when to call it a day, when to let things go and move on — not to a new life but to a new stage of the only one you've got. And that sort of thing was becoming my specialty.

The kitchen light went out and the door opened and closed.

It would've been easy, lying there with the memory of his skin still on my hand, to think only of what I was losing, only of what had slipped away, come too late, been not quite right enough to be perfect. It would've been easy to cry.

But I wasn't crying. I was grinning and I couldn't stop grinning. "Angel Cantos," I whispered to myself, and full-on guffawed into my pillow. "Angel Cantos. Oh my *god*."

The Key-Touching Guys

I got my name from an uncle I never knew, or hardly knew — Uncle Oliver died when I was six. My mother's brother. He was a mysterious figure to me while I was growing up, partly because I think he'd been mysterious to my mom, too. He was eighteen years older than she was and they spent only one year — the first of her life — living under the same roof. He wasn't a brother she'd fought with or giggled in forts with, he was a brother who brought her trinkets from a place called Korea, who took her at the wide-eyed age of eleven to visit New York City for two days.

Those were the ways I knew him too, from those stories from before I was born, and from stories from when I was a toddler. The one about how Uncle Oliver — never Ollie, always Oliver — held my infant self on his lap in a cake pan because he was afraid he would drop me. The one about how he paced the aisles of Toys R Us for an hour choosing a birthday gift for me, and settled on a remote control car I was too little to operate. He didn't know about kids, my mother would tell me, and he didn't particularly like them, but he was proud of me and proud that I had his name.

After he was gone — cancer, 1986 — and there were no

new stories, Uncle Oliver still loomed large for me, the way I suppose namesakes always do. A hat he had worn when he was in the Army turned up in my grandfather's attic and then didn't leave my head for a year. Photos he'd taken during the war turned up, too. For me an Uncle Oliver grew from the grave of the one I'd been too young to know. Mine was a soldier Oliver, a forever-young Oliver who never bothered to get old. A world traveler. An adventuring hero in a family where people rarely left Massachusetts. I was happy for my namesake to be that. Every little boy likes that. But as I got older and started to know I was different from other boys I started to look for something more from Uncle Oliver, something from a part of his life I hadn't thought much about until then, something more mysterious than what any battlefield relic or shadowy Army self-portrait could tell me.

Since his mid-twenties Uncle Oliver had lived with a man named Anders. They had met in high school, or college, or the military—no one was sure, exactly, least of all my mother, who would've been learning to ride a bike at that time. And maybe everyone forgot to imagine a time before Anders because Anders seemed to have always been there, a part of the family. My own few memories of my uncle included Anders. He was there when the remote control car was given at my birthday. He was probably there for the cake-pan incident. He was always there.

As I got older I thought about this more and more. I must've thought that if Uncle Oliver had been gay, and had survived and grown up and found Anders, there was some hope for me. But it was hope for hope, because I didn't know what exactly their relationship had been, and it felt too hard to ask. Anders had kept in touch with my family for a few years after Oliver died, but time and the passing of my grandparents frayed the connection. By the time I was old enough to want to talk to him it had been years since he'd last been in touch.

A few months after I came out to my parents and thus was free to bring up the topic I asked my mother if Uncle Oliver was like me. It was winter, we were in the car on the way to buy supplies for my spring semester at UMass. She sighed and looked at me, and pushed her sunglasses up over her hair.

"I don't know, Ollie," she said reluctantly, sounding a little defeated. I had never asked her the question before but it seemed as though it hadn't been terribly far from her mind.

"OK."

"When we learned about you, it made me wonder about Oliver and Anders. I hadn't ever thought about it, if you can believe that. They never said anything. But of course they wouldn't, not in my family. We weren't— We weren't known for talking about things like that; you know how stiff and English your grandparents were. Anders was always around, but— I guess we all just assumed they were friends." She paused. "I don't know if he was like you, Ollie. I'm sorry."

"OK."

After that we were quiet for a few miles of winding, snow-lined road. Finally we turned into the parking lot of Bradlees, a department store that was having a sale.

"Oh, it's crowded," my mom said, though many of the spaces were filled with piles of plowed snow and not with cars. She parked and shut off the car. With the keys in her hand, she said, "You must think I'm stupid for not knowing, Ollie, but it was a different time, it wasn't on the radar. People certainly didn't ask about it. But I think if he was, he would've told me. I guess that's the reason I think he wasn't." She pursed her lips, then looked at me apologetically. "Ollie, I really think they were just friends."

"OK."

"He would've loved you, though, even if he wasn't like you."

"I know." I cleared my voice. "Let's go shop."

When I got back to school after winter break there was a letter waiting for me from my mom. She must've mailed it a day or two after our conversation about Oliver and it beat me to Amherst. It contained Anders' contact information from her address book, the most current phone number and street address she had. *In case you want to ask him,* she'd written. I did want to ask him, but this was my mom's past more than it was mine, and if it wasn't something she wanted to seek out herself, I didn't think I had a right to dig into it. Oliver may have been my namesake, but he was her brother.

For years I put the mystery out of my mind—or at least toward the back. I went through college; I graduated; I lived in Amherst and took photos of people in silly costumes; I moved to Boston and started a freelance photography business thing. The Oliver question always nibbled, but whenever I pulled out the letter with Anders' information (more likely to have grown outdated with each passing year), a little voice inside me always whispered, *Better not to mess in this.* I knew that things that were merely unspoken had a way of needing a framework of full-on secrets to *stay* merely unspoken. For example, it hadn't slipped past me that if Oliver was gay, it lent questions to the circumstances of his death. A gay man who died from a drawn-out disease at age fifty in 1986 maybe did not really have cancer. Things I wanted to know might be tied up with things I never wanted to find out.

It seemed better just to wonder. After all, wondering has a lot of upsides. No one who's made peace with wondering can ever really get disappointed.

When I was twenty-six something unexpected happened that took it out of my hands. An email came through the website I had set up for my freelance photography.

> *Dear Oliver, "Ollie,"*
> *I wonder if you remember me. You were just a boy the last time I saw you. My name is Anders Verity and I was a great friend of your Uncle Oliver. I'm an old man now and I'm on my way to pushing up daisies and I wonder, might I call you some time? Or you can call me. I do hope to hear from you.*

He left his phone number and signed it, *Anders*.

I stared at the email for so long my screensaver came on. The screen seemed to pulse, or maybe it was my heartbeat behind my eyes. I thought about deleting the email and forgetting about it. Then I showed it to Shelley. I decided not to let it go any further than her. Then I changed my mind.

"That's so odd," my mom said over the phone when I told her. "It's been fifteen years at least. What do you think he wants?"

"I don't know."

I could almost hear her thinking. "There was a ring," she said, "of your uncle's. Anders wanted it, I never knew why. He said he would leave it back to us in his will."

"Well he said he's ready to start pushing up daisies. Maybe he's getting an early start."

"Are you going to call him?"

I tried to judge from her tone whether she wanted me to. All the stuff with Abbey had taken a toll on us, and we weren't as close these days as we used to be. I found her harder to read.

"Yeah," I said, "I think I am. Is that OK?"

She didn't say yes or no. "Let me know what he says," was all she said.

The next day after holding my phone in my hands for a while I dialed the number Anders had given me; it was the same one I'd had on paper all these years. I was fidgeting. I felt that by acknowledging his email I was opening a box that didn't belong to me, and I wasn't sure why it had been offered.

There was a click and a pause, and his voice, when he answered, was familiar. It had the soft Worcester twang my grandmother's had had, the speech equivalent of the soft filters they used to put on the lenses of movie cameras.

"Anders? This is Ollie Wade calling. I got your email."

There was a long pause. "Oh Ollie, I'm so glad, how wonderful."

"How are you doing? My mom says hello."

"Oh, how nice, I'm so glad to hear from you both."

"It's been a long time."

"A very long time."

"How are you, Anders?"

"I'm good, I'm good! Well I'm dying, but I'm good!"

He laughed.

"Oh, I'm— I'm sorry."

"Don't be sorry, I'm old, it happens." And he added, "Tell me about yourself! You do photography? I typed your name in Google and I saw you do photography."

I gave him a rundown, a flash-fiction version of my stories: how I got started taking pictures, the kinds of things I photographed. All the while wondering what the real reason for this call was, and if I could steer it toward the question I'd wanted answered since I was like fourteen.

"You sound just like your uncle, Ollie, do ya know that?"

"I do?"

"I would've thought—" He laughed. "Well, you sound just like him."

"That makes me feel good."

"I'd recognize Oliver's voice anywhere. We were— We were very close, your uncle and me, very close. There were no secrets between us." His voice trailed off, almost as if into memory, or maybe just into the unspoken.

I wondered if he was steering, or trying to, and if I could help him. "You may have seen I photograph a lot of gay weddings," I blurted. "It's because I'm gay." I wanted him to know that if he was like me, he could tell me.

"Oh," he said, and he was quiet for a minute, and then when he spoke again there was a new warmth in his voice. "And I'm glad you do. Men like us need to stick together. Oliver and me, we—never had a ceremony."

So just as easy as that, almost nonchalantly, a question I'd had half my life had an answer. And when I knew the answer I almost had to remember that it had ever been a question.

"I'd just love to see ya, Ollie," Anders went on.

"Yeah, I'd like to see you too!" Could he hear that I had tears in my eyes?

"Your Internet says you live in Boston?"

"Brighton, yeah."

"I don't know that I can drive all that way anymore. I'm on the Cape. Harwich. Know it?"

"I think so, yeah. I can come to you, that's no problem."

"I'd like that. I have some things of your uncle's, I'd like to give them to you. It's why I looked you up."

We chose a Saturday and said goodbye. I put down the phone and looked out the window, my arms crossed on the sill, watching cars go by, thinking.

After a long time I picked up my phone and called my mother. I told her I'd talked to Anders. I said, "They were — together. They were a couple."

I had never outed anyone before but I recognized the same void I felt whenever I told someone who'd known me a long time that I was gay. The words, once uttered, hung there between us, and then, once understood, ricocheted backward into memory, recoloring the past.

When she replied her voice sounded hard, annoyed. "I don't know why he didn't tell me."

"He just— I don't want you to feel like you didn't really know him, or anything—"

"Did he think I wouldn't approve? That I would turn away? He was my brother, I only had one."

"Something tells me he didn't think he was actually hiding much from you. He always brought Anders around. That was his life; you saw it. You knew they went together like bacon and eggs — that was probably all he felt he had to tell you. I think to tell you they were *together* would've been to him like telling you what they did in the — like, privately. It was a different time, like you said. He shared his life with you."

"It must've been so *hard* for Anders. After Oliver died, we went through their house, your grandparents and me, and we sorted Oliver's things — and my god, they were Anders' things, too. But we didn't know. Why didn't he tell me?"

Shortly after I hung up with my mother, my father called me. His voice was muffled, as if he had a hand against the receiver.

"Ollie, Jesus, think twice about all this. This isn't your history to be fucking with here."

"How is Mom?"

"Well she's been crying, Ollie." His voice had gotten too loud and he brought it back down to a whisper again. "When Oliver died — You don't remember how it was for her. She worshipped him."

"You're saying she can't worship him anymore now that he was like me?"

"You know damn well that's not what I mean. It hurts her to know he was different from the Oliver she knew. You can't keep *taking* things from her, Ollie. Her granddaughter, now her brother. You just — I have to go."

***

It was a long drive from Boston to Harwich. Several times I thought about turning around, but never seriously. I hadn't talked to either of my parents since just after Anders' call but my father's words were still

clanking around in my brain. Half of them I understood:
I get that it hurt my mom to learn that Oliver was
different from what she knew. But half of them were
wrong: This *was* my history. And Anders had reached
out to *me*.

I found the house. He lived in a little ranch house
shingled with sun-bleached wood. Snow from a recent
storm was piled high on both sides of his seashell
driveway and lay in drifts against the shrubs around the
house. It had navy-blue shutters and a yellow front door
that opened when my Jeep crunched over the seashells. I
shut off the motor and waved.

"Oliver?" Anders said as I got out of my Jeep. He
shielded his eyes from the snow-blinding sun and
peered at me.

"It's me," I said. "You look just the same!" But of
course it was a fib; he looked older. He looked like a
grandfather, though I knew now that in a different,
better world he would've been my uncle.

He had snow-white hair, thin but not balding, styled
with Brylcreem or whatever type of stuff men of his
generation put in their hair. He had on a pale blue
cardigan over a green polo; pants that would be called
slacks. Orange Crocs.

He laughed and said, "Look at your *hair*, Ollie!"

"I know!" I brushed my hand over the bristly crest of
my mohawk.

Holding the yellow door wide open, he told me to
come inside.

After I'd kicked off my shoes he showed me into the
living room. We sat on little sofas facing one another
across a coffee table covered with crystal dishes filled

with M&Ms and jelly beans. Antiques all over, lots of photos on the walls. I glanced over the photos really without looking at them—I was nervous to look. "Throw that pillow on the floor if it's in your way," he told me, and although it was, I didn't.

"Does the house look familiar?" he said.

"I don't think so? Was I ever here before?"

"Sure you were, sure, we had all of you down one summer. You were probably yay high." He placed his hand three feet from the floor.

"Cool, no, I don't remember."

Nervously I pulled some photos out of my shirt pocket and handed them to him. They were of an anniversary party for my parents, of all of us at my UMass graduation, of me holding Abbey the day she was born. Anders looked at them with polite interest but asked few questions. It was becoming clear to me that he'd invited me here so he could do the talking, and that was fine with me. I leaned against the uncomfortable pillow and listened.

For a while he talked about the snow, and how his last Social Security check got delayed by the storm, and how he almost missed a recent episode of *Law & Order* because they changed the time. His voice was soothing and continued to remind me of my grandmother, and I was content because banalities like these held no secrets and threatened no one's memories.

Then, with all this as the strange prologue, he was into it.

He told me he and Oliver met in the mid-1950s outside a gay bar in downtown Worcester. (So not high school, college, or the military, I observed with a twinge. One sentence in and he'd already diverged from the story I knew.) Anders had been standing on the sidewalk waiting for friends; my uncle walked over and introduced himself. It was a brief chat and nothing came of it, Anders said, and they went their separate ways that night.

A few days later Anders was in a drugstore buying shoe polish and Oliver, who happened to be there too, walked over and said hi again. "I thought he was quite handsome," Anders told me. "And that was it." He leaned back in the sofa, remembering. "We moved in together. Which was pretty rare in those days."

Those were the days when, among other things, the owners of gay bars would make sure everyone knew where the escape routes were, for when the police raided.

"We were always running from the police," Anders told me with a laugh, and with a glimmer of nostalgia I couldn't relate to in the slightest. I thought, but didn't dare say, *I attended an LGBT prom in City Hall.* It made me want to cry—out of guilt, out of luck. He said he and Oliver sometimes went to a particular bar where the drinks were expensive because the bar owner bribed the cops to stay away, a tax they paid to be left alone.

"Would ya like some tea?" Anders asked suddenly.

I nearly slipped off the edge of the sofa, where I'd been perched during his stories of running from cops.

"Sure, yeah. Please."

"Coming right up!"

He got up slowly and I heard his knees crackle and pop, and he ambled into the kitchen, holding on to each nearby chair, table, and appliance for balance as he passed it. I got up and followed him, padding across the hardwood floor in my socks. I stood awkwardly with my hands on the back of a kitchen chair.

"Oh, my cardinal is back," Anders said, looking out the frosty window over the sink while water glugged into the silver kettle. A dot of red was hopping around on the snow. "He's pretty, but mean." He laughed. "Isn't that always the way!"

He put the kettle on the stove and took a few steps away from it before remembering to turn on the burner. "I'd forget my head if it wasn't screwed on," he smirked. He sunk his hands into the pockets of his sweater and sighed contentedly. "So. Since you don't remember — shall I give you a tour while the water boils? See if anything jogs?"

He took me around the little house, dragging his hand along the wall wherever we went, partly, it seemed, for balance, and partly, I thought, out of love. He obviously was proud of the house. There wasn't much to it but each room seemed of a different era of renovation, as if he'd been tending the same garden for, what, fifty years? Twenty of it alone since Oliver had been gone.

In his bedroom (there were two, and I guessed one had been for show) Anders opened the top drawer of his dresser and withdrew a small framed photo of — me? No, not me, my Uncle Oliver around my age. It felt funny to see this near doppelganger. He would've been just back from Korea around then. His dark hair was slicked back like a greaser. No, not *like* a greaser — *a greaser*.

"This," Anders said, tapping the glass, "this is Oliver for me, this is how I still think of him." He paused. "I'd give you this picture but I need it. I talk to him. He keeps me out of trouble." He put the photo back in the drawer.

There were more photos in the hallway, including a couple of famous ones of Oliver my mother had copies of. And of Anders with kids at various stages of their lives, from infanthood to my own age—his nephew and nieces.

"We had a lot of fun in this house," Anders said, leaning in the doorway of a small, cluttered room he used as a library, "and we always had someone staying with us!" There were friends from Argentina, a couple from Quebec who visited often, and "for a while George Murphy, who we buried." The last one gave me chills. I assumed George was an AIDS victim and it renewed my fears of uncovering secrets.

The kettle whistled.

Anders was telling me about Atlantic City—had been for a while without yet coming to a point. He wasn't easy to follow sometimes. His stories rambled and twisted and he often left out key information that only surfaced five minutes in. I spent a lot of time confused. Sometimes I was afraid of asking for details that might uncover something I didn't want to know.

He was telling me how he and Oliver would go down to Atlantic City, and my uncle would leave him sitting on the boardwalk for hours at a time while he— what? Anders went on and on about the boardwalk without revealing why he was there alone. The weather on the boardwalk, how he would sometimes get ice cream cones on the boardwalk—all while I was wondering what my uncle was busy doing while Anders waited on the boardwalk. I thought, *He was visiting male prostitutes, buying drugs, playing in sex clubs, being scary.*

Eventually Anders revealed that Oliver was playing the dollar slot machines in the casinos while Anders, who didn't like the smoke, hung out on the boardwalk. My breath escaped in a puff of nervous relief. *Gambling, thank god, just gambling.* I'm sure my worries would seem silly to anyone who actually knew my uncle, but since I never really did, I had no way to judge. So all I could do was judge.

The crux of all my nervousness was my own internalized homophobia, baggage from a time way before mine: the suspicion that men who lived closeted lives must have, *had to have*, spent those lives doing unsavory things. Coming out for me had not been the easiest experience but still, at twenty-six, it was hard for me to imagine that simply being gay, simply being a man in a relationship with a man, could ever have been any man's biggest secret. There had to have been other secrets. It was silly of me, and ignorant both of history and of too many places and families in the present (I had, after all, been with Johnny), but I couldn't help feeling it. I was afraid there was more to it. I was afraid something Anders told me would topple my uncle's pedestal.

"He was a gambler?" I said, still giddy with relief that it was gambling and nothing else.

"Oh, he loved it," Anders said. "He never really won. But he never really lost, either."

"I didn't know."

He smiled. "Oliver Donaldson had many sides," he said. "All of them were good."

Of course they all had been, I told myself. Of course.

"I don't know how he got it," Anders said sadly, and though it caught me off-guard it didn't feel like another of his non-sequiturs. His stories had been confusing, yet I knew this thought had come from his thinking of Oliver's good sides—a direct line from love to loss. "I don't know how he got it," he said again.

And I thought, with a crushing regret as though I were lingering on the boardwalk again, *No one talks about cancer that way, which means it wasn't really cancer, it was AIDS like I've always secretly feared, it was AIDS because he was a gay man who died young in the 1980s, and oh my god I don't want to know if it was AIDS.*

I was shaking—and why? Would it have been such a terrible thing to know, that my uncle had been one of the countless, history-moving losses my generation owed so much to? It was terrible because it was not what I had known and been told. And now I could see why my mother could be so hurt to find out Oliver was gay—because it meant she'd never been able to participate in the truth.

But still I couldn't say it. "How he got *it?*"

Anders tapped his head. "The brain cancer."

"Brain cancer," I breathed.

He told me how it had started in the stem of Oliver's brain, rooted up and in and then bloomed like a weed behind Oliver's eyes. All of what Anders said, all the terrible symptoms, lined up with what my family had always told me.

Sometimes the truth is just the truth.

***

After I'd been there two hours and I was thinking it might be getting time to head home, Anders asked if I wanted to go out for lunch. I said yes. I thought maybe he'd want me to drive, but after wrangling into his boots and his coat he led me through the kitchen into the garage. A big boaty Cadillac sat under the glow of a single yellow light bulb.

"I don't get to drive much anymore," he said, fumbling with the keys. "My niece won't let me."

I whispered, "I won't tell."

With minor reservations about being chauffeured by an eighty-something with whatever he had — what could happen to me in a car this sturdy, anyway? — I climbed into the passenger seat. My jeans glided across the well-worn leather.

Anders pressed a button on a keyfob and then watched in the rearview as the garage door lumbered upward. He kept his eyes on it until it was fully open, with the focus of someone who maybe once backed through it halfway and was determined not to repeat the mistake.

Then with a crank of the key and the last efforts of a nearly depleted battery the Cadillac burst to life. "There's a pub I like. Sound good?"

"Sounds great."

Off we went. Anders drove slow and got tooted at a couple of times, once for not noticing a light had turned green.

Over lunch he asked questions. About my life, about Abbey, about my parents. He must've felt by then that he'd said what he wanted to say, and now he could listen.

When the remnants of our sandwiches were cleared away we ordered dessert. He had a dish of vanilla ice cream he ate slowly with tiny scoops while I talked. He paid for lunch with a crisp fifty-dollar bill. The waitress clearly thought he was my grandfather.

Driving back to his house, there was silence between us for the first time since I'd arrived. It wasn't an awkward silence but it seemed to me that it must be a wasteful silence. I kept thinking, *What else do I want to know? What else do I want to ask?* In a way I felt like I knew what I needed to know, though; at least the big things. So I wondered what I would ask in a better, more perfect world where nothing had ever needed to be secret—what I would ask on a day like today, in a world like that.

"Anders," I said, "tell me more about that mean cardinal."

***

"This has been such a nice day," he said as he was steering the big Cadillac back into the garage. "I've had a lot of fun today."

"Me too. Thank you for telling me your stories. It means a lot to me. I wondered about you and my uncle for a long time. I wasn't sure—no one was really ever sure. My mother, I mean. But I really wanted Oliver to have been like me."

"It's always good to know you're not the first," Anders said. And he added, "And not the last, too."

He didn't expect to live much longer. He said he'd already had a few close calls but didn't elaborate on what exactly his illness was, only that his brains were leaking out of his ears, which I thought was probably just a figure of speech. But I had a sense that this day was something he'd been meaning to do and was happy to cross off his list.

"Now I want to make sure you get some of Oliver's things so they won't get lost in the shuffle when I'm gone," he told me as we reentered the house.

He took me down the hall to the cluttered library and sat down at a desk. "Pull that chair over," he said, pointing, and I did, and sat down. A bulging orange envelope sat on the desk. With fingers swollen from arthritis he turned the envelope over and unfastened the clasp.

Inside was an ivory shoehorn, some gold cufflinks, an emerald tie-tack, and my uncle's diamond ring, which I supposed was the one my mother had mentioned.

The ring fit me perfectly on the same finger Anders said Oliver wore it on. "Oh, you have your uncle's hands," he said, so matter-of-fact, as if he'd noticed me wearing Oliver's hat or using his wallet.

Also in the envelope were a scattered cluster of photos, including a copy of the one of my uncle at my age with his hair slicked back. Most of the rest were photos taken by Oliver—landscapes of places he had seen in the Army, pictures of their house, their garden. I thought I'd gotten my picture-taking from Wesley; I liked that it came from even farther back.

The last item in the envelope—Anders had to shake it out—was a keychain and two house keys. For a fretful second I thought Anders was giving me his house.

"I'd have to say these were his prized possessions," Anders said, running a finger along the metal teeth. "He was very proud of our house. He saw a lot of the world but he was always most proud of this house. He always said that your house key is a little piece of metal that stands between you and the place you belong."

Anders started to get up, and tapped my knee. "Don't lose that, young man."

The afternoon light had faded to a dusky dusk. Anders stood in front of his living-room window, his hands in the pockets of his sweater, while I put on my shoes and my coat. I straightened up and hugged him quickly.

"Need to use the head before you go?" he said, in such a grandfatherly way.

"Nah, I'm good."

He followed me outside and stood on the front porch as I walked to my Jeep. The seashell driveway crunched nicely under my sneakers. He hadn't given me his house but I could imagine myself living in a place like it someday. All these snowbanks wanted a coffee cup.

"Sometimes I like to come out and stand out in the cold for five or ten minutes," Anders said, watching his breath. "Changes the air in the lungs." He waved. "Give me a buzz when you get home, so I know you got home OK."

***

Anders had told me that when my uncle was in hospice and the cancer had wreaked havoc on his brain, his arm slipped off the bed and was dangling against the side, paralyzed. My uncle noticed his arm missing but had no sense of it having moved, and he said to Anders, "Where's my arm?" And Anders said, "It fell off the bed. Want me to put it back?" And he did.

"I still love ya, Andy," my uncle said.

For all my worry about poking around in the past, it had uncovered only one life-changing piece of new information: that my Uncle Oliver had been in love. I was glad to tell my mom that Oliver hadn't been different from who she had known, not at all, he'd simply been more, and the more was nothing more than that he'd been in love—for a long time, for most of his life, to the day he died. And what a wonderful thing to find out.

"Do ya have someone of your own, Ollie?" Anders had asked while we were eating ice cream at the pub.

"I guess I've had a lot of someones," I said. "A lot of near misses. I've fired off a lot of arrows but I haven't hit the bull's-eye yet."

Anders laughed. "It'll come," he said, "it'll come. And I hope you'll be as happy as we were."

Before I had driven too far from Anders' house I started to cry, and when it became clear that this wasn't a passing thing, that it needed to be let out, I pulled into the parking lot of a gas station and sobbed. I didn't even know what I was crying for, really. Maybe for the bigness of the day, for my awareness of my part in it. Maybe I was crying for a secret that outlived my uncle by twenty years, and for the world that had demanded the secret in the first place. Or for what had been built in spite of that world.

I wiped my tears and got myself together. The orange envelope was sitting on the seat beside me. I shook Oliver's keys out of it and put them in my jeans pocket.

While I drove I touched the keys through my jeans, pressed the metal against my thigh. Still there. I touched them again. Still there. At a stoplight I pulled them out of my pocket and attached them to my own keyring. They swung there from the ignition, clinking against the steering column. A chime, a note that would've been familiar to him. Every minute or two I'd touch them with my finger. Still there. Just to make sure. Still there.

Still there.

And — still here.

We All Go Back to Where
We Belong

The first time I saw Fletcher I must've looked like crap;
it's a wonder he even was interested. I was sweaty and
tired and my feet hurt. My lips were dry and my nose
stung from sunburn. My mohawk was down and
hanging in my eyes. It was evening then, and still hot.
Sweat was running down my ribs and my shirt clung to
my belly.

I'd been walking around Boston all day, listening to
R.E.M. on my iPod all day, walking my way through
what felt like a lifelong time warp, and I had forgotten to
think about looking like anything — good or bad or
anything. My ears were probably red from the earbuds.

It was a day almost everyone remembers now, for
one big reason or another. I remember it for a lot of
reasons. Partly I remember it as the day I first saw him,
and partly of course for what happened that night. But it
started as the day my favorite band broke up.

I saw the news on their website that July morning. I was
drinking coffee and eating an English muffin and
browsing the news. Such a mundane way to learn

something so big. Shelley had left for work already and I needed to be leaving myself. I had a boss again, a job to lose, cameras to sell and passport photos to take. Instead I just sat. Nothing mattered now except the news that the band that got me through high school and college and the post-college-whatever had decided to opposite themselves: they were disbanding. As I digested the news I felt my eyes leave the screen and creep across the apartment. Everything was looking crooked—the blinds, the picture frames, the cabinet doors—even though I long ago made sure nothing was. I pushed the laptop away from me, folded my arms on the table, and put my head down. My eyes filled with tears.

There's a line in "Drive" where Michael Stipe sings my name. *Ollie. Ollie. Ollie Ollie Ollie.* I was sixteen when I first heard it. I was in my childhood bedroom mourning a lost love, feeling as lost as I'd ever felt, even more lost than I felt now. And then: *Ollie Ollie Ollie.* The sound was like a welcome and a wake-up call all at once—and this I promise you is the best mix of anything you can have in your life, something that gives you a refuge and pushes you out of it, all at the same time. This is the giving of confidence. That was what R.E.M. always did for me; they gave me confidence. It seemed in every moment they were there. You know. You know my stories have had a soundtrack. I marked time with new albums, new songs. They were part of all my memories. I guess I thought they always would be. I thought it right up until I found out they wouldn't.

The words on my laptop screen said in no uncertain terms that after almost thirty years together the members of R.E.M. were moving on to pursue other things, and thank you, and goodbye. At the bottom was a link to one final new song, a farewell, one last hurrah. I hurriedly downloaded it and clicked play. As the first notes came through the crappy laptop speakers I realized my elbow was resting on a cold English muffin, the butter thick as sludge against my skin. I didn't want to listen this way, with sleep-skewed hair and crumbs on my lips. This was not the way to listen to the last new song. *Ollie Ollie Ollie.* After all this time we all deserved more.

I called in sick at the camera store, which was not quite a lie since my stomach felt crumpled and hard as a ball of tinfoil. I showered and dressed. I put on my sneakers, grabbed my phone, wallet, and keys, put in my earbuds, and, with my iPod loaded with the last new song and all of the old ones, I left the apartment and started walking.

I started with *Murmur*, their first album. 1983 — I would've been three. I started along the river, going in the direction of downtown. My sneakers slapped the sidewalk silently. I continued with *Reckoning* and *Fables of the Reconstruction* — I would've been four and five. I stopped for an iced coffee at Dunkin' Donuts. The air was fresh. The sun moved across the sky.

What do you lose, really, when your favorite band breaks up? None of the songs that made you love them go anywhere. Nothing is erased or taken away. It all still belongs to you. "Nightswimming." "Everybody Hurts." "Find The River" — the most beautiful song I'd ever heard, the song that once made Wesley cry. These songs were rooted in my past, and nothing could ever uproot them. No — What you lose is the future, and the future is a scary thing to lose. The expectation of landmarks and signposts evaporates. Concerts, new albums, things to mark your progress — they disappear. "That's all.

Goodbye." I'd heard it before and now I was hearing it again. I had heard it so much, it seemed. I guess when your favorite band disbands it's like the end of any relationship. Maybe, for me, Michael Stipe was just another guy.

***

I walked all day, working myself up for that last new song. Fifteen studio albums, 691 minutes. I walked along the river into Back Bay, across the Common, through the North End to the Harbor. The city had a weird energy that day, almost a crackle, as if it were on the verge of something. At least that's what other people say; I'm not sure I felt it myself at the time. I was my ears and my heart that day, and not much else. I thought of all the guys I'd met, loved, lost. I thought of my Uncle Oliver and little Abbey and two young knights, whose photo I still carried in my wallet to remind me to hope. There had been a song for each of these. And this is why the disbanding hurt so much: When I met him, whoever he turned out to be, there would be no song for him.

There were two albums left in my playlist when I decided to head home. My feet hurt and my shirt was soaked with sweat and my hair was in my eyes. I didn't want to walk anymore. I caught an inbound train at Haymarket station. It was rush-hour now, and crowded, and I made my way slowly toward the back of the car as commuters churned in and out. The stops ticked by, almost in time with the remaining songs. Then, somewhere underground between Boylston and Arlington stations, a funny thing happened. As the last album faded out, the train glided into sudden slow silence, as though the same power had been powering both the music and the subway and now was lost. The lights dimmed, flickered, became yellowish with a hint of emergency.

We sat that way for a few minutes. The last new song was queued up on my iPod, and all I had to do was click play. The timing felt right—a time of silence and expectation and in-betweenness as the train sat mysteriously idle— but I couldn't bring myself to play the song. When is the right time to have a last time? How do you know?

I felt lost. I was having internal arguments with myself. My lips may even have been moving, silently acting things out. Suddenly I felt self-conscious. Someone was probably watching me wag my thumb back and forth over the iPod buttons, lips moving like a freak.

And I was right: a guy was staring at me. A few feet away, standing in the accordioned space between two train cars. His dark brown hair was freshly buzzed and his eyes were bright. He was cute. My type. My age. But I didn't really care. He had a baby, a boy, strawberry blond, slung across his chest in one of those carriers, hanging there like a chubby little gargoyle. I didn't really care about that either.

I gave him a nod and he nodded back, but his was less of a greeting and more of a twitch, embarrassed that I'd caught him staring. He blushed.

"Kiddo seems pretty content," I said, removing one earbud.

"He's a good kid."

I smiled. The kid-holding guy smiled back. From his eyes he looked too smart for his own good; there was a mischievousness in them.

"Yours?" I said.

"No. Yeah. Long story." He smiled again but it was more bashful this time.

"Sounds like," I said.

I put the earbud back in and pressed play. The last new song, the farewell song, was slow, quiet, beautiful, almost like a lullaby. Soothing. I didn't cry. I thought I would but I didn't. When the song was done the iPod screen returned without ceremony to the main library, and I switched it off.

"Color me curious," I said to the kid-holding guy as I wound the earbud cords around my fingers.

"Curious about what?"

"His daddy issues."

"His daddy issues," the guy repeated, and smirked. "OK...."

His story seemed cautious, or maybe just unrehearsed; the kid was young and he had probably not been telling it for long. I had trouble following. Something about his roommates, their kid, the father wasn't really the father, not quite, and this kid-holding guy belonged in there somewhere but I didn't catch where. He was cute, though, and had nice teeth, and there was something inviting about him.

"Quite a story," I said when I sensed he was done, though I also sensed there was more he'd decided not to say. I took out my uncle's keychain and jangled it at the kid. "I have one of my own," I said.

The kid-holding guy looked surprised. "How old?"

"Four. She's biologically mine but they live near Seattle. I donated to my friend and her *lesbian lover*." Harriet would've smacked me, the way I said it. I couldn't help it.

"Wow," the guy said. "That was cool of you."

"Well, when they put a cup in—uh—well, never mind."

He smiled. "I saw you," he said, or more like blurted. Then he seemed to try to dilute it with uncertainty. "I think. About a year ago, I guess. On the T. Around Brighton? It was a really hot day and I was grouchy and I saw you touch your pocket to make sure you still had your keys. It was a little thing but for some reason I've always remembered it."

"Just me checking for my keys?" I asked casually. Because he was cute I chose to be flattered rather than weirded out. I thought about where I might've been going last summer when he saw me. That was the summer Anders died and my fear of losing my keys had been at an all-time high.

The guy looked down at the kid's hair. "It sounds weird now that I say it."

"I do that a lot," I said. "Compulsively. I'm always nervous about losing them. It would be so difficult to replace them and meanwhile, how would I get into my house?"

He smiled. "That's what I thought."

I remembered what Anders had told me about how my uncle felt about his keys. And I added, "It's a little piece of metal that stands between you and the place you belong."

After a while a guy with a good cell signal spread the news that the power was out in all of Boston, not just in the subway. There seemed to be no word yet on when it might be restored.

I said to the kid-holding guy, "We might be down here forever."

"This guy's going to poop a lot sooner than that."

"So am I," I laughed.

I wondered what was going on aboveground, above us; what a powerless city would look like. I hadn't ever seen a place so big have to rely on the momentum of civilization. How long would that momentum last? Would there be car accidents? Looting? I wanted to believe something sweet would come out of it, something beautiful and full of color, like a rainbow after a storm. But I was primed to feel that way today — all my senses and emotions were on high. And maybe it was enough that everyone on the train started clapping wildly an hour later when the lights came back to full strength and the floor beneath us started to hum with power.

"Here we go," I said, grinning. "One big happy family for a change."

The train lurched to the next station and the doors opened and a platform's worth of waiting commuters tried to pile in. The kid-holding guy and I were squished together; between us the kid pulled at my shirt.

"I need to transfer to a B train up ahead," I told the guy. "I guess I should start making my way out."

"Good luck," he said. "It was nice spending the blackout with you."

"Same." I reached for the hand rail and turned to leave, then turned back to him. "Would you be interested in grabbing a coffee sometime? You could bring your little friend here."

His face lit up. "That would be cool. Yeah. I'd like that."

"I think I have my, uh, card around here somewhere. — That sounds so pretentious of me." I pulled a business card out of my wallet and the photo of the knights came with it. I pushed the photo back in and smoothed the card a little before handing it over.

"Ollie Wade," the guy read. He looked up. "Freelance photography, huh?"

"Ha. Well, no. Formerly freelance. These are leftovers."

"I'm Fletcher. This is Caleb."

"Fletcher? Do you make arrows? Zing!" It had seemed witty coming out of my mouth but now I felt like a dork. "Sorry, I bet you get that all the time."

He smiled. "Just once before, actually."

Over the speaker came the muffled announcement of my stop.

"This is me," I said. "So I'll talk to you later?"

"Yeah, definitely."

"Cool. Call me. Normally I'd say don't forget, but if you remembered me after a year, I don't guess you'll forget me by tomorrow."

For everyone else—for me too, ultimately—that became the day henceforth known as Paint Day, the big reason everyone remembers that day. After the blackout, through whatever means you find yourself willing to accept or believe in or find true, old graffiti art long painted-over reappeared on walls and vehicles and monuments all over Boston. On the wooden concert bowl of the Hatch Shell, on the white spires of the Zakim Bridge, on pretty much everywhere a guy could reach to put it—and some places no one knew how he'd reached. For weeks we all would talk about nothing except that day, and how the paintings had bloomed with the return of light after the blackout. No one would forget that day because of it. The kid-holding guy would not forget that day. But afterward I waited for his call, and I waited.

And I began to realize that he'd forgotten me.

Summer moved on in ways large and small. Boston and its magical paintings filled the news worldwide. I turned twenty-eight in August and soon afterward found a gray hair in my mohawk, and then one on my chest. I worked, I dated, I took pictures for pay and for fun. There was lots to take pictures of after Paint Day. The city went to war with the paintings at first, scratched at them as if they were an infection on its skin. But they were more like tattoos than infections—they couldn't be removed, and they vanquished any attempt at whitewashing by turning the cover-up paint into dripping gray goop. The city found no cure but acceptance, which grew over time into a sort of mysterious love. I took special pride in photographing the paintings because I knew something about them that no one else knew. And I loved them, too—had maybe loved them first.

Summer turned to fall, turned to winter. R.E.M. stuck to their disbanding, and I wore out my brain on that last new song. And spring. Shelley moved in with her fiancé and I traded the apartment Angel had helped me choose for one I chose all by myself. And summer again. One year.

***

I didn't recognize the phone number. It was local, though. It lit up my phone on a Thursday evening. I was home cleaning the cage of the rabbit Shelley had bought for me because she worried I'd be lonely in my new apartment. Bruno was sitting on the couch lazily gnawing a carrot, dumb and endearing as my old friend and his namesake; a woodchip clung to his silky brown ear. I switched off the vacuum and answered the phone.

"Ollie Wade?" A guy's voice.

"Yes?" I picked the woodchip off Bruno and flicked it away.

"Hey Ollie, this is Fletcher Bradford. I don't know if you remember.... We, uh, met on Paint Day, on the T. During the blackout?"

I was surprised, to say the least, but tried not to show it. "I remember."

"Oh, cool! Yeah, you gave me your business card. You asked if I wanted to grab coffee sometime."

"That was a year ago," I laughed. "I sort of gave up on you, Fletcher, to be honest."

A long pause. "I'm sorry," he said. "Yeah. You're right. It's just that, after Paint Day my life got pretty complicated. My family life, I mean. And I just— I needed some time to sort things out. I haven't dated since then, Ollie. I never forgot about you."

"I seem to be pretty unforgettable to you somehow."

He laughed nervously. "Anyway, I was wondering if you'd still want to get together sometime?"

"Actually," I said, "I'm married now."

There was a longer pause, which I didn't interrupt. I guess I was punishing him for making me wait a whole year. I didn't know why I was, and I didn't like that I'd done it.

"Oh," he said. "You are?"

"No, I was teasing, I'm sorry. I'm single. What did you, uh, have in mind?"

"You had me going there for a second."

"Sorry, Fletcher."

"Are you doing anything for Fourth of July?"

"Not that I know of."

"Ever been to the Esplanade, for the fireworks?"

"A couple years ago. My old roommate Shelley and I went."

"Oh, nice. Did you find a good spot to watch from?"

"It was OK. We were pretty far away from the action. We couldn't hear the Pops concert at all." I grabbed my laptop and opened Facebook, typed *Fletcher Bradford* in the search; I'd never known his last name. He was there at the top of the results.

"My friend Jamar will be visiting his brother Robbie with our son for the weekend," Fletcher went on, "so it's just me around here. I want to go to the fireworks and I was hoping you wouldn't make me go stag." He paused. "Sorry, is this weird, after all this time?"

As I clicked through his Facebook profile, I said, "It's not weird. Are you still as cute as you were during the blackout?"

He laughed. "I guess I look the same, for whatever that's worth."

"Then I'd like to go."

"Awesome," he said. "I like to be right up front, near the Hatch Shell. That cool with you?"

"It's cool but I imagine we'd have to get there pretty early to get that close?"

"We need to get there about sixteen hours early, actually."

I laughed. "*Sixteen* hours?"

"Is that too much commitment for a blind date? This is basically a blind date, it's been so long."

"If you're no fun I'll just slip away into the crowd."

He laughed. "Fair enough. Let's say 4:30 a.m. on Saturday at the Hatch Shell?"

I agreed to it and we hung up. Bruno was still eating his carrot. I looked at him and whispered, "What the fuck?"

***

The subway wasn't running so early so I had to take a cab. Although Fletcher had texted to make sure I was awake I had a hunch he wouldn't actually show up. This had to be some kind of weird joke, though I couldn't imagine why he'd play it. But it was a holiday and I had nothing else to do, so why not.

The cab let me out at the corner of Beacon and Storrow, on the sidewalk in front of a Shuster College dorm. With a trail of other people I walked across that funny orange footbridge to get to the Esplanade, where the Hatch Shell, already decked out in red-white-and-blue bunting for the Pops concert, loomed in the dawn. The air was cool and moist but it probably wouldn't stay that way for long. I had a backpack of supplies for a full day in the hot sun. Everyone else was weighed down with survival gear, too. They were gathering around the outside of the oval of lawn in front of the Hatch Shell. The oval was cordoned off with segments of metal fence. A few cops stood inside the fence, talking to each other and to the people on the other side waiting to get in.

I didn't see Fletcher. I pulled out my phone and texted, *I'm at the Hatch. Are you?*

He texted back, *I'm lined up near the fence. Sorry, I can't move or I'll lose our place. Walk the perimeter & you'll find me.*

This time, for a change, I saw him before he saw me. He was standing at the back of the oval, looking across the grass, his thumbs hooked in the shoulder straps of his backpack. His arms were thin but nice. His hair was longer than last year and he had yellow sunglasses perched on top of his head. He was wearing a white sleeveless t-shirt with the Brazilian—I was pretty sure it was the Brazilian—flag on the chest, which seemed odd because everyone around him was decked out in America's colors. He also was wearing khaki shorts and black sneakers that reminded me of Angel.

I called his name. He turned and grinned as his eyes swept the crowd. I waved.

"Ollie! Hey!" He motioned for me to come over, and I did, though I felt funny moving past people who'd gotten there earlier, as though I were cutting in line— though it was more of a cluster than a line. It seemed no one knew exactly where the fence would open and they were hedging their bets.

For a second Fletcher and I looked at each other, sizing each other up, comparing reality to memory and Facebook. He looked more casual than I remembered, looser, somehow more exotic, more sure of himself.

"You lost your mohawk," he said with a twinge of disappointment. He moved in to give me a hug that was awkward just until we touched, and then felt nice.

"Yup, it's history." I ran my hand through my hair. "I had it five years, that was long enough. Time to grow up, you know?"

"I liked it," he said. "Not that you're less cute without it." He nudged my arm with his elbow and I noticed a row of letters tattooed on his inner forearm.

"I'll take that as a compliment," I said. "So should I, uh, be concerned about that shirt of yours?" I leaned closer and added, teasing, "Aren't you worried they'll tar-and-feather you for wearing that flag on a day like this?"

"For Brazil?" he laughed. "I don't think so? Maybe if it was England's, that might be a little treasonous." He patted his chest. "I got it last winter. I went to visit my friend Vinicius in São Paulo." There was an unmissable sparkle in his eyes when he said it.

"Is Vinicius a — special someone?" I said.

He laughed. "Oh, he's very special," he said with a touch of sarcasm. "We've gotten so close I'd think it was icky if I ever saw him naked."

"Oh. Gotcha. Good to hear."

Behind us the crowd was building. So many people. I could barely believe it, because it wasn't even 5:00 a.m.

"So what exactly is about to happen here?" I asked.

"Well first," Fletcher said, looking down at my feet, "can you run in those flip-flops?"

"I've run marathons in these flip-flops."

"But seriously. We'll need to run."

"Oh. OK. I guess so?"

"Everyone here, all these people, they all want that spot up front. Front-row center." He pointed. "And when this gate opens at 6:00 they're all going to be running for that one spot. But trust me, Ollie, we're the ones who're going to get it."

A lady next to us wearing a Statue of Liberty hat, green foam spikes drooping in the dewy air, shook her head and said, "Nuh uh, honey."

Fletcher had a blue blanket strapped to his backpack. He unbuckled it and shook it open between us. It had the Shuster College logo embroidered on one corner and was worn thin in the center, as if from too many picnics.

"Now the goal," he told me, "is to cover as much grass as possible when we get to our heaven spot up there." He pointed again to the front row. "Whatever square-footage we can claim will be our territory for the whole day. The more space the better, you know? I'm sure you don't want me to have to sit on your lap all day."

I smirked to indicate that wouldn't be so bad, and he smiled.

Meanwhile one of the cops standing inside the oval had approached the fence about ten feet from where we were standing.

She cupped her hand to her mouth. "We're going to open the gate momentarily," she shouted. "Please remember, folks, there ain't nothing you can see from the front row that you can't see from where you already are." And that was true, technically, but it wasn't really the point, was it? No one had gotten here when it was still dark for the tenth row, or even for the second row.

Fletcher and I put on our backpacks and took firm holds of opposite ends of his blanket.

A moment later two cops pulled open a gap between two segments of fence—narrower than probably anyone was expecting, but lucky for the lady in the Statue of Liberty hat, who happened to be right in front of it. She barreled through with a blanket over her shoulder and a suitcase on wheels that bounced in the grass behind her.

"Go go go!" Fletcher yelled, laughing, pushing me after her.

I slipped through the gap with him on my heels a blanket's distance away. A wave of people flooded in behind us, all racing for the front row. I could feel my flip-flops sliding around between the grass and my feet. I knew that if one fell off I'd never see it again.

"Liberty lady can *move*," I shouted, and Fletcher laughed. She was maintaining her lead.

Tethered by the blanket between us, Fletcher and I moved toward and away from each other as we ran, sometimes tugging at the blanket's extremes, sometimes bumping together with a twisted pile of it between us.

Thirty feet from the front row, Liberty lady tripped and lost her balance and seemed to career for like fifteen feet before finally crashing on the grass. The impact popped the pointy green hat off her head and it zinged away like a foam ninja star.

I started to stop but Fletcher yelled, "Leave her leave her!" And he and I literally jumped over her as she was pounding the grass angrily with her fist.

I arrived at front-row center and dropped the blanket and tagged the crowd-control fence there in front of the Hatch Shell with a slap of my hand, feeling like I'd won the race, forgetting we still needed to claim our turf. Behind me Fletcher was scrambling on his knees, yelling "Ollie Ollie Ollie!," frantically spreading the blanket on the grass.

I dove past him onto my stomach onto the blanket and pushed the fabric to the farthest reach of my fingertips, just as another dude slapped his own blanket down. It covered my forearms and a portion of my blanket and I said, "Beat ya!" And he frantically yanked his blanket away to claim grass in the other direction.

When I turned around again Fletcher was already lying on our blanket, on his side with his backpack still on, breathing heavy, and he looked sexy with his bare arms and shoulders shining with sweat.

"Nice work, Ollie," he gasped. He held up his hand and I shook it, hot and slippery.

Around us, as far back as I could see, in what had been green lawn sixty seconds ago, there wasn't a blade of grass left visible. The Esplanade was a patchwork quilt of blankets. Liberty lady was ten feet back. She'd managed to spread her blanket to the size of a bath towel and was sitting in the middle of it opening her suitcase. Fletcher and I had the best seat in the house. What had he called it? Our heaven spot.

***

The sun rose. To our left the Charles River glimmered along the Esplanade, sending popinjays flitting across the huge wooden bowl of the Hatch Shell.

Our blanket — today our whole world — was five feet by seven feet. We organized ourselves and settled in; it was like playing house. Here was the corner where we put our shoes, here was the end where we opened Fletcher's umbrella to cast some shade, here was our supply of water and snacks; our backpacks became pillows. At the foot of our blanket was one segment of the waist-high metal fence that separated the crowd from the walkway in front of the Hatch Shell. Behind us was a young family who had pitched one of those lean-to tents people use at the beach. On our left was a young girl and her middle-aged father working a crossword (the girl made me think of Abbey, as most of them do), and on our right a young straight couple in matching Red Sox t-shirts dumped ice into a cooler. I took out my camera and snapped a few photos of the stage, of the big rolling TV cameras, of the patchwork quilt behind us, and of Fletcher when he wasn't looking.

"So you're a writer?" I said, snapping the lens cap back on my camera. "I saw on Facebook."

He laughed. "I knew a writer, once. It's hard to call myself a writer after knowing him." He was lying on his side, leaning on an elbow. "Let's just say I've written. And I sometimes write."

"And what have you written, Fletcher Bradford? Anything I might know?"

"*Porcupine City*? That's the only thing that's been

published."

"I haven't heard of it. Sorry."

"It's OK."

"Actually, I don't read all that much?"

His eyes bugged. "This date is over." He sat up and pretended to start gathering his things.

Laughing, I yanked his backpack away from him and said, "Nope!" Then we were quiet for a minute, maybe to rein in the playfulness.

"Sometimes I fantasize about writing a book," I told him. "Is that weird? I feel like taking pictures is a good way of documenting things but it's not very useful for resolving the past. Like with pictures you can only see what the past actually was, not what it might have been or what it meant. You know? Plus, you never have a camera in the really important moments, so cameras leave holes. The really important moments happen in the dark, under the covers—or in restaurants, I guess. A lot of important conversations involve food."

"That's astute."

"I guess I wouldn't know where to start, writing a book?" Absently I pulled my foot onto my lap and wedged a finger between my toes. "Where do *you* start?"

He thought for a minute. "With an image, I guess. Then it grows from there. *Porcupine City*, it opens with a blanket lying against a guy's hip. He's sitting up in bed—you know, the morning after."

"Was this from personal experience, Fletcher?"

He grinned. "It just always stuck in my head. And eventually kicked off a book."

"I have this image in my head of a steaming coffee cup sitting in a pile of snow. My first roommate, this guy Wesley, he put it there."

"Wouldn't the coffee cup melt the snow?"

"Hm. Yeah, I guess. Let's say it lurches and some coffee spills out."

"OK. What happens after it spills?"

"Um. Coffee-slush leaps away from the cup?"

"Then?"

"I guess I don't know. What should happen?"

He reached under our blanket and plucked a blade of grass. Closing his eyes against the sun, he tickled it against his lips. "What makes you hurt? What needs figuring out? That's what happens after the coffee cup." He pursed his lips and pushed the grass between them.

"I guess I've had a lot of people leave, in my life," I said. "Loves, friends—family, even. I guess— I don't know, maybe I'd want to imagine what would happen if one of them came back. Like, maybe if he randomly showed up. Like poof, right in the middle of a blizzard or something."

"I'm kind of doing the same thing," Fletcher said. "This guy I was with—Mateo. He left us. Under, let's say, mysterious circumstances. He and I weren't dating anymore but I thought he'd always be in my life in some capacity. I wanted him to be." He added gently, "His son is my son."

"I thought you said the other dad was— Was it Jamal?"

"Jamar. Yeah. He is." He laughed. "Mateo is the bio father. Jamar and I are— We're— I know it sounds so complicated."

"It's OK. I understand, believe me."

"That's right, you have one."

"I do."

"Anyway," Fletcher went on, "I'm sort of working on this book that'll let me bring Mateo back, in a way. At least for myself. I started it when I was flying home from

São Paulo."

"You can write on planes? I would think you'd need a special place. Don't writers usually have a special place?"

"I used to use an old typewriter my friend Cara gave me. Now I just use a little notebook and I whip it out whenever. I like it better. I like knowing I can give everything I have in the grocery store waiting in line. Or while I'm waiting for pasta to cook. I like that I don't need a special place to be at my best or to write the line of my life. That it can just happen in any random moment."

"Deepness follows."

He laughed. "What?"

"Nothing, it's an old thing. What's the book called?"

He said, bashfully, "*Surfboy Forever*."

"Was Mateo a surfer?"

"No. No, I don't think he ever surfed. But there's something about how surfers describe connecting with a wave, that I think is very Mateo. I guess I feel like I can conjure him up through that, even if it's not something he actually did."

He passed me his blade of grass and then sat up and took a water bottle out of his backpack.

"Funny," I said, touching the grass to my own lips, "I've always taken pictures to keep people as they are, maybe to keep them from leaving. You write stories to try to bring them back."

***

Later in the morning we snoozed, side by side on our backs with our heads in the shade of the umbrella, its stem and hook-shaped handle angling down into the space between our sides. I looked down the length of our bodies. He was, I thought, the exact same height as me, and our bare feet rocked side to side beside each other against the hot metal bars of the fence.

I sat up feeling groggy and flushed from napping in the heat. And I needed to go to the bathroom. I'd spotted a parade of Port-o-Potties lining the Esplanade, but I would have to step on a lot of blankets to get there.

Fletcher opened his eyes and leaned up on an elbow when I was scuffing back into my flip-flops.

"Pee break," I said. "Want to come?"

"Someone needs to protect the turf," he said. I might've laughed, but after seeing the race this morning I guessed he wasn't joking.

I picked up my camera as I was leaving and swung it over my shoulder. I didn't want Fletcher to scroll through the photos and find out how many I'd taken of him sleeping—of his long eyelashes and of the bead of sweat on his throat and of the tattoo on his forearm that said *Arrowman Is*. I wondered what it would say when it was finished.

It was well into morning now, a time for breakfast and cartoons on any other Saturday. I walked along the seams of the giant patchwork quilt, in the places where blankets met. It seemed the only semi-public part of a blanket, that inch along the edge, and it was like walking a tightrope trying not to invade people's space.

"Hi, hi, excuse me, sorry, hi, sorry, excuse me." Crossing from tarp to bedspread to beach blanket, one borderline after another. Stepping around coolers and beach chairs and toddlers. I waited in line at the Port-o-Potties, and when I was done I stood at the edge of the Esplanade where the blankets began and watched

Fletcher. He was standing on our blanket leaning against the fence, looking, not at the Hatch Shell but at the Paint-Day painting at the base of it, one of the ubiquitous paintings. This one was of the pink-and-white flowers that cover the Esplanade in springtime. I had seen it earlier without noticing it. But Fletcher was looking at it. And I thought I saw his lips moving.

Noon was harsh and hot. The temperature crept past ninety and the sun pummeled the Esplanade. Fletcher and I huddled together under the umbrella to keep in the shade. It was arousing being so close to him, touching him. Time passed and a beam snuck under and striped my ankle.

"Is the sun getting on you?" he said, holding his hand out to stop the beam from hitting me.

I didn't say anything, didn't move my leg, didn't want to. I remembered Angel saying that same thing to me once. It wasn't because Fletcher sometimes reminded me of Angel that I liked him; it was that he and Angel shared something I liked: they made me feel looked-after. I lifted my hand and touched my palm to Fletcher's, and threaded my fingers through his fingers, and he squeezed, and he smiled.

We played *Go Fish*. We took macro photos of a caterpillar we spotted crawling along the fence. We had a sword-fight with blades of grass while the little girl on the blanket next door cheered. We played that game where you try to slap the other person's hand before he can move it, and I saw Fletcher had blue paint under his fingernails.

Around 1:00 he said to me, "We're more than halfway

now. Seven hours left."

I was pouring water on my head; rubbing my hair still felt funny with my mohawk gone, even all these months later. "Think you'll make it, Fletcher? You getting sick of me yet?"

He held out his hand and I passed him the water bottle. He took a quick drink and passed it back. "I'm hanging in there," he smirked. "I do have to pee, though. Need anything while I'm out?" He kicked his bare feet into his sneakers and stood up and stretched. He had sexy, agile-looking legs, a sprinter's legs.

"Maybe a hotdog?" I pointed to a food cart parked near to where we'd lined up that morning. "Can I give you some money?"

"I got it," he said, and he walked away on the tightrope of borders.

It rained around 3:00 for a few minutes—a sun shower that felt like a gift. We stood and stretched out our arms like kids in a lawn sprinkler. It was the first time I really wanted to kiss him. Soon after the rain stopped we were dry again.

We dozed again with our heads under the umbrella and our legs in the sun. I think I slept for an hour. When I opened my eyes Fletcher was sitting beside me with his hand hovering over my crotch—no, not my crotch, my pocket. My keys. I heard him murmur, "The key-touching guy." And I remembered how he'd once seen me checking for my keys. I'd meant something to him long before today, before I even knew he existed.

I yawned and he moved his hand away and looked over at the Hatch Shell, where the concert equipment was being set up. Brass instruments were blinding in the sun.

"Fletcher," I said, leaning up.

"Hey, sleepyhead," he said, as if he was just noticing me. "We're getting close now."

"What time?" I rubbed my eyes.

"Four-thirty."

"You called me your key-touching guy."

"I— Sorry, is that creepy?"

"No. You can call me that." I reached across the blanket and held his foot in my hand, circled my thumb around the hard skin that ringed his heel—it was a presumptuous touch, I suppose, but it didn't feel that way to me. "Fletcher, I want to ask you. Are you still, like, hurt?"

"Hurt how?"

I let my hand skid up his calf as I sat up. "I told you I've got hurts. They're named Boyd and Johnny and Angel and Wes, and they have a lot of other names, too. I was sort of mean to you when you called me the other day, with the *I'm married* thing, and I think it's because I've been hurt. But I'm realizing I'm not so hurt that I can't ever— I mean, they're not the kind of hurts that have left scars. You know? They felt like that at the time but that's not what they are. I was watching you sleep earlier and now I know that's not what they are. They were hurts like how it hurts to lift weights. Do you know what happens, when you lift weights? Your muscle fibers tear. That's why it hurts. But when they heal they heal thicker and stronger. And you tear them again with more weight. And they heal stronger. Again and again, stronger. My hurts didn't leave scars, they left muscle."

"I don't know if I'm following, Ollie...."

"This Mateo guy. I can tell he's still on your mind a lot. I think he always will be. And if anything happens between you and me — and I'm starting to really hope it will, Fletcher — I know Mateo is going to be there with us. So I want to know how much he hurt you. I want to know if he gave you scars or muscle."

"He hurt me a lot. And I hurt him." He looked down at his hands in his lap, and his eyes flicked across his tattoo — *Arrowman Is.* "Muscle," he said. "I would never doubt it. Definitely muscle."

"Fletcher, did Mateo die?"

The question hung in the air for what seemed like a long time. It took my own breath away and I didn't know why.

Finally he started to say something, something that must've been more than he wanted to say right then, because he stopped. He looked at me. Behind his eyes, I knew, were a million stories I someday wanted to hear. He didn't answer except to say, "Not yet, OK?" Tears came to his eyes and when he wiped them away he laughed at himself for crying.

"It's OK," I said, "I guess everybody hurts. I guess I learned that a long time ago, from a wise dude in a wise song. Of course you're hurt, and I'm glad you got muscle from it. The better question is, are you ready? Because I'm ready. I've shot a lot of arrows, Fletcher, and —"

"Ollie, *I* called *you*, remember? *I* remembered *you*."

He reached out and rubbed my arm, my tricep, which for much of my youth had been so hard and thick, but which now felt like only what I needed it to be.

"What were you doing that day?" he said. "When we met during the blackout. Where were you coming from?"

"I was sad," I said. I told him about R.E.M. disbanding that day, how I'd been walking the city with their songs, how I had listened to their last new song on the train when he was standing near me.

He said, "You like R.E.M., huh?"

"Since I was a kid."

"What were you like as a kid, Ollie? You must've been a cute kid."

"I was a lonely kid."

"Did you have a mohawk back then?"

"I would never have had a mohawk back then. The mohawk came later. That's a story of its own."

"Tell me." He lay down on the blanket and stretched out, his feet on the bar of the fence, his head cradled in the crook of his elbow. "Come on, Oliver Wade. Tell me everything."

***

So I told him everything.

I told him about the graduation dance and about how my friend mysteriously stopping talking and, ten years later, died. I told him about my roommates, the good ones and the tough ones. I told him about my uncle and my parents and Abbey. I told him about my youth and young loves.

In the beginning my stories were choppy, I guess, because that's the way distant memories always seem to be. Little details can stand in for so much in memories. An itchy chin is how you remember a friend. A green-eyed boy on a subway platform is how you remember a life-changing day. A pair of worn corduroys is what you remember about being in love. The sound of a dial-up modem connecting. The tips of your dad's fingers at the small of his back. These details are like pulses, like heartbeat spikes on the cardiac line of memory. *BeepBEEP, beepBEEP, beepBEEP.* I think memories are like that for everyone. One day stands out in a hundred, five stand out in a thousand. A few events in a lifetime of nothing-days can build you, just like how atoms are made up mostly of empty space and yet can build the world.

There was more to tell as I got older. My memories were more vivid and the details piled up. They didn't necessarily bring clarity, though; sometimes details only made things more confusing. Maybe things were simpler when they were choppy. I remembered telling Wesley how I'd been confused growing up as a gay kid, and the confusion hadn't ended in college or afterward, even with clearer memories.

Telling Fletcher all these things, I was worried he would think I was a dumb-ass. I'd made so many mistakes in my life, and in the telling of it they all seem so obvious. Why did I accept an invitation to a dance I didn't want to go to? Why did I smother a boy who needed someone just to be there? Why did I not realize how my parents would be affected by Abbey? It was stupid, all of it, and looking back it's easy to criticize. I'd have every right to be hard on myself. But I know that in the moment I was always just doing the best I could. I was working with what I had, with what I knew, and sometimes that was not very much. But I was never trying to be a bad guy. Everyone I met along the way, everyone who contributed the little hurts that gave me muscle—they all were doing the best they could, too. And I guess I owe them for it. I owe them for the muscle, and I owe them because each one, one by one and stacked together, got me here. The foundation of everything I'd ever be, whatever that might be, was here now, watching fireworks with Fletcher.

***

It happened naturally, and I don't think either of us was completely aware of it, but by the time the fireworks started I was lying on my back with my head in his lap. People were seeing us but nobody said anything. The little girl smiled and I smiled back. TV cameras on cranes swept back and forth overhead, their red *Live from Boston* lights glowing. I understood I was on television with my head resting on a guy's lap, and I was OK, and I thought, again, *Dear young Ollie, you won't believe this but it'll be true.*

"Ba-boom," Fletcher whispered, and he put his hand on my chest, and I didn't know whether he meant the fireworks or my heartbeat.

I told him everything over those past few hours, except one thing. There was something I was saving; it was something I always saved. I hadn't told him what I saw the night of the blackout.

I hadn't told him that after I said goodbye to him and got off the train, I didn't go home. I crossed over to the inbound side of the tracks, got back on, rode to the end of the line and looped around. I hadn't wanted to be home yet and my feet were too tired to walk anymore.

I sat on the train with my arms folded and I looked out the window, through the scuffed, scratched glass, at the fuzzy shapes of the city drifting by. My mind was silent. I had listened to R.E.M.'s last new song, "We All Go Back to Where We Belong," a dozen times but now my earbuds were tucked away in my pocket again. I watched through the window as the sunlight dimmed and disappeared, as storefront lights and headlights and signs lit the worn glass with blurs of color, like watercolors rubbed on the window.

Night had fallen fully and for the last few stops I'd been almost alone in the T car—at the other end a man dozed with his head against a handrail.

I was looking at the window, at the colors, not thinking, just being. Clear of everything else my mind's eye started conjuring the picture that boy on the subway platform drew with his finger so many years before. That two-stroked heart and the line that flowed away from it, made when my train started to pull away from him— while I'd watched unbelieving that I'd lost him forever. I didn't know what made me think of that now, what made the image so clear in my mind. I could almost see the heart fading onto the window, clear lines growing in the scuff, like the reverse of breathing on glass. If I held my head just-so, if I tricked my eyes, I could almost see—

With a jolt I leaned forward.

I got up and went to the window, knelt on the seat in front of it. Two strokes were there now, two parts of the heart, one curved, one curved with that flat line—two strokes clear in the scuff, glowing with the colored lights of the city. I touched the glass. How? But it was there. Tears came to my eyes and electricity seemed to buzz along my hair.

My heart started thumping in my chest, reminding me it was there, and that it was strong.

I thought, If I decide to tell Fletcher about that heart that showed up on the night we now call Paint Day— If I tell him that I know who the Painter is, that I know what he looked like as a teenage boy, with emerald eyes and space-black hair— If I tell him that when I mouthed to the boy that I loved him he *smiled*— If I tell Fletcher those things, and if he believes me, if he is the kind of person who would believe a thing so unbelievable, I swear I'm going to marry him. If he believes me, I'll know this is where I belong.

Fireworks were crashing overhead, faster now, and louder. Then louder. We were close to the grand finale. I wanted to tell him. I was afraid he would laugh at me and the day would be ruined, but if ever there was a time to risk everything, it was underneath fireworks. I felt as though they'd push things my way. And anyway, if he laughed, I was strong.

With my head still lying in his lap I looked up at him. "Want to hear something pretty weird, Fletcher?"

"Yeah, tell me, Ollie," he said, watching the sky. Colors lit up his face and he looked beautiful. "I can handle weird, believe you me."

"Let's find out if you can," I said.

So I told him the last thing, and slowly he looked down at me while fireworks exploded beyond his head, forgotten. My story had made him forget about thunder and fire. Although his eyes were wide enough for me to see myself looking up into them, there was no doubt in them. There was confusion, maybe, but even in the confusion I knew I belonged. What can love ever be but confusing? Even when you know every detail, it's something to figure out, day by day, a perpetual discovery. You wouldn't want it any other way.

The sky lit up with sound and sparks. *Ba-boom, ba-boom.* Deep, thunderous, loud enough to set off car alarms in the distance. I could feel the sound in my chest.

Fletcher leaned down and kissed me and said, "I believe you."

I laughed, and at long last I knew I belonged. It was a sweet word, *belong*. Once upon a time I had said it to my daughter, but I had said the wrong thing. This was what I should have said to her that day, when I told her not to be like me: "Yes, be like me. When a path isn't laid out for you, find it. Find the place you belong."

Belong. Do you hear it? *Belong.* It was an orange word, warm, warm as a whisper in a noisy bar, warm as a bed with the blankets held open for you, warm as a kiss that ends a fight, warm as plans, warm as future, warm as fireworks on a summer night.

Belong, belong, belong.

You know?

AUTHOR'S NOTES

A few things before you go:

First, if you liked this book, please rate it, tweet it, whatever it! This helps other people discover the book — and let's face it, given my poor marketing skills it's basically all in your hands. I'll be grateful forever for your help!

Questions, comments, complaints? Email me at cranberryhush@gmail.com. Tweet me @benmonopoli.

Second, fans of R.E.M. and doers of careful math will note that in this book the band disbands in 2008; in real life it happened in 2011. Otherwise I've mostly stuck to the actual dates of their album releases and such. I wish I'd been able to show Ollie at a concert, but the band's tour dates never quite lined up with the timeline of the stories. It's safe to say Ollie saw a concert or two between stories, though.

Last but not least, I need to thank the usual suspects. Particularly Maggie, for reading and encouraging a lot of these stories when they were still just snippets in emails. Jake, for designing me a fancy new lighthouse logo. Tom, for helping with the blurb, which is always the hardest part for me. Enriquez, for answering all my questions about Army enlistment. Chris, for continuing to be where I belong. And you, of course, for reading.

— Ben

ALSO BY BEN MONOPOLI

The Cranberry Hush: A Novel
The Painting of Porcupine City: A Novel
Homo Action Love Story! A tall tale

Printed in Great Britain
by Amazon